Stolen Tongues

Felix Blackwell

Stolen Tongues

This is a work of fiction. All names, characters, locales, and incidents are products of the author's imagination and any resemblance to actual people, places, or events is coincidental or fictionalized.

All artwork by the brilliant Lorinda Tomko.
www.lorindatomko.com

Published in the United States in 2017 with CreateSpace.

ISBN: 1533240418
ISBN-13: 978-1533240415

Dedicated to the real Faye

There are many things that make me afraid to sleep.
You, on the other hand, make me afraid to stay awake.

With special thanks for making this novel possible:

Jeff Mumaugh
Rory Collins
John DeSantis
Saurabh Dutta
Jesse Laabs
Laren Lee
Michael O'Brien
Tanya Quarry
Gina Baird
Daniel Parco
Molly Walker
Colin J. Northwood

Stolen Tongues

Prologue

Deep in the Rocky Mountains, at the top of a howling peak, sits a cabin. It is a lonely and unremarkable thing, nestled at the end of a winding gravel road and surrounded by a crescent of woods. There are no other houses nearby, and if not for the distant town it overlooks, a visitor to this cabin might get the impression that she was entirely cut off from the world.

It is at this site that my life descended into a surreal nightmare. What happened on that mountain left permanent scars on my body and heart, but it also threw light onto seemingly unrelated events that occurred long before. And so, this story begins years prior to the incident at that wretched place.

I've known my best friend Colin since we were little. On his ninth birthday, his mom bought him a bird for a pet – an African grey parrot. They're quite smart and good with kids, so the bird ended up being wildly amusing to both of us. Naturally, we tried to teach her swear words, but her first word ended up being "carrot," so we named her Carrot the parrot.

I never realized it until I was much older, but Carrot did a whole lot more than just learn words and repeat them. She recognized people and greeted them uniquely; she learned to speak politely to Colin's mom but addressed Colin's little brother via "*Hello, twerp!*" Sometimes she'd even try to comfort people when she heard them arguing or crying, usually by saying things like "*Don't cry*" or "*I love you.*"

The bird knew people by their faces and voices, so she would sometimes get upset when she saw an unfamiliar person. When we were twelve years old, Colin and I put on Halloween masks and spoke to Carrot. It was amazing watching her try to reconcile our familiar voices with the strange new faces. You could actually see in her expression how puzzled she was. In response to some Halloween masks, she'd even shriek "*Ugly! Ugly!*" and flap her little wings.

I came to know Colin because we lived on the same street. Whenever I'd head up the walkway to his front door, Carrot would shout "*Knock-knock!*" before I arrived, obviating the need to ring the bell. At times she'd play games with us; if I walked away from her cage, she would say, "*colder...colder...*" and as I walked toward it, she would say, "*warmer...warmer...*" At the time I never appreciated how sharp she was, but in retrospect, Carrot was cognizant of everything going on around her. And that is what made her so frightening.

When I was a senior in college, I started dating a woman named Faye. Colin had just recently gotten married, and asked us to look after his pets while he and his wife Gabriella went on honeymoon. At that time, they lived up in the mountains in a rather impressive old house, left to Gabriella after the untimely death of her father. It was only a forty-five-minute drive from our campus, so Faye and I happily obliged. I was thrilled to see the parrot

2

again, and to get away from school for a few days with my new girlfriend.

I could hear Carrot's trademark *"Knock-knock!"* as we fumbled with the old door, and she lit up when we walked in. Although she hadn't seen me in a few years, the bird still recognized me, and was even curious about Faye. There were also two excitable huskies named Boomer and Chewie, so we had plenty of animals to keep us entertained.

The bird's cage sat in the breakfast nook, which overlooked a little grove of trees outside. There was a glass door that slid open in that room, leading out to a deck. Whenever Faye and I left it open for fresh air, Carrot would shout *"Up yours!"* and *"Damn liberals!"* at the hummingbirds that flitted by. Colin had taught her all kinds of silly phrases to embarrass Gabriella whenever they had company over. Faye and I spent the first evening on the couch watching movies and laughing at Carrot's ridiculous prattle.

Later that night, I found myself alone at the table, working on a paper. Faye was asleep on the couch; I could see only her strawberry curls dangling just above the snoring dogs on the floor. The TV was off. Carrot had relaxed and was watching me quietly from her cage, and in that moment I realized how dreadfully silent it was. Not just the animals, not just the house, but the entire forest outside had fallen utterly still. The quiet lulled me out of focus and crushed my will to be productive, so I woke up Faye and the dogs and we headed upstairs to the guest room.

There is a brief moment at night when the brain is neither awake nor asleep, but somewhere in between. In that moment, I sometimes hear things – distant voices or odd sounds. Normally I dismiss them as the wisps of dreams, just barely taking form at the edge of consciousness. So when I heard a noise on this particular

3

night, I ignored it as long as I could. But the sound kept invading my mind, over and over. Eventually I sat up in bed, trying to determine whether the noise was real. After a moment, I heard Carrot chattering downstairs. As I recalled from my childhood, she almost never speaks when she's by herself, and virtually never makes any noises at night. But now she was mimicking laughter and saying *"Hello! Hello!"*

I assumed the bird was trying to get my attention, so I went down to check her food bowl. When I flipped on the light, Carrot was staring up at the ceiling, captivated by something I couldn't see. I figured she'd spotted one of the many moths we'd let in earlier while taking the dogs out. The bird refused to speak to me at all. I shrugged and went back to bed. She grumbled a few more times that night as I fell asleep, but I couldn't make anything out.

The next morning, it was brilliantly sunny outside, so Faye and I took the dogs for a hike in the woods. We explored for a bit and returned home around lunchtime. As we approached the sliding glass door in the back, I could hear Carrot yelling *"Knock-knock!"* and *"Hello!"* from inside. She flapped her little wings in salutation as we entered and whistled excitedly. The day carried on with more of her nonsensical jabbering, but as twilight descended, the bird's behavior changed. She appeared fixated on the sliding glass door, and on a window in the kitchen, occasionally cocking her head to study them intently. Faye was the one to notice this time, but she dismissed it as Carrot hearing owls or catching glimpses of bats near the porch.

That night as we lay in bed, Boomer and Chewie seemed agitated. They kept getting up from their doggy beds and looking around, sniffing in the direction of the hall, and jolting awake shortly after settling down. The jingling of their collars began to drive me insane, so I led the dogs into the master bedroom with the intent of locking them in. As I did, Carrot called out from downstairs, "*Knock-knock! Knock-knock!*"

Feeling a little creeped out, I went down and checked on her. She was again engrossed with the glass door. There was nothing to see out there; it was just a wall of soupy darkness. Even when I flicked on the porch light, only an empty deck and the faint outlines of nearby trees could be seen. I closed the blinds, hoping they'd pacify Carrot, and trudged back upstairs.

The moment I hit the second floor, the bird shrieked, "*Knock-knock!*" This time her call positively unnerved me. I jogged down the flight and stormed to the front door, glaring out the peep hole with the wild expectation that a madman would be standing there clutching a knife. Alas, there was no one, just an empty footpath that led down to the dark street. As I pulled my face away from the door, Carrot mimicked growling noises, then laughter.

My heart fluttered in my chest. Was this a trick that Colin had taught his bird to play on me? I circled the first floor, turning on every light and investigating every room, but found nothing out of the ordinary. I sighed with defeat and sleepiness, told Carrot to shut the hell up, and went back to bed. While closing the bedroom door, I heard her call out softly, "*Don't cry. Don't cry.*"

Faye laughed at me when I told her of the previous night's events. She spent that Saturday playfully mocking my credulity and baby-talking the parrot.

"Did you play a trick on Felix?" she'd ask while scratching the bird's cheeks. Carrot reveled in the attention and mumbled her pleasure. "Yes you did. You scared him good! What did you see? You see those bats on the porch?"

We barbecued on the patio and took the dogs for an afternoon romp through the forest, this time much farther out, and barely found our way back in the dying light. Strange noises emanated all around us from deep in the woods, prompting eruptions of frenzied barking from the dogs every few minutes. By the time we got back to the porch, the gloom had deepened to nearly black, making the glowing lights of the house look warm and inviting.

Carrot, however, was not as welcoming. She cowered at the bottom of her cage beneath her perch and behind a swinging rope. She looked up at me, apparently relieved, and cautiously edged out of her hiding place. Faye opened the cage and coaxed the parrot to step onto her hand.

"What's wrong, pretty bird?" she asked in a motherly voice. "You hear a scary noise?" Faye stroked Carrot's head, trying to calm her, but the bird kept glancing over to the sliding glass door.

"She's shaking," Faye said, turning to me. "Scared to death."

I checked to ensure that the door was locked, squinted into the darkness beyond it, then drew the blinds and joined Faye in her attempt to soothe the bird. Eventually, Carrot relaxed enough to be returned to her cage without a fuss, but the bird's disposition only added to our growing unease. There was definitely something strange up here on the mountain.

That night, as Faye and I were lying in bed watching a movie on my laptop, there came a commotion from downstairs. It sounded like utensils being spilled in the kitchen, but I realized after a moment that it was Carrot's cage. The bird shrieked and the dogs started barking. I leaped out of bed and flew down the stairs to find Boomer and Chewie snarling at the patio door. The bird's cage lay on the ground, Carrot flapping around inside it.

I raced over and set the cage upright, then yanked the blinds open. The porch was empty, and a breeze set the nearby woods fluttering. I pulled at the door to ensure it was still locked. Satisfied that no one had come through it, I searched the house once again, and once again found nothing out of the ordinary. When I passed a large portrait of Gabriella's late father, thoughts of his ghost shuffling through the halls drifted into my mind. I wondered if he was still here – then shook the idea from my head.

Faye called out from the top of the stairs, asking what had happened.

"The dogs heard something outside and started freaking out," I said. "I think Carrot got upset and knocked her own cage off the table." The explanation didn't satisfy either of us, but it was the only one I was willing to consider.

"Bring her upstairs," Faye replied. "We can put her up here tonight. See if that calms her down."

I laughed.

"Are you kidding? She'll keep us up all night."

My protest fell on deaf ears; Faye had already descended the stairs and walked up behind me.

"We'll keep *her* up all night," she said, stabbing a finger into my ribs. I immediately abandoned my resistance and nodded in agreement.

"Dogs too," she said, grabbing the cage and whistling at Chewie and Boomer. They trotted up the stairs behind her, overjoyed to be allowed back into our bedroom. They, like Carrot, did not like to sleep alone – especially not downstairs, for some reason. I shrugged helplessly and followed everyone back to the guest room, closing the door and locking us inside.

It was nearly 2 A.M. when I awoke to the bird chattering in the dark.

"*Don't cry...Don't cry...*" she repeated from across the room. I reached over a sleeping Faye and grabbed my cell phone off the nightstand, using it to illuminate the room in a faint glow. Carrot was sitting on her perch, facing the bedroom door. She craned her head to the side, listening intently to something I couldn't hear, and opened her mouth as if considering what to say. Chewie dug her snout under the door and sniffed around while Boomer sat rigid, ears perked, head jerking back and forth as he tried to hone in on whatever Carrot sensed.

Faye mumbled something in her sleep, but I could barely make it out. It sounded like, "...where they find...it's where he is...no, no..."

Boomer whimpered, and Chewie withdrew from the door. She retreated to Boomer's side and sat down next to him. The bird called out, *"colder, colder,"* reciting the words to the game we used to play as kids.

I shook Faye awake and motioned to the scene before us, then pressed my finger to my lips. She remained quiet but her eyes screamed in terror; even in the dark I could see their whites. She huddled there under the blanket as I got out of bed and slipped my jeans on.

Carrot flapped her wings and called out, *"Warmer...warmer..."* The dogs stood up defensively, but did not bark or growl. They only listened, and occasionally glanced at each other and back at me.

"Warmer! Warmer!" the bird cried, beating her wings faster. After a few seconds, she ceased her movements and looked up at me, then back at the door, and said in a softer voice, *"Knock-knock."*

I stood rooted to the floor, breath caught in my throat. The door rattled gently in its frame, as if someone had pressed an ear against it. The silence was only broken when Faye whispered, "Don't open it."

Her words didn't register in my brain. I reached out and pulled the door open slowly. It issued a loud creak that echoed through the house. There was no one there. I felt

8

the dogs brush past my legs as I stood in the doorway. They stood before me, motionless, gazing down the darkness of the hallway. At the far end, the master bedroom door was open. Inside it was pitch black, but the dogs peered in as though they could see something.

"What is it?" I whispered, patting Chewie's head. She didn't move a muscle. Her entire body was rigid, ready to attack. But neither dog made a sound. I waded through the dark of the hall to peek inside Colin's room, but I was stopped by a powerful wave of nausea. The walls spun around me and my legs went rubbery. I caught myself on the handrail next to the stairs. As I regained my sense of balance, Carrot said from behind me, *Warmer...*" and then shrieked, "*UGLY! UGLY!*" Her cage rattled again, and Faye screamed.

I bolted back down the hall, nearly tripping over the dogs, who were now barking and snarling wildly. I flicked the light on in the guest room to see Faye sitting at the far end of the bed, knees pulled to her chest, terror in her expression. Carrot's cage was on the floor again, and the bird was flapping around inside, still shrieking.

"Someone was in here," Faye choked out, trying to hold back tears. "It felt like someone was standing right there." She pointed directly at me.

At this point I'd seen enough. We got dressed, threw our luggage together, and ushered the dogs out the front door. We all piled into the car and sped down the mountain. A full moon lit our path. All the way home, Faye and I traded stories of all the creepy and unexplainable things that had happened to us in our lives. Most of mine involved the sounds I hear at night, and most of hers involved sleepwalking as a child. Carrot watched our conversation from her cage on Faye's lap, but never uttered a word the entire drive.

When Monday rolled around, Colin and Gabriella were

surprised to hear that they had to come pick up their pets from my apartment. In the coming years, I learned from them that Carrot never spoke again.

PART I

Chapter 1

I hadn't seen snow in decades. Fresh powder dusted the road, and our rental car struggled to make it up the hill. It was hard to take in the beautiful view while trying not to plummet off the cliff, but I managed. To the right, an icy pine forest drifted past, and to the left, far below, lay an enormous valley. A big town rested inside it. All around us, dozens of other snow-capped mountains jagged the rim of the horizon.

Faye was my copilot. She pushed a stream of fiery-gold hair out of her face and studied a map on her phone.

"Half a mile to go!" she said, glowing with excitement.

It was Thursday afternoon and we were on our way to her family's cabin, high up on Pale Peak. The mountain was about a two-hour drive from her parents' house in Avonwood, Colorado. We'd set out that morning after her mother surprised us with the key. Faye and I had just gotten engaged a few weeks earlier, and her parents had flown us out to celebrate.

This month marked our fifth anniversary as a couple. I was a graduate student working on a Ph.D. in English, and Faye had recently begun her career as an animal keeper at a wildlife sanctuary. We had always talked about taking a trip, but life never stopped flinging new hurdles at us, and somehow that talk of escape never came to fruition. The time we spent together faded to brief moments before bed.

It took an engagement ring and a war with our bosses to pull it off, but at long last, we were finally on vacation: a romantic cabin getaway, totally unexpected, and far removed from the humdrum of California living. On the plane I'd imagined a week with Faye's waspy parents in their immaculate house, but I was delighted when they lent us their cabin for a few days. I pictured myself and Faye wrapped in blankets by a crackling fire, sipping hot chocolate and whimsically debating the terms of our marriage. She'd demand regular back rubs, and in return, I'd be allowed to buy video games whenever I wanted.

"Oh my God," Faye said, interrupting my train of thought and swatting my thigh. "Felix, look!"

As we rounded another corner of the winding road, a little house came into view. It wasn't much more than a cottage tucked against an idyllic tree line. The whole scene might have climbed straight out of a Kinkade painting.

"Damn," I mumbled.

The car practically died in the driveway. Faye jumped out and raced in a circle around the cabin, taking it all in.

"Oh my God, it's *adorable!*" she yelled from behind the building. I could hear her laughter as I unloaded the car. "And look back here, Felix! A hiking trail, right out the back door!"

I followed the tracks she left in the snow. There was barely a half-inch of it, just enough to tint the earth white, but a boyish giddiness brimmed inside of me at the sound of each crunching footfall. As I rounded the back of the cabin, a brown and white snowball pelted me in the neck.

"Faye!" I shouted, "that had rocks in it!"

Faye peeked out from behind a pile of firewood

with a huge grin on her face. As I reached down to make a snowball, she burst into laughter and took off running. She darted across the little field that constituted the backyard, then slipped into the dark woods behind it. I rushed after her but stopped short of the tree line.

"Uh, babe," I called out, "are there like...wolves and bears up here?"

Faye popped out of the woods about twenty yards away.

"There's a whole bunch of hiking trails!" she replied, motioning for me to come over.

I turned around and headed for the car.

"Hike tomorrow, sweetie," I said over my shoulder. "Unpack today."

"Ugh, and look at the view from here," she said, framing the cabin with her fingers and peeping through it. "I'm gonna draw the shit out of this place."

"Pencils are in the luggage, babe. Gotta take it in first."

She huffed in defeat and followed me back.

The inside of the cabin was white and modern, and had obviously been remodeled over the years. It didn't quite match the rustic exterior, but at least it had a fireplace. There was a combined living room and kitchen, and a short hallway that led to the bedroom and bathroom. We dropped our bags on the floor and explored the place; Faye headed to the bedroom while I inspected the entertainment center. There was a newish flat-screen TV, a stereo unit from the early 90's, and a little DVD player.

"Why didn't you tell me to bring movies?" I called down the hallway.

"I didn't know they had a TV up here," Faye replied. "Hey, come feel this bed. It's like, space foam or something." She groaned in relaxation.

"What do you mean you didn't know?" I said, fumbling

15

through the drawers in search of DVD's. "Haven't you been up here?"

"Not since I was fourteen, and I was only here once. A lot has changed."

"Only once? You visit your parents almost every Christmas...you guys never spent one up here?"

"They haven't come here in years. I think they wa—"

"Oh my *God*," I blurted out, staring down into one of the cabinets of the entertainment center.

"What?" Faye called.

"Oh Jesus," I said, reaching a hand inside.

Faye stormed down the hall into the living room.

"What's going on?"

I pulled an object out of the cabinet.

"It's...it's a Super Nintendo," I said, barely able to form the words.

"Yeah? So?"

I turned to face her directly.

"A *Super. Nintendo.* Faye."

She rolled her eyes.

"My dad was obsessed with it when I was little," she said dismissively, then walked back toward the bedroom. "He bought it for Becca but she never got into it. I guess he brought it up here to rot."

"Oh *Jesus Christ!*" I said, stopping her in her tracks.

"*What,*" she snapped, cracking a smile.

My lips trembled.

"It's...it's *Donkey Kong Country 2*," I said. I held the game cartridge to my chest, embracing it as a childhood friend.

"For God's sake," Faye grumbled.

"It's my all-time favorite game. It took me forever to beat. Best soundtrack ever."

"Huh. Becca liked the music too, actually," she said.

"I'm marrying the wrong sister," I muttered.

"Excuse me? I didn't quite catch that."

"Leave us," I said, tossing the car keys at Faye. They bounced off her chest and fell to the floor. She remained motionless, unimpressed. "You can go home," I continued, sliding the cartridge into the Nintendo and taking a seat on the couch. "I...*we* need some alone time."

I heard the keys sail across the room, and felt them smack into the back of my skull.

The sun set, and a deep cold swept over the mountain. I rummaged through the food we'd brought, trying to figure out what to cook for dinner, and Faye relaxed on the couch with a few of the magazines she'd picked up at the airport.

"Wow, Garden of the Gods looks neat," she said, holding up a picture for me to see. It was one of those must-see travel destination magazines for tourists. She wanted me to look at a spread of some weird rock formations, but my attention was drawn to a photo of a Native American headdress on the opposite page.

The Rocky Mountains are rich in Native American history and lore. Virtually every place you can visit here used to be home to an Indigenous community, and there is some effort to preserve that fact in the local economy, for better or worse. It is possible to find "authentic" Indian wares in any of the thousand gift shops that dot the region, but finding portrayals of Natives as anything other than fantastical heroes or mysterious savages is quite difficult.

Pale Peak was no different. While buying groceries in town, the cashier eagerly regaled us with stories of magic and war. There is an industry here that sells a certain picture of the people who once inhabited these mountains: mysterious Indians who performed rituals and fought with cowboys, then vanished altogether, leaving behind only arrowheads and legends about constellations. But that enthusiasm for all things Native American, however commercial, really does make the land itself feel alive and humming with memory.

I leafed through Faye's magazine after she passed out, scavenging for less sensational tidbits of the area's history. As the crackling of the fire died away, other noises came to my attention. The wind whispered across the mountain in short gusts, and new snow battered the windows. A few sounds rang through the forest, probably from animals, but I couldn't make them out. They were eerie and forlorn, like the howls of dying wolves. The longer I listened, the more my skin crawled, so I took out my laptop and tested the cabin's ancient WiFi. The connection was weak and repeatedly dropped while I browsed the internet. I gave up after a half hour and went to bed, leaving Faye on the couch. Waking her up from a dead slumber didn't always end well.

Sometime around midnight, I woke to the sound of Faye's voice.

"Felix, babe, get up. Get up. Someone's outside."

She stood there in the doorway with a blanket wrapped around her. She'd been on the couch the whole time.

"Wuh...what?" I said, rubbing my eyes into focus. It was dark. The only light in the room came from the moon; it poured in from the window and bathed Faye in cold silver. Her ghostly appearance and the fear in her voice frightened me.

"I heard someone outside," she continued. "Someone calling for help."

I kicked the sheets off and shuffled to the living room in my boxers. It was even darker here. All of the curtains were drawn.

"Uh, I don't hear—"

"Shh!" she said, grabbing my arm and holding me still.

Eventually, I did hear a sound. It was the pained cry of an animal, or maybe a person. It sounded more sorrowful than injured. Faye and I exchanged concerned glances.

"Peek out the door," she whispered, handing her blanket to me. I rummaged through the bags on the kitchen counter and found the flashlight that Faye's dad had given us. The cry resounded again, this time louder, and seemed to say *"Leave me alone"* or *"I'm alone."* It was so distorted by wind and echo that it barely sounded human.

The moment I cracked the door open, a blast of frigid mountain air stung my face. It burned the last bit of sleep from my eyes and sharpened all my senses. The light's beam moved across the deck and out into the clearing. It lit up a fluffy wonderland of snow, but revealed nothing unusual. I swept the light back and forth across the tree line, but its glow was too weak to penetrate the blackness.

"Nothing," I said, withdrawing into the warmth of the cabin. "Probably an elk or something. Those things make some frickin' weird noises. Probably even more so when they're hurt."

Dissatisfied, Faye walked around the room, peering out each window. "That was a *person*, Felix. You know it was a person. Maybe a camper got lost."

"Camping? In the snow?" I asked, incredulous. As a Californian, it seemed utterly absurd. "You know, there's this thing called pareidolia. See, our brains come with a kind of software application that's pre-installed when we're born. Facial recognition, pattern recognition, that sort of thing. It helps us recognize our mothers when we're babies, and helps us—"

"Uh-huh," Faye interrupted.

"...Well, sometimes it misfires," I continued. "You know when you're a kid and you see a shadow on your wall at night, and it looks like a monster? Or when you see animals in the clouds? That's pareidolia. And it happens with sound, too. The wind blows through a cave or something just right, and people think they hear a voice. Your brain even makes words out of it, in the language you know best."

Faye shook her wild hair out of her face and exhaled sharply.

"Pareidolia my *ass*."

She climbed back into bed and closed her eyes. She tossed and turned for hours.

Chapter 2

Morning came, and with it a symphony of bird calls. My joy at the brilliant sunny day was tempered once I looked in the driveway. Our rental car was now encased in a brick of ice, waiting to be chipped free by future archaeologists. Restful sleep had only taken Faye around 3 A.M., so she remained dead to the world long after I ate breakfast. I put a good hour into *Donkey Kong*, then suited up in my winter gear to go poke around the property.

Outside, I found no trace of last night's visitor. No footprints pocked the white landscape; it must have snowed earlier this morning. But now the sky was clear and blue, and the sun perched high overhead. It illuminated the woods and made them bright and inviting, so I dashed across the short clearing and took a stroll inside.

The snow now concealed the paths that Faye had mentioned yesterday, so I made my own. I promenaded between the trees, watching the frosty sunbeams that appeared and vanished before me as I moved. I lamented leaving my cell phone and its excellent camera back at the cabin. Faye and I had developed a special fondness for the outdoors; we regularly hiked in the redwoods during our time in Santa Cruz, and I eventually proposed to her while camping.

"Felix!" a voice echoed from far away. Little birds and squirrels jumped around in the trees in agitation, knocking bits of snow off the branches. I doubled back to the meadow and saw Faye's face through the little bedroom window.

"Morning," I called.

"Wait right there – I'm getting dressed!" she yelled. Her voice boomed across the mountain and returned shortly after.

We spent the late morning creating a mental map of the forest behind the cabin. We often did this before embarking upon a serious hike, to ensure we'd not get lost. The path we forged through the half-foot of snow took us to the western edge of Pale Peak, where we could see down into a gorge and over to the next mountain. A river rushed below, snaking between the rocks. The splendor of nature beamed from every direction, beckoning us further into the woods.

On our way back, Faye thought she heard a voice. She mentioned it a few times as we walked, shushing me and spinning around, trying to locate the source of the noise. I strained to hear anything above the whistling of the wind through the trees and the fading gush of water.

"I think you're shaken up a bit from last night, sweetie," I offered. The look she shot at me almost forced the words right back into my mouth.

"When have you ever known me to be paranoid?" she pressed. "I'm not some basket case, Felix. I heard someone."

"What did it sound like?" I asked. We waded through the shallow snow, carefully following our own tracks back to the cabin.

"It was a man," she said. "He was upset."

22

"He must have tried your mom's casserole," I replied. It was a big risk, but it paid off. Faye burst into laughter, her voice reverberating through the woods. I loved so much the way her eyes squinted when she laughed.

We talked about food the whole way back, working up an appetite as we did. As we neared the edge of the wood, I stopped to take a leak. Faye wandered up ahead.

"Felix."

Her voice came out flat and dead. As soon as the word hit my brain, I immediately felt a hot rush of panic. Something was wrong. She sounded afraid.

It's a fucking bear, I thought, imagining Faye standing face to face with a grizzly.

"What?" I whispered, zipping my fly and sneaking toward the sound of her voice. My heartbeat rattled my ribcage.

"Look," she said.

Faye stood a dozen yards ahead of me between two trees. Her hand was extended in front of her, pointing at something I couldn't see.

"What is it?" I whispered, still moving like a soldier behind enemy lines. I rounded a few trees and tried to make out what she was pointing at. Something odd came into view. A dangling, twirling thing.

I moved closer, pushing a few needled branches out of my way as I did. There was an ornament on the tree, just above Faye's head.

"The hell is that?" I said, almost laughing. Relief washed over me, alleviating the sudden terror that we'd bumped into a grizzly.

The thing was made of twigs and bones, expertly bent into strained and taut shapes. Pieces of ragged twine swung from it, some of them tied to hawk feathers. More string was woven through its center in the shape of a mangled spider web. It took a moment for me to figure out

23

what I was looking at, but eventually, I recognized the object.

"Is that...is that a fucking dreamcatcher?" I asked, more to myself than to Faye. She remained silent.

The structure was huge. Unlike the fragile little ones I'd seen in bedroom windows and on rear-view mirrors, this dreamcatcher was over two feet in diameter. Its construction looked frantic; the gnarled branches and twine held each other together in an unnatural, almost menacing way. Some of the feathers and bones had dried blood on them. I imagined a madman hurriedly assembling the thing, attempting to ward off the voices in his head.

"Who the hell put this here?" Faye said, causing me to jump. I was so bewitched by the object that I'd nearly forgotten she was there.

"I don't know," I replied, reaching up to touch it.

"Don't!" she yelled, slapping the back of my head. "Aren't you the one who loves horror movies? You're gonna get cursed or something, stupid."

"I wonder how long it's been here," I said.

"Someone was just here," Faye replied. "Look." She pointed to a set of footprints in the snow. They wrapped right around the tree that the dreamcatcher now dangled from.

I made a print with my own boot next to one of them. They were roughly the same size, but little detail could be seen in either of them.

"They might be mine," I said. "Earlier, when you were asleep."

"And you didn't notice this giant *thing* right next to your head?"

"I don't know – I mean it's possible I just walked right past it. I really don't know."

"Leave it alone, and let's get inside," Faye said, fear on the edge of her voice. "If you take it down, whoever put it here will know. That's probably what they want. To mess with us." She brushed past me and walked into the meadow.

Any relief I'd felt before now washed away in a torrent of dread. I suddenly believed Faye. I believed that someone was wandering around out here last night. Someone who had no business being out here in the freezing dark.

I glanced around the side of the tree to see Faye approaching our cabin in the distance. Whoever put this thing here had a clear view of the building. We'd never be able to see them back due to the shadow cover beneath the trees. Unnerved, I took one last look at the object and trudged off after Faye.

Chapter 3

That evening, Faye and I tried our best to ignore the strange ornament hanging a few hundred feet from the cabin. We agreed that it was probably old, and if someone had indeed put it up recently, it was probably just to scare us. Even so, Faye spent nearly twenty minutes trying to get enough signal on her phone to call the ranger's station at the foot of the mountain. When she finally did, a trooper named William Pike promised to swing by in the morning. He assured Faye that there was a popular hiking trail on the north side of Pale Peak, and that city teenagers would sometimes come up and torment visitors staying in the cabins.

That calmed our nerves a bit. We had a candle-lit dinner to the tune of relaxing world music thanks to Faye's laptop, then we broke out one of the several board games she insisted on bringing from her parents' house. A little smile crept across her face when she pulled out Scrabble. When we'd first met, while hanging out at a big gathering of our mutual friends, she won the game by laying down the letters for "denied" across my word "date."

Between songs, something bashed into the kitchen window. Faye rushed to silence her laptop as I went to inspect the glass. It was unbroken, and the impact sounded muffled, so I assumed the noise was caused by a wayward owl. Flashlight in hand, I headed outside to look for a dead bird in the snow – but found nothing. While closing the door, a faint voice called out from the woods. More snow was beginning to fall and the wind intermittently kicked up, so I couldn't be sure of what I heard. But it sounded like, "Why'd you go?" or "Where'd you go?" I stood there for a long time, listening carefully, but heard only the eerie howls of the wind. As it rushed and seeped through a million branches, it occasionally formed the sounds of a human voice. I shuddered and dismissed the idea that someone was out there.

We turned in early. I struggled to fall asleep, but eventually did, only to be shaken awake not ten minutes later by an agitated Faye.

"*Felix!*" she whispered, rattling my arm. "Get up! Someone's outside again."

My eyes shot open at her words. Without responding, I leaped out of bed and grabbed my pants. Faye sat up, holding the sheets defensively to her chest.

"He's walking around right out there." She pointed toward the front of the house. I held still, trying to listen for movement, but heard nothing.

"Are you sure you weren't dreaming?" I asked loudly, prompting her to shush me. I held still.

The crunching of snow broke our silence. Something was tromping around the side of the cabin, a few yards out. It circled the house, pausing briefly at the back door that led into our bedroom. The footsteps then continued back around toward the living room.

"Son of a bitch is casing the house," I whispered back, "trying to figure out how to get in."

I stormed out of the room and grabbed the flashlight. I threw the front door open and blasted the darkness with the light's brightest setting, only to find a thick blanket of snow gleaming up at me. Snowflakes washed through the air in tidal waves, obscuring my vision and giving cover to anyone who might be sneaking around out there. The footsteps I'd heard a moment ago vanished into the wind, and after a while, even the breeze receded into the night.

Not satisfied, I closed the door and scrambled around the cabin, pointing the light through each window. There was no sign of footprints or their maker anywhere. When I returned to the bedroom to check the back door, Faye was gazing out the window, motionless.

"You see something?" I asked. "I looked everywhere. Couldn't find anything."

She gave no indication that she'd even heard me.

"Faye?"

"Someone was out there," she said, turning toward me. Her voice was determined and sharp.

"Could have been a bear," I offered. I didn't really believe that, but the look on her face demanded reassurance. "They come up to houses and cars all the time when they smell food. I mean come on...nobody's out there playing practical jokes on a night like this."

"What is it with you lately?" she said. Her face set me back on my heels. "You don't believe anything I say. You're telling me that was an animal? Do you have ears? It was walking on *two fucking legs*, Felix. Some freak is coming to this cabin at night."

I sank down to the bed and looked up into Faye's eyes.

"I'm sorry, sweetheart," I said. "I'm not trying to make you feel crazy. I'm just not ready to accept that we're being stalked on a mountain six miles away from the nearest town. In a blizzard. The ranger will be here in the morning, okay? Then we'll get some answers."

Faye slipped into bed and turned her back to me. I touched her shoulder softly, but she shook me off.

"Someone was trying to look inside," she said with finality.

It took a long time to fall back asleep. Faye was restless and mumbled indecipherable things for hours. I lay there in the dark, trying to make sense of her incoherent ramblings and imagining the things she must have been dreaming. My thoughts became more abstract with the passage of time, and eventually they blended into dreams of my own.

I don't know how long I slept.

A cacophony of shrieks and sobs dragged me from my slumber. I fumbled for the light amidst Faye's deafening cries, wondering if someone had tried to get in through the door in our bedroom. When my hand found the light, its brightness silenced her. She covered her eyes, shaking all over. I immediately recognized her state. She'd had a nightmare. I grabbed onto her and squeezed tight, which was my standard remedy, and it usually worked.

"It's okay, baby. It's okay."

She sobbed into my chest, but eventually her breathing slowed.

"What was it?" I asked. "Do you want to talk about it?"

It took Faye a moment to get her bearings. She gazed around the room in confusion, shielding her eyes and pointing at the light. I turned it off.

Faye has an undiagnosed sleep disorder. She regularly talks in her sleep – usually funny things like sassing her coworkers – and sometimes sleepwalks. She even suffers from sporadic bouts of night terrors, which are a bit like nightmares, except the monsters and killers don't disappear when she opens her eyes. Instead, they spill into the room and remain very real for several moments,

29

causing her to freak out while she's awake. All of her sleep disturbances are triggered by stress. Things like job changes or money problems will send her into week-long episodes of terror.

Faye pulled herself away from me and leaned against the headboard. She wiped tears from her eyes.

"I was in the woods," she said, pointing a shaking finger at the window.

I caressed her other hand and nodded my attention.

"I was naked, just standing there watching. Someone was up ahead past the trees. He was digging in the snow really frantic. Digging down into the ground beneath. And he looked up and saw me watching him. Then I was running, trying to find my way back, and he was following me. But he didn't feel like a person. He felt empty. Like he didn't have a soul."

"Jesus," I said, squeezing her hand. "But you're okay. You're right here. You never left. It was just a dream."

Faye squeezed my hand back.

"I think he wanted to eat me," she said. She fiddled nervously with a tangle in her hair. "I could feel this terrible hunger that he had. Like he was hungry for a thousand years."

My stomach churned. Thoughts of the eerie dreamcatcher invaded my mind.

Chapter 4

It was Saturday now, and the morning was not nearly as jovial. Faye and I both awoke exhausted, and were dismayed to find the windows completely caked with ice. More than a foot of snow had dumped down on the mountain during the night, and plenty more was still coming as I opened the front door. The woods had disappeared, completely shrouded behind a wall of falling flakes. I could barely make out our poor rental car in the driveway.

There was something else out there too. A trail had been forged through the snow on the deck; it snaked around the side of the house. I reasoned that it must have been freshly made, given the rate of snowfall, and it was rapidly vanishing even now. Could it have been the ranger? I prayed that it was, but my gut told me that no one was coming to save us in this blizzard. The one road that led up here was an icy deathtrap with zero visibility. Only a crazy person would be outside right now. I winced at the thought and slammed the door shut.

Faye and I stayed inside with the heater on, trying to distract ourselves from the eerie hush that had descended upon the landscape. Our romantic cabin getaway wasn't going exactly as planned, but we still had each other, and I was hoping that was enough to salvage the rest of the trip.

"Do you remember the first time you had one?" I blurted out, breaking an hour-long silence. I fiddled with the router while Faye lay on the floor playing Super Nintendo.

"Had what," she said, distracted.

"You know. Night terrors."

The sounds of little monsters being knocked into a swamp issued from the TV.

"I was a little kid. The earliest one I remember was of my mom leading me down into our basement. My dad had a big entertainment center down there, so I was never allowed to go by myself. They thought I'd break it."

"Sounds rough," I interrupted. "I wish our house had stairs, growing up. In fact I wish we had a house."

Faye took her hand off the controller long enough to flip me a middle finger. We both laughed.

"The staircase was long," she continued. "At least in the dream. I don't remember if it really looked like that. But we fell down it, both my mom and me. As we fell, it got darker and darker. I woke up before we reached the bottom, but I remember seeing a face down there. A really scary one, looking up at me. Waiting for me. When I woke up, it was still there in the room, then slowly faded away."

"You're frickin' scary, you know that?" I said.

"You should see me when we're out of chocolate," she replied.

"What do you think causes them?"

"Night terrors?"

"Yeah. I mean for you. Why you? Why not your mom? Or Becca?"

"My dad had 'em," she said, pausing the game. I gave up my tinkering and slumped onto the couch. Faye joined me.

32

"He doesn't seem the type," I replied.

"Oh yeah. A couple times when I was a kid, I remember hearing him at night. He was a medic in the late '60's. I learned more about him while he was asleep than from talking with him for twenty-six years."

It made sense. Greg was absolutely grizzled, and had all the personality of stone. He seemed out of place in his big, beautiful house.

"Does it still happen for him?" I asked.

"No. It stopped a long time ago. They came all of a sudden and then disappeared shortly after. I guess I'm the lucky one."

"Hm."

Faye hammered away on the game, occasionally swearing under her breath. I had nearly fallen asleep next to her when a wail from outside startled us both. I sat up, listening. Faye had a thousand-yard stare on her face. When the voice cried out again, her brow furrowed in confusion.

"Hello?" it called. I scrambled to shut off the heater so we could hear better. "I give up, I give up. Please." The voice sounded distant, maybe a few hundred feet away from the cabin near the edge of the forest.

Faye jolted straight up from the couch and marched to the front door. She swung it open and stood there, ignoring the wind that battered her face and the snow that toppled onto her bare feet. The voice babbled at length, but was interrupted by gusts of wind. I couldn't make much of it out.

An equally strange noise erupted from Faye's mouth. It wasn't a gasp of fear, but rather one of anguish. It was the kind of sound you'd expect to hear from a family in an emergency room when the doctor approaches with an apologetic look on his face.

"It's grandpa," she said in a horrified voice. "That's my

33

grandpa."

"What? What do you mean?"

"It's him, Felix!" she shouted, clutching the open door's knob like she was going to rip it off. "He's out there! I hear him calling."

I had no idea how to respond to that. It was impossible. I approached Faye and held her from behind, listening to the voice as it sailed into the cabin on violent bursts of wind.

"Where is everyone?" the man called out. Fear and misery hung on his words. "Please, please, I'm lost!"

"Grandpa!" Faye shrieked into the blizzard. "We're over here! I'm coming!" She tried to tear away from me and dart off into the snow. I yanked her back and wrestled her into the house, screaming for her to calm down. I tried to tell her that it wasn't her grandfather, but she fought and screamed.

"Get off me!" She raked and clawed at me like a tiger. "Let me go! Grandpa!"

I managed to kick the door shut with my foot, forfeiting my balance in the process. We toppled to the floor as one, crashing into the bags we'd left in the entryway. I held Faye like a living straightjacket until she finally went limp. She burst into tears.

"What the fuck is going on?" she asked, sobbing. I knew she didn't expect an answer.

I had only met Faye's grandfather once, at her sister's wedding a few years ago. Alfred was a charming old man who loved cigars and muscle cars. We knew virtually nothing about him because he worked high up in the government and never talked about his life, but he was very open about how much he loved his granddaughters. After the reception, he asked me if I was thinking about becoming a member of the family. I told him I couldn't

34

imagine my life with anyone else, and said that my mother was very fond of Faye. This seemed to really score points with him, and he jokingly told me he'd vouch for me. I tried to joke back and said something along the lines of, "Well, if I'm going to be in the clan, there's something I've got to know. I've always wondered about Area 51." Alfred took a long drag on his cigar without taking his eyes off me, and his face became totally void of expression. Through a noxious cloud of smoke, he breathed, "What's Area 51?"

Alfred dropped dead of a heart attack not three weeks after the wedding, and the news of his passing broke everyone's heart. It horrified me to admit that the voice outside the cabin sounded just like him. But unlike Faye, I wasn't willing to risk my life to go outside and rescue someone that I knew to be dead. I kept my eye on Faye as she rested in bed, sipping hot chocolate and shivering with disquiet. A movie played on her laptop, but she ignored it. The experience had shaken her up badly, and now I watched her torturous effort to reconcile the voice she heard with the knowledge that her grandfather was long dead. With each passing second I had the morbid expectation that the voice would cry out again and send Faye into another explosion, but thankfully it never happened.

"It was him," she'd assert every few minutes. "I know his voice. I know it was him."

I alternated between trying to call the ranger station and trying to get online to email them, but both attempts failed. At long last, just as the sky darkened to thrust another terrifying night upon us, I went out to check on the car. In case these odd experiences came to a head, I wanted to be sure that we had an exit plan – even if it was a dangerous one.

Outside, it was colder than anything I had ever experienced in my life. It was early spring, and Faye's

35

parents had assured us that the worst of the snow had passed. But standing there on the porch looking out at the landscape, I felt a ghastly chill even through my winter gear. The cold brought with it the silence of death; not a single animal made so much as a peep for miles. Only the air itself made sounds as it whipped across the valleys and sprayed bits of ice at me.

The car was a popsicle. A two-inch layer of ice glazed its windshields, and icicles hung like jagged teeth down to the tires.

What's the freezing point of gasoline? I wondered.

Even worse, I couldn't make out the road at the end of the driveway; everything was obscured under a blanket of pure white. In this blizzard I wouldn't even be able to see the guardrail that would keep us from plunging to our deaths. There was no way a ranger had made his way up here this morning, and there was no way we were getting off the mountain. At least not tonight.

As I stood there reforming the exit plan, I heard a woman talking. She wasn't far away at all, and seemed to be in a good mood.

"*Oh stahp! Stahp it!*" She said in a thick Bostonian accent. She laughed my mother's laugh. "Look there. Look at the windows!"

My brain instantly cramped. I could almost *hear* the blood waterfalling out of my head. A freezing feeling replaced it, followed by the sensation of all the muscles in my legs clenching up.

"H—Hello?" I said. The word died just outside my mouth. "Hello?" I tried again, louder.

"You are too!" she replied. "Did you see it? Up in the trees!"

I managed to regain command over my legs and circled the car, edging closer to the source of the voice.

"Mom?" I asked, unable to believe what I was hearing.

36

Unlike Alfred, my mother was alive and well – two thousand miles away in Massachusetts.

The woman unleashed a string of phrases, laughing hysterically. She dipped into a language I had never heard before, then resumed speaking in English. I couldn't make most of it out, but it almost sounded like things she'd say at a dinner party.

"They're on their way!" she yelled. Her voice receded further into the distance. I took a few more steps toward it, calling out again. She always responded, but never directly replied to my questions.

Suddenly, I got the feeling that I was being coaxed into the woods.

I turned on my heels and dashed back to the cabin. The little thing seemed too far away; its warm glowing windows felt like lights disappearing at the end of a tunnel.

"Down in the hole!" the voice shrieked behind me. "Put him down there!" A flurry of incomprehensible babble followed. A lightning bolt of fear struck me, giving me the turbo-boost I needed to practically dive into the cabin.

When I was sixteen years old, I smoked pot for the first time in my buddy's garage – and had a full-blown panic attack. That event seemed to unlock a hidden trove of anxiety buried deep within me, and the attacks continued for months afterward. Eventually I visited a doctor, who referred me to a therapist, and together we developed coping strategies that helped me avert the attacks and deal with my anxiety before it pressurized and exploded. By the time I was twenty-two, I had my demons under control, and the panic attacks disappeared. I was even able to get stoned like a normal college kid.

But standing there in the living room of the cabin, listening to the impossible voices outside, revealed to me that I had not at all learned to cope with my anxiety in a healthy way. I had simply learned to bury it deeper, and now, all of those demons came rushing up to the surface. I collapsed to the floor and sobbed. My entire body shook. All my muscles turned to stone. Wave after wave of nausea pounded the back of my throat. I tried to remain silent so as not to disturb Faye's rest, but I knew now that there was something far worse on this mountain than pranksters or Peeping Toms.

I resolved to stay awake all night long, to protect my partner and to prove to myself that I wasn't losing my mind.

Chapter 5

Faye passed out around 9 P.M., leaving me alone with my thoughts and the horrible noises outside. Snow crunched, twigs snapped, trees creaked, and other things went bump in the night. For each unidentifiable sound I heard, my mind invented a grotesque creature to cause it. I tried to keep myself busy at the kitchen table with grading and student evaluations, but my thoughts never converged on the task at hand. Instead they wandered out the windows of the cabin, through the meadow, and into the mysterious woods. My desperation to leave Pale Peak was only matched by my desire to know who or what was out there lurking around in the dark.

I filled up on oven-baked pizza and soda, plotting to remain caffeinated and cheesed for the remainder of the night. Just after midnight, nature called, and I crept to the bathroom so as not to wake Faye. I poked my head in as I passed by, and was relieved to find her sleeping soundly under a pile of blankets. The door beside her was sealed and locked. The curtains were drawn. A glimmer of moonlight pierced them and lit up the room just enough to act as a nightlight.

While standing at the toilet, I gazed out the window beside me. The sky had cleared a bit, revealing a thousand glittering stars. My eyes scanned the tree line, which was just barely visible, and my brain parsed the significance of our experiences up here on the mountain. What did it mean that both Faye and I had recognized the voices outside as those of our relatives? Were we having some kind of shared hallucination? The possibility of radon poisoning crossed my mind; many old buildings in the mountains were susceptible to toxic gases that seeped out of the ground. Did the dreamcatcher have some relationship to the sounds we'd heard? Was there some weird cult operating up here? As a skeptic, I didn't believe in ghosts or curses or literal "evil," but those explanations were now a lot more sensible to me than anything else I could think up.

Something moved outside.

Just past the first row of trees, something moved slowly, purposefully, like a person looking back at me and slinking through the forest.

A muffled voice rang out. I couldn't discern the words, but it sounded desperate.

I slid the window open just an inch and put my ear beside it. The freezing air that seeped in felt like a death sentence. There was no way anyone could survive out there tonight without some serious, military-grade winter gear.

A burst of cackling laughter erupted from nearby. It was a woman's voice, but not one I recognized. She sounded elderly – and angry. Her laughter came out dry and condescending.

"Where is it?" she demanded.

I shut off the light in the bathroom, hoping to make out the shape of a person by the trees, but the moonlight was too faint.

"Is there…forget…his name?" Some of the words were lost before they ever reached the window, but I could make some of it out.

Then, another voice spoke. This one was much closer, maybe right beside the cabin – and it was familiar.

"Not mine. Not mine. Just a few days."

My heart raced. I cycled through the faces of relatives and friends in my mind. It was a young woman.

"Mom and Dad's."

I fell back from the window and caught myself against the sink. My body went cold. It was Faye. For a moment I feared she was outside, but when she spoke again I realized her voice was echoing from behind me. I moved through the hall and pushed the bedroom door open.

Faye was still in bed, asleep on her tummy as usual. She hadn't moved an inch.

"Why…" she asked, drunk with lethargy. "Whose name?"

The woman outside cackled again, and muttered something I couldn't make out.

Faye responded, "But I don't know. Yes, yes, With me."

Every inch of my skin crawled. Someone was outside, having a conversation with my fiancée in her sleep. Drilling her for information. Asking for my name.

I wanted to scream but I couldn't. The insanity of it all, the incomprehensibility, numbed my brain. All I could do was fall heavily onto the bed and shake Faye awake. Just as I did, she altered the pitch and tone of her voice, imitating someone else entirely.

"Don't let them in," she said. The sounds were otherworldly; they did not belong to her. They could not even have been formed by her vocal cords. "Don't let him in."

A scream finally burst from my mouth, bringing her back into consciousness.

41

"What...what's going on?" she asked. Faye instinctively retreated from me, as she had many times when coming out of a nightmare. If ever I wake her up instead of allowing her to come out of a dream or a night terror on her own, I risk becoming a part of it. From her perspective, waking up to a dark figure sitting in front of her, reaching toward her, is horrifying.

Normally I'd have reassured her and said, "It's just me, sweetie, it's just me" and rubbed her arms. But what Faye had just done was something totally beyond her normal behavior. "What the fuck is wrong with you?" is all I could blurt out.

It took some explaining, but eventually Faye realized what she'd been doing.

"Who were you talking to?" I pressed. "It's important."

"I don't know, Felix," she replied, rubbing her face. Her hands were shaking.

"What was she asking you?"

Faye looked to the window, then into my eyes. It was so dark I could barely make out her features.

"I don't know. I don't remember anything."

I grabbed her hands.

"Try, Faye. I need you to try."

She swatted my hands away and distanced herself from me.

"*I don't know.*"

We argued a bit. Faye struggled to believe what I'd heard, and it took me a while to realize that she wasn't doubting me. She was trying to block out the possibility that something supernatural was happening. Faye was raised Catholic, and although she only attended mass around the holidays with her folks, she still retained a strong belief in the existence of bad spirits. To her, there was another world behind ours, obscured only by the veil of death. Right now, outside, something seemed to be piercing that veil and calling out to us.

"This place is haunted," she said, more of an admission to herself. "We need to leave. We need to get into the car and just drive. Right now."

I tried to explain why that was impossible, but her expression turned to that of a cornered animal. Faye was scared to death, and she wasn't going to be able to take much more of this mountain and its strange inhabitants.

Just as I went to hold her, a new sound interrupted our conversation. It was one we did not expect. Both of us froze there on the bed, listening intently. It was another voice, weak but melodious, somewhere near the front of the house. Faye stood up first and followed the sounds into the gloomy hallway. I followed close behind.

We stood there in the living room for a moment until she gasped in realization.

It was a child, singing in the dark.

I tried to make out the words, but much of what we heard was in some strange language.

"Ahhh soul me ah do, soul me ah do, I'm a naked soul me ahhh dooo…"

Faye cursed and swore, terrified and outraged and trapped on a frozen mountain with the songs of Hell emanating from the woods. She stormed up to the kitchen window and threw the drapes open, searching for the kid.

"Oh Jesus," she said, clasping her hands to her mouth.

I ran over and gazed out the window from behind her.

Standing there, about two hundred feet out, was the dark form of a person. It was an adult man, devoid of detail in the shadow of the woods. He stood just outside the tree line with his back facing the cabin. He appeared to be gazing up at the tops of the trees, and never moved.

"What the hell is that?" Faye breathed. She still clasped her mouth in horror, trying to avert a scream.

This was the first moment at the cabin that I felt we were truly in danger. My senses sharpened into razors. My brain shut down all complex tasks and diverted full power to a primal survival mode. I grabbed Faye and dragged her down to the floor.

The unseen child sang louder. He recited common nursery rhymes, but his pitch wavered off-key like a melting record player. He stuttered and mispronounced many of the words, but not in the way a person might if he were practicing English. It was as if this boy were learning how to speak altogether. It almost sounded like a computer program mimicking a child's voice. Every few seconds he'd burst into hysterical laughter, or begin humming a particular refrain over and over. Sometimes he'd blurt a random string of nonsense, like *"Pile up the twigs, gather the lambs, tie up the hogs, burn up the hags"* and then continue singing.

Faye crawled away to the bedroom, then returned with her cell phone. After a few tries, there was a faint ringing against her ear.

"Dad." Faye swallowed hard, holding back tears. She sniffled and cleared her throat. "Daddy, when you get this, please, please come pick us up. We need help. As soon as you get this, get in the truck. Come get us right now. Don't wait."

The boy called out again.

"When do we go insiiiide? When do we go insiiiide?"

I flicked on the front porch lights and then headed to the back door in our bedroom, hoping to discourage anyone from approaching the cabin. As I hit the switch for the back porch, the distinct silhouette of a person glowed through the window curtain. It looked like a woman. She pressed herself against the glass with her hands cupped around her face, trying to peer inside. I approached the window, but the person ran off before I could yank the curtain open.

"He's still out there," Faye said from the kitchen. "He's just *standing* there."

Chapter 6

Faye and I spent the remainder of the night hiding in the bathroom with the lights on. She huddled in the tub with blankets while I sat against the door, clutching the dusty magnum her father had left on a shelf in the closet. I had never fired a gun before, but just having it with us brought me some sense of control over the situation.

Faye was a talented artist, and always had a sketch pad and graphite pencils somewhere nearby. Her busy work life had dulled those skills this past year, so she intended to sharpen them on this trip. But instead of filling the book with Colorado mountainscapes, she now jotted down the voices we heard and sketched the man we saw. By dawn, her notes read as follows:

Adult man's voice:
"Hello? Oooooh God, look at it! Look look!"
"Don't. Don't. They see in the dark."
"I'm...I'm lost. I'm lost. Show me the way." (could also be "throw me away")
"Wachu, wachu, wachu, wole my...wole my..." (guttural, growling)
"It's dark out here. I see those lights! Yeah, I see 'em!"

"I'll come down there! Don't think I won't!"
"Don't smile. Don't smile. He'll see you."

Teenage girl's voice:
"The goats led me here." (could also be ghosts?)
"Lay it on the ground...and burn it." (laughing)
"I can't feel my fingers anymore...I can't climb up." (crying)
"Ooooh! She talks in her sleep! Did you hear? I found a friend."
"Lalalala....lalalalala..." (flat and monotone)

Child's voice:
"Eat eat eat!"
"Soul me aaahh dooo...souuul me aaaahh doooo..."
"Don't tell him your secrets. He found mine." (crying/whining)
"Rooock-a-bye baaaaby...iiiin the tree top..."
"How do we get in there?"

Grandpa Alfred's voice:
"There's bodies still in the ground there. Never found 'em. But they're there." (laughing)
"Right here. Right here. Ooooh they found it. Theeeey fooouuund iiiiiit."
"Ah, I'm always standing in the same goddamn place. Twenty years! You believe that?"
"Dig 'em up an' burn 'em. All you can do. It's what a sane man would do."

The chattering would disappear for hours, then start back up again. By dawn on Sunday, I was at the end of my rope. I hadn't slept well since we'd arrived at the cabin, and my insides were all knotted up with stress. Faye was even worse. Her face had paled from hours of dread, and she

47

gazed around listlessly with bloodshot eyes. She anxiously twisted the engagement ring around her finger and never looked at me. As soon as the sunlight poked through the bathroom curtains, I checked the house and encouraged Faye to get some sleep before she cracked. I ran my fingers through her hair as we lay on the bed, promising that I'd keep her safe. She forced a little smile. We fell asleep holding each other.

It was after 2 P.M. when I woke up. Dazed, I snuck out of bed and went outside to see if Faye's dad or the rangers had come up the mountain. My heart sank at the view of the undisturbed road; no one had even tried to check on us.

There was evidence of last night's strange activity outside. Dozens of tracks cut through the snow. They all meandered erratically. Some zigzagged to and fro as if made by a drunk person, while others appeared to have been made by someone making enormous leaps across the field. Two pairs of tracks circled the cabin five or six times, then separated and re-entered the woods in different places. One set of footprints moved in a straight line from the trees to the place I stood on the porch, and never turned around.

I had the thought to go out to the edge of the property to see if that dreamcatcher was still there, but the forest seemed a thousand miles away now. I was worried that if I entered it, I'd never come out alive. Moreover, a part of me was too afraid to even look at the strange object. At Faye's behest, neither of us had touched it, and yet I now wondered if simply being near the thing had put us in danger.

Back inside, Faye slept deeply in a bright pool of sunlight. The clouds had vanished, leaving a crystal blue sky that promised better cell reception. I kept the bedroom door cracked so that I would hear her if she began talking in her sleep again, then grabbed the phone. Faye's dad didn't answer, but someone at the ranger's station did.

"Rocky Mountain National Park Service," an older man grumbled, "Pike speaking."

"William, this is Felix, up here at the Spencer cabin—"

"Oh, hey there," he interrupted, "you folks alright? Hey we tried to get up there yesterday but the ice—"

"I need you to come up here *right now*," I said, walking out onto the porch to avoid waking Faye. "Get a damn snowplow or whatever you need, and get up here."

"Everything okay?" he asked, taken aback. "Y'all need medical? I can call the hospital down in Orchid Valley. 'Em boys got a helicopter."

"Nobody's hurt. Not yet. There's somebody up here on the mountain with us. Walking around in the woods at night, tapping on our windows, calling out to us. We want out. Right now. We've waited long enough."

The ranger paused for a moment. His tone noticeably changed.

"We got a snowcat on the fritz, but it's gettin' worked on as we speak. Had to take it to the north face to go get some dumb-shit nature photographers lost in 'em woods. Main center across the valley's got the big 'cats though. I can call 'em if you think it's an emergency and they'll come out pronto."

I took a deep breath and sighed in disappointment. A huge cloud formed as I exhaled.

"It's...it's not exactly, I mean, I don't know what these creeps want. Seems like they're screwing with us, but we really feel in danger."

"Tell you what," the ranger said, "I'll call 'em up there by sundown if we don't get ol' Crunchy up and runnin' beforehand. How's your power?"

"Good."

"And your water?"

"Fine."

"Heat?"

"Yeah." I booted a clump of ice off the porch and watched it roll into the snow.

"Just make sure you kids—"

I waited for him to finish his sentence, but it never came.

"Hello?" I said, taking a few steps into the driveway. "William?"

The call had dropped. I didn't bother trying again.

Dusk fell rapidly. The sun dipped behind the mountain across from Pale Peak around 4 P.M., and I began to dread another night trapped in this god-forsaken cottage. I mulled the idea of suiting ourselves up in our winter gear and hiking down the road before dark, but I shook the thought out of my mind. It would have been suicide to miscalculate the trek or the light. And who knew what was really lurking around in the forests that covered the mountain? We had to stay put.

Faye eventually woke up and complained about a stomach ache, turning down the sandwiches I'd made. Instead, I heated a bowl of soup for her, but she ran to the bathroom and vomited it back up after a few minutes. Her forehead was cool to the touch, so I figured she was just stressing herself out. We watched one of the many movies saved on her laptop. Eventually, she fell asleep again, leaving me alone to watch the last glimmers of twilight die to black.

I sat at the kitchen table and forced myself to grade a stack of papers that were due the day we returned to California. Perhaps it was the flicker of the candles still burning from my lonely dinner, or the soft music seeping Faye's laptop, but there came a wash of heavy relaxation that compelled me to lie down on the couch. I committed to resting my eyes for only a few minutes, but soon disappeared into dreams of brighter places.

A ticking sound woke me up. For a moment I froze there on my back, struggling to put an image to the noise. Something caught my eye out the nearby window. A faint light pierced between the edge of the curtain and the wall, illuminating the mud mat near the front door. The beam went on and off in patterns of five. My stomach leaped into my throat as horrifying thoughts flooded my mind. I imagined some kind of creature standing in the darkness of the cabin, flipping the porch light switch up and down with a menacing grin on its face.

The moment I got up, the lights flickered five more times and went dark. I peeked out the curtain near the front door and didn't spot anyone. As I stared into the darkness, a groan erupted from far off in the distance. My first instinct was to check on Faye to ensure that she wasn't talking in her sleep again. I wondered if she somehow attracted the voices by calling out in her slumber, and if she drew attention to herself with her babbling. The thought sent ripples of goosebumps across my arms as I made my way down the hall.

"Faye?" I whispered, creaking the door open just enough to peer in.

The bed was empty.

I shoved the door open and looked around, finding only a vacant room. The sheets had been tossed off the side of the bed, as though she'd been dragged off in her sleep. I ran to the old door that led outside from that room and tugged on it, but the deadbolt was secured.

Faye was an accomplished sleepwalker and had been doing it all her life. During the five-year span of our relationship, I had seen her descend stairs, open boxes, and try to operate her cell phone while unconscious. She was even capable of having semi-coherent conversations while milling around the house. On one such occasion, I heard a noise downstairs and went to investigate. I found Faye opening cabinets, taking things out of the refrigerator, and searching for her car keys. We chatted a bit about how she was late for work and how she hated her manager. To the uninitiated, Faye might have seemed totally cognizant of her actions. If not for the fact that she was completely nude and trying to heat up a couch pillow for breakfast in total darkness, even I might have been fooled. But I knew what she was capable of, and I knew that stress was the catalyst.

It wouldn't be too far a stretch for Faye to sleepwalk right out of the cabin and lock the door behind her. I ran out onto the porch and was met with the stinging winter breeze, but didn't see any tracks in the snow.

"Faye?" I called out, just loud enough for her to hear me if she was nearby. I didn't want to risk our creepy forest friends realizing I was outside.

There was no response. I ran back into the cabin and out the front door where the porch light had been flickering. I suddenly realized that it might have been Faye toggling the switch. Simple, repetitive actions like turning on lights are a common behavior of sleepwalkers.

The icy wood of the deck seared my bare feet. There was no one out here.

"Faye?" I called out again. Panic surged through me when I didn't hear a response. Branches crackled in the woods across the street. My eyes searched for the source of the noise, and they landed on the rental car in the driveway.

Something shifted near it.

I squinted through the gloom and made out a figure sitting atop the roof of the car.

"Who's there?!" I shouted.

It was a woman. She was naked, and her back was turned to me. Long, curly hair draped halfway down her back, and although it was silver in the pale moonlight, I immediately recognized it.

"Faye?"

She didn't reply, but one of her shoulders dropped and the other raised. She cocked her head back as if to gaze at the stars, then looked down again. All of her muscles flexed, no doubt a reaction to the biting cold.

"What the fuck are you doing out here?!" I yelled, confounded that she had slipped past me. It suddenly felt like someone had tightened a belt around my chest. I thought I'd drop dead of a heart attack right there on the porch.

Again, she didn't respond. I turned to quickly grab my boots just inside the door, but as I did, Faye leaped off the car and dashed away from the cabin. She bounded through the snow toward the forest, limping as she did.

"Faye!" I screamed. My voice shook the entire mountain and returned to me a dozen times. I dropped the boots and took off after her, instantly cursing the electric cold that sliced into my feet like razors. Faye had already made it to the tree line, and the darkness swallowed her whole as she entered the woods. A terrible dread replaced my surprise. I knew then that she'd freeze to death before I ever found her in there. Her only hope for survival was to wake up.

"What are you doing?" a weak voice called out from behind.

I slid to a stop just past the car and whirled around.

It was Faye. She stood there in the doorway of the cabin, wrapped in heavy blankets. Her eyes drooped under the weight of exhaustion and illness.

I looked back at the woods, then again to the cabin. The stupefied puzzlement on my face further confused her.

"Felix," she repeated, "what are you doing?"

It took me a long moment there in the driveway to gather my wits. The sensation of cold vanished from my limbs, replaced with a numbness I could ignore. The realization dawned on me that I was being drawn out like a rabbit from the undergrowth. I stood motionless, staring out into the dark forest. I couldn't help but feel like it was staring back.

"Clever motherfuckers," I said breathlessly.

Chapter 7

In my masculine crusade to protect her, I had forgotten to check the one place a sick Faye was most likely to be: the bathroom. I wanted to lie to her and tell her that I'd chased some elk away from the car, but instead I spilled my guts. My wide-eyed tale seemed to compound the misery of her stomach bug, and she lay there on the bed with a pillow over her face, begging me to get us out of the cabin once and for all.

As if to answer her prayers, the unmistakable crunch and clank of a snowplow resounded from outside. She took heart at the sound and quickly threw on a jacket. I raced around, gathering our things and peeking out the window.

It was just before dawn on Monday morning, and Ranger Pike had finally arrived. Behind him was a cavalcade of happy sights: a police SUV and Faye's father Greg in his old pickup.

I threw the door open as the men approached the porch.

"I'm so sorry 'bout how long it took," the ranger said, offering up his hands. A bushy brown mustache clung to his face and accentuated every movement of his lips.

"Right on time, actually," I responded.

"Where's Faye?" Greg said, stepping between me and the ranger. He was a bear of a man, a few inches taller than me with a chest you could chop wood on. His chin looked like a brick, and on it grew a gray and perpetual five-o-clock shadow – probably for striking matches.

"Dad!" Faye called out from behind me. She rushed over and threw her arms around him.

"Christ, sweetie," he said into her shoulder, "are you okay? What happened?"

Faye and I exchanged knowing glances, and when I opened my mouth to explain, she cut me off and said, "Long story. We'll talk in the car. Let's go."

"We need to keep her warm," I said, holding my hand toward the truck in a 'please get in' gesture. "I'll grab a blanket."

"And maybe some trash bags," Faye added.

"Young miss need a doctor?" the ranger asked. He shifted his bulk into the path of the plow's headlights, throwing a gigantic shadow over the snowy meadow.

"Just ate some of Felix's fancy cuisine," she replied, clutching her stomach. Everyone laughed except me.

Greg ushered Faye back to the truck while the ranger and I collected handfuls of half-packed luggage. While inside the cabin, he asked me what was really going on. I took only a moment to elaborate on what I'd said over the phone: there was a weird object dangling in the nearby tree, and a lot of movement and voices in the woods, some in a strange language. On at least one occasion, someone approached the windows. I left out the little detail of the woman sitting on top of my car. As I rifled through the room, throwing clothes into a suitcase, the ranger sat down on the bed.

"There's been some...activity reported up here," he muttered. "Weird shit. I dunno." He seemed almost apologetic, and I realized he had deceived me by assuring us over the phone that it was pranksters causing all the mischief.

"Weird shit?" I echoed, halting my rampage through the closet.

"Well, nothin' real serious," he offered.

"Go on."

"I mean... it's a mountain," William said. "People gone missin' up here. Some of 'em end up dead. Hikers say they hear things out there from time to time. Occasionally folks stayin' up here call us up, tellin' they heard all kindsa hubbub in the wee hours."

"Hubbub," I said, hurling a shirt into the suitcase.

"Ain't nobody ever been murdered up here, Mr. Blackwell," William replied, smiling and ticking a thumb on his badge. "Not since I been here. Damn sure of it."

I circled the bed and approached him.

"You ever had a doppelganger of your wife try to coax you into the woods by sitting naked in your driveway?" I asked.

William gazed up at me, completely lost. I grabbed the suitcase and left the room.

Outside, the two officers from the SUV were on either side of Greg's pickup, speaking to Faye and her dad. The red lights from the trucks cast across the snow, making for a surreal view in the twilight.

"Mr. Blackwell," one of the policemen called out, "you ride with your family. Officer Kennedy here's gonna follow you in your rental."

"Be careful," I said, tossing the keys to the officer. "That thing's a death trap."

"One more trip and we'll be ready," William called out. He carried two bags out of the cabin and stuck them in the plow.

"Ranger Pike, you lead," the officer replied.

The ride down the mountain was enormously relieving, and so beautiful that all our dark experiences momentarily vanished from my mind. I took the back seat so Faye could be next to her dad. Greg sat at the wheel, grumbling about the icy roads from time to time. I didn't mind the slow journey as much as he did. At least we were getting the hell away from Pale Peak.

Surprisingly, Greg didn't ask much about the cabin. Instead, he kept the conversation on us. In his usual leathery voice, he asked, "So Felix, you tried to kill my youngest child?"

I huffed in shock. I had no idea what he meant until Faye intervened. I thought he was talking about this little vacation.

"He's raggin' on your cooking, babe," she said, exhaling slowly in pain.

"Oh, right," I laughed. "Normally your daughter's like a trash compactor. Eats whatever the hell she wants and still looks like a twig. Probably made a deal with the devil for that talent." I tickled Faye's side, but she winced and protected her stomach.

"Not even Satan can protect me from your tacos," she moaned, rolling the window down. I instinctively jammed my fingers into my ears and ducked for cover behind Greg's seat. I'm a lifelong emetophobe, and cannot stand to be near someone vomiting – or even the sounds of it. Faye, in all of her good nature and selflessness, kept that in mind as she puked her guts up into the freezing mountain air that swooshed by. She tried to keep quiet so as not to freak me out. Afterwards, I rubbed her shoulders in support and thanks. Through the rear-view mirror, Greg shot a disapproving glance at my cowardice.

"We left a bunch of stuff," Faye said in a weak voice.

"I didn't get all my clothes. None of the groceries."

"I think I got most of your stuff," I offered. "Didn't open every drawer, though."

"We can buy you new clothes," Greg added. "Just forget about that stuff."

The purplish gloom in the sky gave way to deep reds and oranges, the first heralds of dawn's brilliant crest. The sunrise chased out the darkness and glinted off the snow in a million places, bringing the entire landscape to life once more. My relief swelled with the growing light. The snowcat in front of us picked up speed a bit, sending plumes of white powder into the air and over the cliff. They glittered like diamonds as they fell.

"So Greg," I said, once more trying to redirect the conversation to him, "when was the last time you stayed up here?"

He snorted and adjusted his grip on the wheel.

"'Bout uh, a decade or more."

I waited for him to elaborate, but he didn't.

"Why so long without visiting?"

"Never liked the cold. Metal in my knee and arm."

"Ah," I said, "why not in the summers?"

Faye stuck her head out the window again, this time unleashing a horrible sound. I was too late to cover my ears, and Greg seemed happy with the disruption.

"Seem to be gettin' worse," he said, rubbing her arm. "Should take you to the hospital back home."

Faye covered her face in embarrassment.

"At least Felix didn't make chili," she replied. "That always comes out the other end."

They both laughed. I didn't.

PART II

Chapter 8

Avonwood is a lily-white suburb about thirty minutes outside the Rockies. Tucked safely within it is the home Faye and her older sister grew up in, a place that is now too big for her aging parents. We got there after a visit to the ER; the doctor ran a few tests and deemed Faye's condition to be the result of extreme stress – not food poisoning, as she had jokingly insisted during the lulls of her nausea.

That night, the four of us sat around in the huge living room. We propped Faye up hospital-style on the couch with pillows and blankets. Greg was sprawled out in his three-thousand-dollar recliner. A relaxing fire crackled nearby. Faye had managed to keep down some soup, only after being repeatedly assured that I had no hand in its preparation. After the three of them grew tired of mocking me, the conversation became more serious. Lynn, Faye's mom, was horrified at the stories we recounted of our trip. Greg barely showed any emotion at all.

"Did you guys ever experience anything weird up there?" Faye asked, point-blank. "I mean, there must be a reason you haven't been in years."

Initially, Lynn avoided answering, but Faye cornered her mother with direct questions and eventually she caved.

"I was just never comfortable up there," she replied. "I'd heard a few things and that was it for me. Nothing ever happened, not like what you're telling us."

"What do you mean, heard?" I asked. "Heard stories from other people? Or you heard things outside?"

I watched Lynn's eyes closely. They darted all around but never at me. She glanced quickly at her husband, who cleared his throat and removed his reading glasses.

"Bed time for me," he said. "Sorry kids, you woke my old ass up too early."

Greg kissed Faye on the forehead and then abruptly retired for the night, leaving the three of us alone downstairs.

"I'm so glad he was able to get up that road," Lynn replied with a smile, trying to change the subject.

Faye sat up with a grunt and cast her impatient eyes onto Lynn.

"*Mom.*"

"It was nothing," her mother whispered. She set down the mug of hot chocolate she held and wrapped herself tighter in a blanket. "Just, you know. Creepy things about the place. That's all."

After a few more minutes of our prodding, Lynn became visibly upset. Tears welled in her eyes, and a look of guilt swept over her face. She kept picking at her fingernails and apologizing to us, swearing she never thought anything bad would happen. Then, out came a story that horrified us.

Nearly thirty years ago, in the youth of their marriage, Faye's parents bought the cabin from some old friends. Those folks were named Jennifer and Tom, and they lived in Orchid Valley, deep within the Colorado Rockies. When their daughter died in childhood of leukemia, they couldn't bear to live in the same house anymore. The couple bought land on nearby Pale Peak and built a cabin.

Tom was a big outdoorsman, and was especially fond of the mountain for its solitude and its astonishing views of the Rockies. He collected arrowheads and all sorts of historical relics he found on his hikes, and made friends with all the locals. He seemed to be healing from the loss of his only child.

But after a while, Jennifer began complaining to Tom about weird experiences in the cabin. She suffered recurring dreams of her husband being dragged out of the bedroom and off into the woods at night. The dreams grew more bizarre and horrific with time, until she began to question her own sanity. Eventually, Jennifer's nightmares culminated with her walking barefoot into the woods, where she'd find Tom's flayed body pinned up in the trees like some macabre work of art. The dreams led to insomnia and a fear of sleep, which exacerbated the depression she already bore.

Then things got worse. Sometimes when Tom was at work in the valley, Jennifer would hear her daughter calling out to her from the edge of the forest. The voice terrified Jennifer and slowly drove her mad, until she suffered a breakdown and begged her husband to leave. He resisted for a while and the psychiatrists changed Jennifer's medication several times, but nothing stopped the horrible dreams or the voice outside. Tom finally requested a transfer to Las Vegas, and the couple hastily sold the cabin, never to return. Two years later, he unceremoniously hanged himself in their garage. He never left a note.

Faye and I were shocked to hear such a dark history of the little place. The grim tale had me momentarily doubting my conviction that ghosts did not exist, and Faye reacted with unmitigated anger toward her mother.

"How the hell could you send us to a place like that?" she hissed, trying to keep her voice down.

Lynn cowered in her seat.

"Honey...We stayed there many times over the years. It was our vacation house for a long time. And I never experienced *anything* like that. No voices, no dreams, nothing. If I didn't think it was safe, there's no way I would send you up there."

Faye's glare did not relent. Her mother pressed on with her defense.

"Jennifer and Tom were dealing with the death of their child, sweetheart. Of course weird things happened to them. It's a traumatic experience. It can drive you crazy. There aren't any ghosts on that mountain. Just the painful memories that people carry around with them."

"Then why did you never feel comfortable there?" Faye asked.

Lynn shrugged.

"Once you know the story, it's just...a little creepy, I guess. You're always expecting something to happen."

"But you guys bought the place knowing that story?" Faye replied.

"No. No. We didn't know for a long time. Tom and Jen never even told us. We had to find out from the locals."

"What about Greg?" I asked, trying to cut Faye off before she could chastise her mother any further.

Lynn sighed and slouched deeper into the ludicrously cushy sofa. I was almost angrier at the decadence of their home than their decision to send us to Pale Peak.

"Your father doesn't like it there either," she replied, looking directly at Faye. "Remember when you were little, and dad was talking in his sleep a lot?"

"Yes."

"Well, it kind of started up there at the cabin," Lynn said. She dropped her gaze to her lap.

The admission reignited the fire in Faye's eyes.

"Just like Jennifer," she said angrily.

"No. Not like that. Your dad always had nightmares

before you were born. But his were gone for a long, long time, and came back on the mountain for some reason. I always say it's because he confronted Tom about what we learned. It just... *affected* him. I think Jennifer's story reminded your father of his own bad dreams, that's all. And that's hardly a reason to prevent our daughters from using our vacation home."

Faye became quiet and pensive, probably recalling her own nightmare at the cabin. The fire suddenly popped, causing all three of us to jump. After a moment, Faye and I caught eyes.

"What did he dream?" we both asked at the same time.

Lynn hesitated and looked over her shoulder at the staircase. After a moment, she said, "You can never repeat this to him. He'd be embarrassed. And furious, of course."

We nodded.

"One night when we were staying on the mountain, he started screaming in the dark. When he woke up, he told me that all his buddies who got killed in the war, well, they were inside the room with us – all maimed and rotten. Just sitting on the bed or standing over him, watching us sleep."

A cold, tingly feeling spread down my back. I tried to hide the goosebumps that popped up on my arms. Faye looked as if she already knew, corroborating what she'd told me at the cabin about his sleep-talking when she was little. She hugged her knees to her chest nervously.

"He was so upset he didn't talk almost at all the next day, and didn't sleep the next night," Lynn continued. "So we left. And that was the last time we stayed the night. We made day trips to do upkeep and remodeling from time to time, but your father refused to ever sleep there again."

"But he was fine with us going?" Faye asked loudly, incensed over this whole conversation.

"No, he wasn't," Lynn replied. "But you know your dad. He doesn't like to talk, and didn't want to explain himself.

Plus, he knew you had Felix there to take care of you. I'm so sorry, honey."

"Lynn, if you don't mind me asking," I said, again trying to head Faye off, "why did you guys keep the cabin all this time? If you never use it, why not sell it?"

"Well," Lynn said, "property value around Orchid Valley has quadrupled in the last fifteen years. Greg always says it's gonna be the new Aspen. Probably wise to hang onto the place until we're ready to liquidate it when we retire in a few years. I'm really sorry, both of you. I don't know what really happened up there, but I'm so glad you're okay."

With that, Lynn touched my hand and cupped Faye's cheek. She gathered herself and went upstairs to bed.

Faye was still furious with her parents later that night, but was also creeped out by the story her mother had told. She insisted on me staying in her old bedroom with her, despite my offer to sleep on the couch. I wanted Faye to get a full night's rest and be on the mend as soon as possible, but she refused to be left alone. For an hour she vented her frustrations to me behind a closed door, but soon became nauseous again and fell into a restless sleep.

While I scrolled through the news on my phone, Faye began mumbling her dreams out loud. Instead of waking her up, I listened quietly, hoping that she'd reveal something useful that might explain what was going on in her mind. Instead, she answered more questions, just like at the cabin when she sleep-talked to the strange figure outside:

"Never. No. No. I wouldn't."

"In the snow. Up there."

"I can't."

"Why...his name?"

"I don't know you. Why, why?"

"Down in the hole."

"No it's Felix...Felix, yes."

The feeling of being naked and exposed came over me. Someone was coaxing Faye into divulging things about herself and me – someone in her own subconscious mind. This freaked me out so much that I felt the urge to shake her awake and demand an explanation, but I knew that she'd never remember what she was saying or who she was talking to. I convinced myself that letting Faye rest was the best way to distance her from the experiences on Pale Peak; hopefully the terror she brought home from there would be washed away by a week of good sleep.

But hours later, near the approach of dawn, Faye sat straight up in bed and sucked in a huge breath. The sound woke me up, and I instinctively grabbed the trashcan I'd set near the bed, preparing to catch a volley of barf. Instead, she grabbed my arm with surprising strength. With her eyes still closed, she looked right into my face, and said,

"Tell the man in the hall...he needs to leave."

Petrified, I slipped away from her grasp and peeked out the door into the long hallway. There was no one. For the first time in ages I thought of Carrot the parrot. When I shut the door and turned around, Faye was horizontal and snoring. I was so weirded out that I couldn't fall back asleep. I read the news on my phone for hours, quietly waiting for the sun to come up.

Chapter 9

Greg was up bright and early the next morning. I could hear him shuffling around downstairs, talking softly on his cell phone and moving back and forth between the garage and kitchen. He mentioned something about Pale Peak. Faye was out cold and hadn't budged for hours, hopefully because her illness had passed. I crept down the hallway and tried to pick up on Greg's conversation.

"Nothing in particular," he said. "Just, yanno. Poke around. Make sure it's all locked up. Don't need anybody fuckin' around in there." After a few moments he chuckled and added, "It burns down, it's on you. Ten-four, buddy. Owe you one."

I descended the stairs and headed to the pantry for cereal as if I hadn't been listening, but the stupid look on my face instantly gave me away. Greg was a mindreading, black-ops kind of guy anyway. He knew what I was up to.

"Ranger," he said, dropping the phone into his bathrobe pocket and taking a sip of coffee. "Just gonna check on the place. I figure you kids got loopy on a gas leak up there. Pipes were laid in the 'seventies, you know?"

I didn't bother pretending to agree.

"Wasn't a leak," I said, shoveling Kix into my mouth.

"There's someone up there in the woods."

Greg palmed the lighter that was sitting on the counter near me. He shrugged and headed toward the patio door.

"Whoever it was," I called across the room, "they were talking to your daughter from outside the window. In her sleep."

Greg stopped at the door, just for a moment, then pushed it open and went outside.

Faye and I spent our last day in Colorado with her parents. We watched movies, traded cheery stories, and generally tried to pretend that our visit had been an unremarkable one. That evening, Greg and Lynn dropped us off at the airport.

Faye slept the entire flight home. Despite her lifelong parasomnia, she was adept at falling asleep virtually anywhere. I, on the other hand, am a nervous wreck on airplanes, and barely managed to operate my iPod. I clutched her limp hand for the duration of the trip and occasionally looked at her eyelids. Beneath them, her eyes rolled and darted to and fro, up and down, toward me and away. Again, I found myself wondering what was going on in her sleeping mind. Her lips trembled and mouthed words from time to time, but any sounds she might have made were lost in the din of humming engines.

We arrived at our house after midnight and went straight to bed. I had never felt so overjoyed to be in our old, familiar bed, away from the frigid air and dark memories of the cabin on Pale Peak. Perhaps Faye felt the same way, because from the moment she crawled under the blankets until noon the next morning, she didn't make a sound.

I woke up around 9 A.M., which is sleeping in, for me. There was a missed call on my phone from Greg. When I

71

called him back, he notified me that Ranger Pike had investigated the cabin with his partner, and it appeared as though someone had tried to break in. It was probably a simple burglary, and most likely committed by some teenagers from the high school down in the valley. He made me promise to tell Faye in order to settle her nerves, then bade me not to worry about what had happened.

Something in Greg's voice made me think he was lying. It was too friendly, too warm. His insistence that we try not to focus on such an odd series of events didn't help either. It was too urgent. The moment he hung up the phone, I called the ranger station at the foot of Pale Peak.

"Rocky Mountain National Park Service, Pike speaking."

"William, it's Felix," I said.

"My favorite tourist!" he replied in his thick Southern drawl. A muddy laugh slid out of his mouth.

"Hey listen," I said, cutting straight to the point, "Can you tell me about the burglary?"

"The wha—? You talkin' 'bout Hemsville?"

"Um, no, I mean the cabin. I just got off the phone with Greg. He said you told him someone broke into his cabin."

"Uhhh..."

"He said some teenagers were messing around up there. Told me not to worry."

William paused for a second too long.

"Oh, right, the burglary! Yeah. Yep. Sorry, coffee maker's out. Ain't woken up my brain yet. Cabin's fine, I just—"

"It's bullshit, isn't it?" I interrupted.

"No, it's true! Karen knocked it over this morning when she was pullin' files. Damn carpet's been—"

"I want to know what you found up there, and I want to know why everybody's acting like I'm fucking crazy."

William sighed and asked if I could hold for a moment.

The phone beeped, and then he came in much clearer.

"Had to take this in my office," he said. His voice softened to just above a whisper. "Look Felix, I don't want any trouble with Faye's daddy. He's a good man, and I gotta see 'im a couple times a year. So whatever I tell you, you can't go tellin' around."

"I won't say anything," I replied. "I just want to know what's going on."

William cleared his throat.

"I respect Greg, but I think you have a right to know, seein' as how y'all went through what you did. He wasn't lyin' about the break-in, only they didn't take nothin'. You know, I been on this mountain for eighteen years, and before that I worked all over the Appalachians. I ain't never seen anything that made me believe in ghosts. But I was weirded out up there yesterday."

"What are you saying?" I asked, glancing up the stairs for any signs of Faye.

"I'm tryin' to say I believe you," William responded. "I mean I don't think any UFO's been touchin' down up there, but I believe that somethin' happened. I don't think y'all are lyin'. Or crazy."

"Tell me what you found." I tried to sit down on the couch but immediately found myself standing again, nervously awaiting William's reply.

"Well, uh, we come up there about noon. My buddy and his son come with. They live over on the Indian reservation, other side of the mountain. Big hikers, helped us on a few search-and-rescues in the past. Cabin was fine outside, no smashed windows or nothin', but somebody's been in there. I don't know how."

"How do you know?" I asked. Faye coughed upstairs.

"I was in that bedroom with you when you were packin'," he said. "Y'all had stuff in the closet. You only grabbed what you could. But I remember how that room

73

looked when we left, and it wasn't like that when we visited yesterday. Them clothes were all over the ground, some on the bed. Like somebody was smellin' 'em, or maybe even tryin' 'em on.

"We also found some big black stains on the carpet, in both the living room and bedroom. Smelled ungodly. Still can't figure out how they got in."

"What do you mean 'they'?"

William sighed again.

"My buddy found tracks outside in the snow. 'Bout a dozen of 'em. Wanderin' all around, like they were all lost, weren't goin' in no specific direction. Wandered up to the windows like they was tryin' to look in, back and forth to the woods over and over. He never saw nothin' like it before. Couldn't explain it."

My knees went weak and I finally felt like sitting. I dropped onto the couch and rubbed the back of my neck. My hands were freezing. Pins and needles of anxiety climbed up my limbs.

"Is that it?" I asked.

"Mostly, yeah," William said. "Couple other things were odd. Silverware drawer was taken out and dumped all over the kitchen counters. Dirty dishes on the floor too, but none of 'em broken. Nothin' stolen from the house, looks like. Not even the food. Maybe somebody was searchin' for somethin'. I gotta tell ya kid, this one's got me stumped."

A door opened upstairs, and I heard footsteps across the ceiling. Faye was awake.

"Look uh, I ain't sayin' I believe much of this," William added, "but there's a lot of old legends about the mountain. Real old."

"Like what?" I whispered, trying to keep Faye from overhearing. I now understood why Greg had lied to me. Neither of us wanted to scare her any further.

"Stuff about uh, the old mines. People gettin' dragged

deep down into 'em. Strange things comin' out. Stuff about spirits of the woods, things livin' up in them trees. Shit like that. I don't know much more but if you wanna talk to my buddy, he'd probably be willing. I told him about them voices you heard in another language, and he was real interested. He thinks he knows what it is."

"Did you tell him about the dreamcatcher?" I asked.

"We didn't find one," he said.

I rushed to the kitchen and grabbed a pen.

"Okay. Go ahead."

"Alright so that's *Tee-Way*, he's the father. Guy I've known a long time."

"Uh, can you spell that?" I asked.

"T-i-w-e. One of them little Frenchy flairs on the *i* and the *e*."

William gave me the number and I quickly hung up, just as Faye descended the stairs. She looked at me with a blank expression, almost as if she didn't recognize me, then smiled and walked past me to the refrigerator.

Chapter 10

For much of the day, Faye appeared to have returned to her cheerful and feisty self. She blared hard rock and danced around doing chores, occasionally winking at me and batting away my attempts to annoy her by pulling on her curls. We were back home in Northern California, unpacking the few things we'd managed to grab during our escape from the cabin. Our shared relief was palpable; we laughed and joked all afternoon.

But as night settled in, I noticed a few odd things in Faye's mannerisms. We ordered a pizza and she wolfed down most of it, despite her common objection to greasy carbs. I chalked it up to her lack of appetite while she was sick, but I'd never seen her eat like this. She was absolutely ravenous, like a pregnant woman – or a wolf.

Faye also began to grow anxious. The darker it got, the more on-edge she appeared, until she abruptly suggested we not go to bed, but instead watch a funny movie. When I resisted, she grabbed my hand and pulled me close to her, pretending to pout. I could feel that she was trembling, so I agreed. She fell asleep in my arms about fifteen minutes into *Wedding Crashers*, and twitched and jerked throughout its duration.

The movie ended just before 1 A.M. It was only then in the darkness and silence of the house that I realized I still felt very fearful about our experiences at the cabin. Each little sound outside tripped a wire in my brain, triggering flashes of creepy memories. I tried to remind myself that we were nearly a thousand miles away from Pale Peak, safe at home and surrounded by watchful neighbors, but no amount of rationalizing could calm my nerves. My mind kept returning to the woman on my car and the man standing at the edge of the tree line, facing away from us and gazing up at the trees. Those images will be burned into my retinas forever.

When the movie ended, I quietly snuck away from the couch to get a drink. As I passed the stairwell, a soft noise came from upstairs. It sounded a bit like a man sighing. I dismissed it as the heater, which occasionally whooshed and clanked – but hurried back to Faye and woke her up.

She looked up at me with a puzzled expression, then glanced around the room.

"I had a weird dream," she said, touching my hand as I caressed her face.

"Oh yeah?" I said.

"There was a man."

"Better looking than me?"

"He was carrying something," she said, closing her eyes again. "It was heavy. I offered to help him. But when I spoke, he ran away."

"Ran away? From *you?*" I said, tugging on a lock of her fiery hair. "Why didn't I think of that?"

"Because I only date dumb guys," she replied with a yawn. We both chuckled.

"Weird dream," I added.

"After he was gone, I looked at it," Faye continued. "It was a big bag. Like a body bag. But when I opened it, it was just a bunch of snow and twigs and stuff."

"...Huh."

"I stuck my hand inside. Like there was something else in there, something underneath. I just knew."

At this point, I was intrigued. Faye's dreams were often complex and metaphorical. Even when neither of us could understand them, I always got the sense that her dreams – even her nightmares – carried a deeper meaning.

"What did you find?" I asked.

"I never saw what it was. You woke me up before I could find out, you jerk." She laughed and pushed me away.

We headed upstairs to brush our teeth and then climbed into bed. Faye was out before her head even hit the pillow. I tossed and turned for a while, still a tad afraid to fall asleep. I had the irrational fear that I'd wake up back at the cabin, our escape having been only a desperate fantasy.

"What the hell are you doing?" Faye blurted out in the darkness. By the stilted way she spoke, and the unusual tone of her voice, I knew she was sleep-talking.

I rolled over and watched her face in the moonlight that filtered through the curtains above our bed. Her eyes were closed but rolled all around against the lids.

"Do you want some help?" she said.

Perhaps she was reliving the dream from earlier this evening. I held my breath.

"Oh my God," she panted. "What is this? What is this?!"

I instinctively reached over and ran my fingers down the length of her arm. Being touched usually soothed Faye, and helped to weaken the nightmare. Being touched – I liked to think – reminded her on some subconscious level that I was nearby, and that she was safe. She settled back down and mumbled a few more sentences, but there was nothing I could make out. In a few moments, Faye returned to peaceful sleep.

I lay there for a long while, gazing into the softness of her face. The chaos lurking beneath those gentle features astonished me. If only I could know what plagued her thoughts in the murk of sleep. But the fleeting nature of dreams sometimes hindered her ability to recall them, and abruptly waking her guaranteed that they'd vanish like shadows hit with a flashlight. Whatever mysteries lay buried in Faye's head, they would not be unearthed through interrogation.

At least not by me. Twice now, Faye had answered questions to someone else, or some*thing* else, in her sleep. I remembered the woman's voice outside the cabin, how it lit up with menacing glee when Faye replied to it. Had there really been some dark force on that mountain that took unnatural interest in her? Was it still with us? Or was Faye simply talking to a dream of that memory – to a creation of her own mind? Anxiety and despair crept through my muscles, causing them to tense and twitch.

I just need sleep, I assured myself. *We both do. Lots of it.*

Eventually, I found a bit of rest. Faye giggled a few times and said the names of two of her coworkers, and this actually made me feel better. On a normal night, she babbles about mundane things and people from work, so hearing this sleep-talk indicated that her mind had turned away from dark dreams of the cabin. A new calm settled over me, and all went black.

Much later, I floated up from a dream of grading papers. The first thing that came into focus was the alarm clock across the room. Its glow read 4:01 A.M. I tried to remember what day it was, thinking that the paper stack was due in a few short hours, but my thought was interrupted by a voice.

"Shhh...yes. Yes."

It was Faye.

She was whispering.

I held perfectly still, feeling every hair on my neck bristle at the quiet words she spoke. Normally, Faye giggled, cursed, argued, and even shouted in her sleep. But in five years of sharing a bed with this woman, never once did I hear her whisper. Faye was lying on her side, facing away from me, and whispering one half of a very strange conversation. I imagined a person crouching in the darkness at the edge of the bed, smiling up at her and whispering back.

It was impossible to make out much of what she said, but I thought I heard "wolves," "beneath it, down there," and "not allowed."

"What are you saying, Faye?" I asked, loud enough to wake her. She didn't respond. I reached over and nudged her. "Who are you talking to?"

She jolted under my touch, and whispered "Don't."

Exhausted and annoyed, I yanked the sheets and rolled over, trying to get some rest. As sleep crept its way back over me, I imagined the man from outside the cabin, lying beneath our bed and staring up at the mattress in the dark. In my mind, he had a big grin plastered across his face.

Chapter 11

At about 5:45 A.M., I was awoken by Faye. My eyes cracked open just as she came into the bedroom. She walked stiffly, as if she had muscle cramps in both legs. Faye clambered back into bed and covered herself with blankets, making little effort not to wake me. Her green eyes were big and full, as though she'd been up for hours, and she stared right into mine for just a moment. Then she rolled over and faced away from me. The rhythm of her breathing was soft and shallow, like that of a sleeping person.

This was another disturbing omen that something was wrong. Despite her tendency to babble in the middle of the night, Faye sleeps like a dead horse. A water glass already rested on her nightstand, so I assumed she hadn't gotten up to get something to drink. Our bathroom is connected to the bedroom, and she certainly hadn't come from there. The most likely explanation was that she had been sleepwalking. This scared me because I always worried that she'd fall down the stairs. But even then, Faye only sleepwalked a few times a year, and I usually saw it coming. I kicked myself for not having predicted that her current stress levels might precipitate an episode. I should have known.

A fuzzy memory popped into my head. I thought I had seen Faye returning to bed at about the same time on our last night at her parents' house in Colorado. I couldn't be sure it was real, but now I wondered how long Faye had been getting up and wandering around in the dark this early in the morning. Did she do it at the cabin? Everything about the past week was a blur.

We woke up late the next morning.

"Yo Monkeytoes," I said, leaning out from the kitchen. Faye was reading something on her phone while I made us some eggs. "You remember anything from last night?"

"Ughh," she replied, wiping her face with her hands. "I think his name was Brett or Brad or something...I don't know. I was pretty wasted."

"Smartass," I said. Faye burst into laughter, apparently satisfied with herself.

"What are you asking, Poptart?" she said.

I told her everything I remembered from last night, knowing that it could trigger a chain reaction. Once Faye was aware that she was sleepwalking and experiencing other nocturnal disturbances, she tended to overthink it and cause more of them. To me, it was worth the risk. She was acting stranger than ever before, and I wanted to get to the bottom of it. Her constant disruptions to my sleep were beginning to drive me insane.

"I don't remember any of that," she said, looking into my eyes with a joyless expression. I knew she wasn't lying. I didn't press her any further.

Faye's work shift didn't start until the afternoon, so when she left, I had the place to myself all evening. In that time, I decided to call Tíwé. I felt hesitant to reach out to him, even after William had assured me that it was alright.

It was probably a reluctance to hear anything that would further terrorize my brain while lying in bed at night. It took some consideration, but eventually I picked up the phone.

Tíwé picked up on the first ring.

"Felix," he answered in a dreary voice, "I foresaw this conversation in a dream."

"Uh...hey," I replied, not knowing what to say to that.

Tíwé let out a disarming laugh. I instantly got the sense that he was a nice guy. A friend.

"Bad joke," he said. "Sometimes it's fun to play the part. For the tourists, you know."

"That was good," I admitted, letting out an awkward chuckle. "All those magazines and gift shops they have out there...I can see why visitors get the wrong impression."

"The industry isn't really fair to us," Tíwé said. "We're not all shamans and wise men. In fact, we cuss and dick around and use Facebook – almost like you humans."

"I'm sorry," I replied. "I felt a little weird calling you, and that's one of the reasons. Is it wrong of me to ask you for help with...uh...whatever this is? Isn't it a bit like asking a random Chinese guy to teach me kung fu?"

Tíwé laughed again. His voice was rich and textured, the kind you'd hear narrating a nature documentary.

"Well," he said, "I guess if he's the one who offered it first."

"Okay. In that case, it's nice to meet you. Can you make my fiancée stop doing Satanic shit in her sleep?"

We both cracked up. For the first time in days, I felt hopeful.

"How's things?" he asked. "I've been meaning to call you. Got your number from William a few days ago. But I figured I'd give you both some time to unwind."

I filled Tíwé in on what had happened at the cabin, and about Faye's unusual behavior since we'd left the place.

83

The conversation became more and more grim as I proceeded down the list of disturbing things we'd experienced. Tíwé listened carefully, and occasionally said "Hmm," or "Tell me more," but did not share any of his thoughts with me. He waited patiently and considered my every word.

After ten minutes of recounting the story, Tíwé finally spoke.

"Felix, this sounds like a really strange situation. I understand why you're upset, and I'm sure what you guys went through would've given me a heart attack. Based on what William told me, I had some idea about what's going on. But now that I've heard it from the horse's mouth, I want to talk to a few buddies of mine – *wise men*, you know. Can you give me a few days? Just to be sure."

My heart sank at the request. I was hoping for a simple explanation for everything, but I appreciated that someone was willing to help at all.

"Sure thing," I said, trying to hide the disappointment in my voice.

"I just don't want to be wrong about this," he added. "It sounds like you love your fiancée very much. Hold onto that. It will keep you both strong, should she get worse."

"What do you mean 'worse'?" I asked.

"I've got to go now," Tíwé said. "But I'll call you soon. Get some rest."

The conversation left me with mixed feelings. On one hand, I felt better knowing that I wasn't alone in my quest for answers, but on the other, I feared that Tíwé was going to come back and tell me that Faye was possessed or some other crazy nonsense. I couldn't understand why *she* was the one who ended up with all the weird psychological problems from the trip; I was the idiot who almost touched the dreamcatcher, and who almost got dragged away into the forest. I went outside into the snow multiple times, exposing myself to God knows what. Maybe the difference was that Faye believed in the supernatural – the world behind the world – and I did not. Maybe her belief that the cabin is haunted was having a psychosomatic effect on her, causing her to feel sick. Intruded upon. Tainted. Maybe it was all in her head.

Then who the hell was talking to her in her sleep? I heard voices up on that mountain. I didn't dream it. Someone was out there, walking around in the freezing dark, calling out to my future wife.

Chapter 12

That night, I came up with a plan. I wanted to test my hypothesis that Faye had been getting up early and sneaking around for the past several days. I set my phone to buzz at 4:15 A.M. and placed it under my pillow. Then, I went to bed before nine, hoping to get in a good few hours of sleep before the alarm went off.

At least my insomnia's gone, I mused, just at the brink of consciousness.

An unfamiliar voice woke me up. I glanced around the room, trying to get my bearings, and saw that it was just after midnight. A dry, raspy voice croaked a few things from nearby. At first I thought there was someone on the floor or under the bed, so I jumped up and used my phone as a light. It only took me a moment to realize that the voice was Faye's, and that she was mimicking another person in her sleep. Just as she had done the night before, she was lying on her side (usually she sleeps on her tummy), facing away from me.

She repeated the sounds "Laaaa... Laaaa... Lalaaa..." as if she were trying to sing, but the words were robotic and monotonous. I could hear her tongue wagging around and flicking against her teeth between utterances, like she was testing a new mouth for the first time. Then, Faye spoke a few phrases:

"Down in the hole."

"He's still up there."

"Where were you? I looked for you..."

Faye's voice had changed, but she wasn't channeling some otherworldly spirit. It was as if she were trying to imitate the person she was speaking to. It frustrated me that this person was in her head, in her dreams, and I could only ever hear one side of the conversation. I found myself beginning to hate this phantom of her mind.

As I stood there clutching my phone, contemplating whether to wake her, there was a noise outside the bedroom window. It sounded like an old man grumbling to himself about something. The night was quiet and hardly any crickets sang, so I knew I hadn't imagined the noise. Whoever he was, he was moving away from my house, muttering his frustrations under his breath as he went.

Because I'm in a Ph.D. program, Faye and I are able to live in a faculty housing complex at the base of campus. It's a quaint little set of neighborhoods surrounded on three sides by a belt of redwoods, and there are small groves of trees separating each neighborhood from the next. Our bedroom window overlooks the street in front of the house. Just across it rests one of these groves, and at night, the faint yellow lights of houses in the adjacent neighborhood twinkle through it. They look a bit like fairies floating in the dark.

I left Faye and quietly pulled the curtain open, hoping to catch someone wandering around in front of the house. Instead I saw the silhouette of a man far off in the distance, meandering between the trees across the street. He'd never have been visible if the houses behind him weren't lit up; each time he passed in front of one, his huge form eclipsed the yellow lights, providing me with momentary glimpses of his body. He must have been nearly seven feet tall, and shuffled awkwardly like a drunken person.

A thousand hairs pricked up on my arms as I stared out the window. The longer I watched, the more bizarre the man seemed. Suddenly, he stopped in his tracks and turned around. His body was a featureless black mass, so I couldn't tell if he was facing toward or away from me. Then, he lurched a step past the tree line. The moon lit him up just enough to reveal that he was wearing a ragged jacket. His back was turned to me, and his head was tilted straight up at the sky. He paused there for only a moment, then retreated into the darkness of the woods and disappeared. I scanned the tree line, trying to spot any disruptions in the lights beyond it, but there was nothing. The man had vanished.

Because I'd opened the curtain, pale moonlight now poured into the bedroom. I turned back toward the bed, trembling with fear – and nearly shrieked when I saw Faye. She was lying there on her back with her neck craned out toward me, head upside-down and dangling off the side of the bed. Her wide, crazed eyes locked onto me, and her mouth hung open. She issued a gurgling, drawn out groan and flicked her tongue around, prompting me to back into the window frame and nearly climb up the wall. Her movements looked like an epileptic fit in slow motion.

Faye watched me with a malice I'd only seen in movies. Her eyes pierced into mine with hateful desire and never broke from their assault. They seemed to drag me down into them, where I'd be swallowed up forever. Faye had opened her eyes while sleepwalking in the past, but never like this. Nothing human remained in her gaze now; I was staring into the eyes of a wolf, and they looked up at me with terrifying glee. She seemed to recognize me, but not in the way that two people who live in the same house recognize each other. It was as though I'd been missing a thousand years, and she had finally found me.

The fear that gripped me mutated into an acute rage. I strode toward Faye and bellowed her name, shattering the nightmare's hold on her. She went limp for a moment while her brain rebooted. Then she clawed her way out of the ungodly position she'd bent herself into and pulled herself back onto the pillows. Her eyes blinked repeatedly until the rabid hunger in them subsided.

"Felix?" she asked. Fear anchored her voice so that only whispers escaped her mouth.

"Please tell me you remember whatever you just dreamed," I said, sitting down next to her. I glanced once more out the window, but couldn't see the tree line from where I sat.

Faye threw her arms around me and buried her face in my chest.

"I was walking," she said. "It was dark."

"What did you see? Do you know where you were?"

She paused for a moment, then turned her head toward the window.

"Out there."

I felt the hair on my arms stand up again.

"I think it's time for another doctor's appointment," I replied, trying to exhale the wave of dread that rose up in my chest. Faye nodded, seemingly afraid to take her eyes off me. I wrapped my arms around her and held her close, trying to ensure that she didn't feel alone in this struggle. Faye was engaged in some internal conflict, and the war was being waged across her subconscious. Fear and revulsion rose within me, but I reminded myself that she was my future wife. My devotion required that I be there for her no matter what – even if I didn't yet know how to help. After some time, the pounding of her heart slowed, and her heavy breathing fell away to a calm rhythm. Her grip on me loosened, and she drifted off into the mysterious world of her dreams, to where I so desperately wanted to follow.

In all the commotion, I had forgotten about my alarm. My phone scared the hell out of me when it vibrated beneath my pillow at 4:15 A.M. By the time I realized what was going on, I had already blurted out a string of curses and nearly woken Faye up. I hobbled to the bathroom.

When I returned, I saw Faye baring her teeth up at the ceiling and gently caressing her face with her hand. As I stared at her through the darkness, a part of me feared she'd suddenly bite off her own fingers as they dragged across her lips. Eventually, her arm flopped back down on the bed.

I sunk down into the old armchair that occupied the corner opposite our bed. It was an ancient thing, discovered by Faye at a garage sale and now essentially a clothes rack, and it was uncomfortable enough that I knew I wouldn't fall back asleep. I waited quietly in the dark for a half-hour, fixated on my sleeping fiancée and the strange movements she made. Every so often she'd twitch, or reach toward the ceiling, or mumble something unintelligible. But I remained silent, wondering if she'd validate my suspicions that she'd been getting up in the wee hours to skulk around the house.

At around 5:00 A.M., my eyelids hung heavy and my limbs tingled due to the awful chair. I stood up and stretched, ready to abandon my mission and crawl back into bed. Suddenly, Faye drew a sharp breath. She jolted straight up in bed, back stiff, and stared into the darkness before her. A mess of tangled curls cascaded down her face and obscured it, but she appeared to be looking around the room.

I felt the words "Faye? Are you okay?" well up inside

my mouth. Before I could blurt them out, she tossed the sheets from her lower body and swung her legs over the side of the bed. She planted wobbly feet on the carpet one at a time and stood, teetering back and forth, then rose up onto the balls of her feet. She tilted her head back and forth a few times as if to empty water from her ears, then tiptoed across the bedroom and pulled the door open with a gnarled hand. Her movements were not cute and clumsy, like those of a sneaky child on Christmas eve. They were robotic. Inhuman. She moved down the hall like a meth-addicted zombie ballerina and stopped at the stairwell. Her breathing remained delicate and hypnotic.

I paused at the doorway, watching Faye's alien movements. She stood at the top of the stairs, peering down into the abyss, whispering something I couldn't make out. She remained high up on the balls of her feet, every muscle in her body pulled taut until her form was stiff as death. The moon peeked through a nearby window, illuminating her from behind. It cast her figure in a ghostly glow, adding to the illusion of an old corpse stalking around my house.

Faye slid her fingers over her face for two or three minutes. It almost looked like she was learning about her own appearance for the first time. She ran a hand over the banister, then the wall, and flicked the light switch on and off in patterns of five. All the while, she maintained her perfectly mechanical breathing.

In my mind, I saw her collapse and fall down the stairs. I wanted to hurry to her side and wake her up before my vision became a reality, but a cocktail of fright and morbid curiosity rooted me to the floor. I looked on as she moved through her disturbing performance.

Faye reached an arm out, stretching and wiggling her fingers. Then she closed her hand and pulled it back up to her face in roughly the motion of a bicep curl. She repeated

91

this behavior for about a minute, and I had the idea that she was testing the limb – as though she'd never used it before. However, after seeing her lips move again, I realized that she was communicating with someone at the bottom of the stairs. Someone in the dark. Faye was making a "come hither" motion, enticing whoever it was to come up here with us.

Recalling the man I'd seen wandering around outside, I strode out of the bedroom and leaned over the half-wall that overlooks the first floor. It was so dark down there that I couldn't see anything but the glow of the clock on the cable box. Beside me, Faye stood there waving, smiling, and touching her face and hair. I gently wrapped an arm around her waist and flipped the light on, blinding myself in the process. She went limp at my touch as if released from a magic spell, and nearly sent us both tumbling down the stairs onto the tile floor at the bottom. I ushered her back down the hall and spoke as softly as I could, trying not to fully wake her. As with every other time I'd discovered her sleepwalking around the house, Faye offered no resistance, and climbed back into bed without so much as a mumble. A part of me felt silly for doing it, but I searched the entire bottom floor of the house – and found no one.

I now had to admit what I could not before. Whatever it was that had found us at the cabin had followed us home.

Chapter 13

That morning, Faye woke up looking terrible. Dark rings circled her eyes, and a deathly pallor had fallen over her skin. She was clammy to the touch, and if not for her ravenous appetite, I'd have thought she'd come down with the flu.

After about ten phone calls, we landed a same-day doctor's appointment. When I notified Faye of it, she hardly looked up from the giant omelet she'd made for herself.

"Doctor in Arvada's gonna fax your blood work over to this one," I said, squeezing her shoulder as I passed by. "Maybe something's changed. You okay with some more tests?" I circled the table and sat across from her.

"Mh," she grunted.

"You never eat eggs," I said. It was more a question than a statement. She paused for a moment, then continued shoveling forkfuls into her mouth. Pieces of onion fell from her lips as she did. I looked closer. It was just eggs with onion. Too much onion.

Faye barely spoke during our drive to the appointment. She answered a few of my questions with one-word responses, but remained disconnected and listless. She watched the world rush by as the car moved, but I couldn't be sure she was even seeing anything. I made a few comments that would normally prompt her to reply with a smartass joke – things like "man, I'm so sore" and "I couldn't sleep at all last night" – but Faye never took the bait.

At the hospital, we were greeted by a man named Dr. Farmer. He was older, with salt-and-pepper hair that looked uncombed for a century. His cheerful demeanor and sincere interest in Faye's health seemed to coax her out of her shell, and after a few minutes, he actually got her to crack a smile.

As I recounted Faye's unusual sleepwalking incidents, the doctor made exaggerated reactions of pretend shock and horror. This elicited a few giggles from Faye, and she eventually began speaking in full sentences again. Dr. Farmer's playfulness, combined with his rather small stature, made him appear more like a cartoon character or a hobbit than a medical professional. But as soon as I mentioned the creepy sleep-talking, his conduct changed, and the gaiety fell away.

"Tell me about your dreams," he said, yanking the stethoscope from his ears and dropping onto the stool in front of her.

She stared into his little blue eyes for a long moment, hesitant to share, then said, "Someone's trying to talk to me."

"Who?"

"I don't know."

"Do you see this person? Or just hear a voice?"

"It's foggy. Hard to remember. I always forget what he looks like. But I saw him a few times. He never looks right at me."

The two spoke a few more minutes, drawn into a conversation about the significance of dreams and whether

94

they reveal anything about the state of our minds. They carried on as if I were not even in the room. Suddenly, Dr. Farmer looked to me and said, "Mr. Blackwell, do you mind if I speak to Faye alone?"

I felt stunned and a little put off, but I understood the importance of his request. If somehow I were the cause of Faye's recent psychological issues, she might be unwilling to speak openly with the doctor. I glanced over at her as I left the room. She returned a little smile to me.

When Dr. Farmer opened the door a few minutes later, he was cheerful again. I felt a warm hand on my back as I passed by him into the room.

"Well, my boy," he said, ushering me to an empty chair beside Faye. "I was just telling this young lady that I'd like for her to see a psychologist if these dreams persist for more than a few days."

"You mean like for a psychiatric evaluation?" I asked. Faye and I exchanged worried looks.

"Oh yes," he said, eyes widening in terror. "This one's out of her mind."

Faye laughed. My face went a bit warm. She hadn't laughed at anything I'd said all morning.

"Nothing official," he replied, then looked at Faye. "I just think you could benefit from talking to someone more extensively about these dreams. Get down to the root, you know. That's the thing about strange dreams, and sleepwalking and so forth. They're like smoke. The fire's even deeper. And as fascinating as I find yours, Miss Spencer, I'm no expert on nightmares."

The doctor prescribed Faye a mild sedative to ensure she got a full night's sleep, and started her on a short course of anti-anxiety medication to see if it helped to calm her nerves. He surmised that Faye was dealing with some kind of trauma and suggested that we spend some time outside to clear her head. We accepted the suggestion and a referral to a psychologist if the medications failed, then went home.

As we left the office, Dr. Farmer poked his cherubic head into the receptionist's area and called out to Faye, "Write them down! Spend some time on it!"

For the remainder of the day, Faye was in better spirits. She went right back to teasing me and joking around as usual, and even agreed to go on a little nature walk on the trails near our house. We grabbed her meds from the pharmacy on the way home, then suited up for the walk. It was about 3 P.M., so we planned to be outside for only an hour. In the redwoods, it gets dark as soon as the sun dips behind the tree tops, and this time of year that's just after three.

Faye came trotting down the stairs in a curve-hugging gym outfit. I pulled her in for a kiss, but she nipped at me playfully and shoved me away. It was relieving to see the fire in her eyes again. It was that fire that I'd fallen in love with. The one that occasionally burned me. She grabbed her water bottle and flung the door open, signaling for me to follow.

Outside, we crossed through the neighborhood toward the trails. The walk required us to cut through the line of trees where I had seen the dark figure the night before. As we moved into the grove, I glanced around, looking for any sign of his presence. I tried not to alert Faye to what I was doing, but she noticed me periodically gazing up into the trees and scanning the ground around us.

"This place," she said abruptly. "I had a dream about it last night." Her remark pulled me out of a memory of the figure. Faye stopped in her tracks and turned around, facing back to our neighborhood.

"What do you remember?" I asked.

"I was just standing here," she said. "Just watching."

She pointed a finger into the distance. A few hundred feet away, our little bedroom window was visible.

"Do you know why? What were you doing all the way out here?"

"I don't know. But someone was watching me back, from our window."

"Was it me?" I asked. I needed to dance around the subject; I didn't want to divulge to Faye that I'd seen a man slinking around out here in the middle of the night. "I uh...that night, I got up and looked outside. Heard a noise."

Faye studied the window, deep in thought.

"Not you," she said, voice lowering to near a whisper. Her brow furrowed in contemplation. "Someone else. He was all dark. He watched me for a while..."

"Was it the man from your dream at the cabin? The one digging the hole?"

"It felt like him."

"Did he talk to you?" I took a step toward her and put my hands on her arms. The symphony of songbirds died away, leaving us alone in the murky shadows of the redwoods.

"No," Faye said, closing her eyes. "He turned around, and looked down at you. He stood over you while you slept."

It was only in this moment that I realized how cold the air felt. But it wasn't just the breeze that chilled me. It was the similitude of her dream to what I had seen through that window while she slept.

"What did you do?" I pressed, squeezing her arms a bit tighter.

Faye tilted her head back and drew in a long breath.

"I turned away. I was so scared. And then I looked up."

She opened her eyes toward the tree tops. They darted around for a moment, and then locked onto something.

Faye gasped, and her knees buckled. We stumbled together, but I managed to catch her before we fell over.

"What is it?!" I asked, clutching onto her and frantically searching the canopy.

"I feel like I'm gonna pass out," she panted. Her face went pale again. "Let's go home. I need to go home."

Faye held onto my arm with both hands as we headed back toward the house. Right as we exited the little grove, she stopped and looked over her shoulder.

"You hear that?" she asked, voice still weak.

"Hear what?"

"Thought I heard a little boy," she replied. "He was singing."

Chapter 14

Back at home, Faye napped a while on the couch. She seemed more comfortable sleeping downstairs than in our room, probably because she had come to associate our bed with all of the awful things plaguing her mind. While she was asleep, a strange thought occurred to me. The child she thought she heard today – was it a memory of the little boy that sang and babbled in the darkness outside the cabin? I tried to recall some of his phrases:

"Burn up the hags!"

"Rooock-a-bye-baaaaby...iiiin the tree top..."

"When do we go insiiiiide? When do we go insiiiide?"

The terrible way he spoke, the simultaneity of joy and emptiness in his voice, painted a gruesome picture in my head. I imagined a little boy in an archaic school uniform, standing in the snow outside the cabin on Pale Peak. His eyes had been gouged out, leaving behind a darkness that yawned from their sockets. Despite his blindness, he stared out at the cabin with a knowing gaze, cheerfully practicing songs and phrases he most likely didn't understand. He was a hollowed-out thing, a desperate mockery of a person. The child's voice reminded me of what Faye had said about the man digging holes in her dreams. They both felt singularly inhuman.

I shook the image from my mind, but could not shake the darker thought that replaced it. What if the phrase *"When do we go insiiiiiiide?"* didn't refer to the cabin at all? Perhaps instead, it referred to Faye herself. I glanced over at her from my chair, watching her chest rise and fall. I wondered when her mysterious visitor would reveal himself again – and what he would ask of her this time.

Faye was hungry when she woke up. She insisted we get away from the house and go out to eat. I obliged, hopeful that being around other people might help to snap her out of the peculiar moods she'd been suffering. She chose our favorite steak joint, Bucky's Smokehouse. There, Faye always orders the same thing, and calls it her "death row meal": a barbecue chicken sandwich with macaroni and cheese, and a glass bottle of Coca-Cola. It's the only soda she'll drink; in fact, her blood is mostly Coke.

On the ride over, Faye again withdrew into herself and barely spoke to me. Instead, she hummed a familiar song, but I couldn't remember where I'd heard it before. When I asked what it was, she said she didn't realize she'd been humming anything, and probably made it up.

At the restaurant, things got even weirder. Faye gulped down two huge glasses of water and said nothing to the waiter about Coke, then proceeded to order a New York Strip, "as rare as you can make it. Just wave it over the fire." I asked if she could order for me too, pretending to take a call on my cell phone, but she appeared to have forgotten that I always order the ribs. I reminded her, then decided to test her further.

"Do you still think about the cabin?" I asked, fiddling with my phone.

"Not really," she replied vacantly. "You?"

"What do you remember about the last time you were there?"

A bit of anger flashed in her eyes.

"You've been fucking interrogating me ever since we left," she snapped. "I feel like I'm on trial all the time."

I was caught off guard by her reaction. "I'm sorry" was all I could muster.

"What do you want from me?" she added. "Really. It was awful. I think about it every goddamn day. Even when I'm asleep. And I *don't* wanna talk about it." She took another big gulp of water. It dribbled down her chin.

"I'm just worried, is all. You've been acting funny."

"I'm fine. Worry about yourself."

An awkward silence fell. It was Faye's nature to be very protective of her inner thoughts and feelings. The entire first year of our relationship felt like an epic quest to win her heart. I would leap one wall only to find another beyond it. Dating her was a bit like the old fairy tale about the knight who scaled the highest mountain – except in this story, the damsel had to rescue *him*. I had nearly given up on my quest for Faye's love when she at last said those three words, and told me I had earned it.

For the past several days, however, she was unusually defensive, even for her. It wasn't just her sleep disturbances that were bothering me; lately, nothing about her behavior felt familiar. I tried a different angle, hoping to find a weak spot in her armor.

"Babe...did anything like this happen when you were at the cabin before?"

Faye eyed me suspiciously, but she restrained herself from another outburst.

"What do you mean?"

"Well, you went there once when you were fourteen, right? Why'd it take you twelve years to go back?"

She took another few gulps of water.

"I've never been to that cabin before in my life."

A steaming plate of barbecued ribs moved in front of my face. The waiter put our food down and asked us if we needed anything, but I was too baffled to respond. He picked up on the mood at the table and immediately left. I watched in awe as Faye wolfed down her steak and chased it with glass after glass of water, never once looking up at me or indicating that she was aware of her surroundings whatsoever. We ate in silence.

On the walk back to the car, I put my arm around her waist and noticed that all of her muscles were tense. When I pulled her close and said "I love you, Noodle," Faye smiled dismissively and nodded.

"You still like it when I call you 'Noodle'?" I asked, sliding my hand down to her butt. I stuffed my fingers into one of her back pockets and squeezed.

"Of course," she replied.

But I had never called her that before. The only nickname I'd ever given her was "Monkeytoes," because of the unusual dexterity of her feet. Faye had earned the nickname at the beginning of our relationship when I saw her use a foot to pluck the TV remote from the ground, and deftly channel-surf with her toes. Conversely, I'd earned the shameful moniker "Poptart" when she caught me shoving the chocolate pastries into my mouth under the cover of darkness one night.

My little tests throughout the evening did not convince me that Faye had been kidnapped by the body snatchers and replaced with an evil duplicate. She still *felt* like Faye, at least some of the time. It was important for me to try to maintain some measure of skepticism. If I put stock in the idea that a ghost had followed us home from Pale Peak, it might cloud my judgment during an emergency. But I found myself vacillating between logical and spiritual explanations for her disturbing behavior, and recognized that my skepticism eroded a little more each day.

It felt like a part of Faye was disappearing. It was as if she would go somewhere else, as we might in a dream, leaving her body behind in the process. She wandered far away, and each time she came back, she returned with less and less of herself. Each time she returned, she brought more of *someone else* back with her – the one who calls out to her from her nightmares. Whoever was whispering to Faye at night, whoever was prowling around outside the cabin and our home, I could now feel him too.

Faye would notice if I called her "Noodle." Faye would remember her favorite drink. And Faye would put five across my eyes if I ever grabbed her ass in public.

When we got home, I headed upstairs to finish writing a paper. Faye cracked open one of the Cokes from her stash in the fridge, then collapsed onto the couch and scrolled through Facebook on her phone. Her weird mood had vanished the moment we'd walked into the house.

As I worked, Faye's gentle humming drifted upstairs. The song was hypnotic and familiar; it resonated inside my head and drove me crazy. Eventually I began humming along, and then the words formed on my lips and hung in the air:

"Soul me aaahhh doooo....soul me aaahhh doooo...Naked souuul.....me aaahhh....dooo."

The lecture I was writing turned into gibberish. A warm fuzziness spread around the back of my head and weighed down my eyelids. Sleep dragged me downward into its narcotic abyss, and the last thing I heard was that wicked song, but not from my own mouth or Faye's. It seemed to come from outside.

Cackling laughter jerked me from unconsciousness. Warm air blew against my face from the laptop. I'd passed out with my head on the desk.

Something moved behind me – something scraping against carpet, like a big dog tearing across the floor at dinnertime. I spun around in the chair and peered into the darkness of the hallway, but failed to locate the source of the noise. There was a faint ray of light cutting toward the staircase. It came from beneath our bedroom door at the other end of the hall.

I walked past the stairs and pushed that door open, but Faye was not in bed. The sheets were neat and untouched, so I assumed she was still watching a movie downstairs. As I turned to leave, an inky form clambered up from the staircase and into the hallway, then moved into the spare room where I'd been working. The thing skittered like a human-sized spider, each limb moving independently and jutting from a rigid body.

I nearly screamed as it darted across the periphery of my vision, but I found the courage to walk after it. The spare room's light glowed against the blackness of the hall. My hand shook so hard that I couldn't find the hall light switch. As I desperately ran my fingers up and down the wall, a head emerged from the doorway. From knee-level, it peered up at me sideways with a malicious grin. The harsh light coming from inside that room threw ugly shadows across its face, and it took me a moment to realize what I was looking at.

It was Faye.

She was crawling around on the floor, laughing and smiling with her eyes rolled back in her head. She gurgled and hacked a clot of phlegm from her throat, then stuck her tongue out and flicked it around, mouthing words I couldn't begin to understand.

"Faye?" I called. "What the fuck are you doing?"

She loosed a wet cough, then dashed out from the room and zig-zagged her way toward me. Her arms and
104

legs flailed wildly in exaggerated lunges and her head rolled about like a bowl on a stick.

"Someone's at the door," she hissed, laughing as she snaked past me into our bedroom. *"Knock-knock!"*

I watched as Faye ducked into the bathroom. The house fell eerily silent.

"Faye," I said in a stern voice, "wake up."

She didn't respond. The bathroom door sat ajar, allowing a beam of light from the bedroom to penetrate. A single bare foot rested in the glow. Its toes curled and tapped rhythmically against the floor. Slow, heavy breathing rose in volume as I approached the door.

"Babe?"

The door squealed as I nudged it with my palm. The beam of light expanded into the dark, illuminating an eerie scene. Faye stood between the toilet and the bathtub, clenching her fists over and over. Her toes wiggled. She swayed gently to and fro. Her eyes were now shut, but she still appeared to see everything in front of her, and watched intently as I stepped into the bathroom with her.

"Tell them," she whimpered. It took a moment for my eyes to adjust, but I could now see tears dribbling from her eyelashes.

"Tell them what, Faye?"

"To leave."

Just as the words left her mouth, there came a gentle *knock-knock-knock* from far off in the house. We'd only been living here for a year, but I knew all of its creaks and squeaks intimately because of how much time I'd spent working from home. There really was someone at the front door.

Baffled, I looked over my shoulder, then back at Faye. How long had someone been standing out there?

"There's a man at the door," she continued, clenching her jaw as she spoke. Her eyes rolled around behind the

105

lids, indicating that she was dreaming. "He whispered to me while you were upstairs. Been doing it for hours. Wants to know your name. Tell him and he'll go away."

Pure rage blurred my vision. I turned to leave, wanting to punish this son of a bitch once and for all – but then halted in my tracks.

"Faye," I said, looking back, "what do you mean, 'them'? Who else is here?"

She rolled her head again. The bones in her neck crunched.

"There's a woman at the bottom of the stairs."

The surge of masculinity that compelled me vanished as quickly as it had struck. I cautiously exited the room and made my way into the hallway, peering over the low wall that overlooked the bottom floor.

The way the gloom hung in the air – the way the frail moonlight seeped in through curtains like silvery sludge – cast the room in a grid of light and dark patches. Wedged into the far corner between a wall and the bookcase, there stood a dusky figure, trapped in place by a blade of pale light that stabbed through the window. It looked like the slender form of a woman clutching herself in the cold.

"Who's there?" I demanded as bravely as I could. "Who's in my house?"

I could hardly focus my eyes in the soupy darkness, and not at all when I looked directly at the figure. Adrenaline electrified me now, and I charged to the light switch at the staircase, throwing it on and bull-rushing down into the living room.

Nausea overwhelmed me as I reached the bottom of the stairs. It was the same feeling that had overcome me at Colin's house all those years ago, when Carrot the parrot tried to warn me about someone lurking around in the dark. The air thickened and soured, and as I pressed into it, the bile inside me washed up into my throat. The couch and table and stairs looped around me in a dizzying whorl, and I nearly lost my balance. The figure seemed to move toward me, but I struggled to keep sight of it. I withdrew from the living room and stumbled to the hall that led to the front door. A plume of cold air drifted past me, drawing my attention to the entryway.

There came another knock, this time louder.

"Hello?" a voice called from beyond the door. It sounded familiar, but in my nauseous daze, I couldn't place it.

"Who the fuck are you?" I growled, leaning against the wall to stabilize myself. "What do you want?"

The man outside knocked again.

"Who are you?!" I shouted.

"Hello?" he asked again. The word sounded identical to the first time he said it, as though it were a recording on loop. Nothing in his voice indicated that he'd heard me at all.

Finally, my legs found the strength to take me the last few steps to the door. As I reached for the knob, a voice echoed from behind me.

"What's going on, Felix?"

I whirled around to see Faye, awake and scared, standing at the bottom of the stairs. Her eyes were open, and a disoriented fear emanated from them. She had no idea what she had done minutes earlier.

I ignored her and yanked the door open, inviting in a rush of crisp night air. There was no one on our walkway, but the faint sound of leaves crunching drew my attention to the little grove across the street. Someone was walking through it, away from our neighborhood. I slammed the door and stormed around the house, flipping on lights and searching for the dark figure. I hadn't had a good night's sleep in days, or maybe weeks; I couldn't even remember anymore. The tendrils of insanity were slowly wrapping themselves around my neck, squeezing off the blood to my brain.

"You're taking the damned sleeping pills," I said, glaring at Faye. I snatched the bottle off the counter and shoved them into her hands. "Now."

Chapter 15

A few days passed, thankfully without any strange activity at night. The sleeping pills Dr. Farmer prescribed appeared to be working, and allowed both of us to get some desperately needed rest. During the day, Faye's anti-anxiety medication softened her up quite a bit. She came home from work each evening looking serene, and after dinner, she busied herself sketching and writing in a dream journal she'd made from one of my notebooks.

Of all the strange and horrible things that had been happening to us over the past few weeks, one thing kept returning to disquiet my mind. Up on Pale Peak, Faye told me she had only visited the cabin once when she was fourteen. But a few days ago, she told me she'd never been there before. I assumed she made the statement out of frustration as a bid to stop me from discussing our trip any further. Faye was trying to process everything that had happened in her own way, and each time I pressed her for answers, it churned the well of those ghastly memories. She just wanted them to settle.

But I had never known Faye to be a liar. Now, because of her capricious and vacant demeanor, I wasn't sure anything that came out of her mouth was true. I wasn't even sure she was still entirely Faye. So, I did the only thing I could do. I called her mom.

Lynn was as disingenuous a person as I'd ever met. I tended to group people into two groups: one that values politeness over honesty, and the other exactly opposite. Faye's mother was doubtlessly a member of the former, and would go to great lengths of insincerity to avoid telling the truth – if the truth were inconvenient, hurtful, or scary. Thankfully, she was also the type of person who was addicted to her smartphone, so she called me less than a minute after I sent her a text saying *Hey, can we talk?*

"What's going on?" she demanded, before I could even say hello. "Is Faye alright?"

I hesitated to tell her much of anything, for fear that it would give her a heart attack. But I realized that if I wanted her to be honest with me, I needed to be honest with her.

"She's gotten worse," I said flatly. "She's been sleepwalking and saying really weird stuff almost every night. She talks about a man. This is gonna sound crazy, but I swear I've seen him."

Lynn struggled to conceal the sorrow in her voice. She tried to tell me that we were both exhausted and sleep-deprived, and that the mind can only put up with so much stress before it starts to break.

"Lynn," I said, fed up with her evasions, "I really need you to cut the crap. For your daughter's sake. Is there anything you're not telling us that we should know?"

She exhaled hard into the receiver.

"Well, no, not that I can think of."

"Faye can't get her story straight about how many times she's been up to the cabin. I thought you might be able to clarify." My tone came out a bit bossier than intended, but Lynn seemed to respond to direct pressure.

"What did she tell you?"

"Don't worry about that," I said. "I just want to hear it

110

from you."

She hesitated for just a moment.

"And don't lie," I added, "or else I'll know." I had no idea where the words came from, and cringed as soon as they left my mouth.

"We used to take her up there all the time," Lynn said, almost an admission. "Took her snowshoeing and stuff. She loved the snow. She was just going into high school last time she went up."

I glanced out the kitchen window, trying to see if Faye was home from work yet. Between her whimsical changes in mood and her mother's penchant for sugar-coating everything, I couldn't tell which of them was the liar. Perhaps they both were. But why would they deceive me over something so trivial? What were they hiding?

"Well, thank you," I said, unwilling to carry on any further. "This has been helpful."

Not long after the conversation with Lynn, I received another call. It was Tíwé. He immediately apologized for not contacting me sooner. We spoke briefly about Faye's condition, and he was disheartened to hear that her behavior had grown more erratic. In the same fashion as the first time we spoke, Tíwé eluded my questions. Instead, he had a few of his own. This time, he made no jokes.

"Is there any way you guys could make it back out here?" he asked.

"Are you kidding?" I replied, choking back a string of curses. "There's no way. That's an expensive trip, and Faye would sooner chain herself to the door."

"What about you?" he persisted. His voice was grave; I could tell he wouldn't ask if it wasn't important. "Could you find a way?"

I was stunned at the request. Going back to Pale Peak was the last thing on Earth I wanted to do. But the urgency in his voice actually made me consider it.

"I...I couldn't leave Faye here. Not like this. It's been a few days, but you should see the way she gets, Tíwé. It's...I can't even describe it. The only thing keeping her down right now is the medication, and that's gonna run out any day now. Doc only gave us a week's worth."

Tíwé paused for a long moment, then sighed.

"You guys aren't the only ones who've been through something like this. It's rare, but you're not the first."

"What do you mean?" I asked.

"There are things about this mountain that my people don't fully understand. I think waiting around isn't going to fix your problem, Felix. You guys did something up here, or something happened to you, and I think it can only be undone here. All the others who have left the mountain – the ones who ran away – it finds them in the end."

The urge to hurl my phone at the wall swept over me. I let it pass.

"What is *it*, Tíwé? Faye talks to him in her sleep. I see him outside my house. Maybe even inside. Tell me what we're dealing with here."

"Would you really believe me if I told you?" he shot back.

He had a point. There wasn't anything he could tell me that I'd readily accept. This entire experience had challenged my most fundamental understanding of the universe. All of those horror films I'd seen over the course of my life, and all of the superstitious nonsense people believed – how could any of it be true?

"I think my mind's a bit more open, given the circumstances," I grudgingly replied.

"Good. Truth is, I don't know much of anything about this stuff. My father and grandfather knew a lot more, but they've been gone a long time. If you can't get back here to talk about all this in person, I want you to see a friend of

112

mine. Her mom knew my grandfather, and I trust her. Name's Angela. She's only a couple hours' drive from you guys, I think."

"Can she help us?" I asked.

"It's not like that," he said, careful not to get my hopes up. "I just want her opinion, that's all. I'll speak to her. Maybe she can come to you."

We discussed the matter a bit further, and I eventually said I'd have to defer to Faye. She already felt that I was treating her like a mental patient under careful observation, and she'd be pissed to have a stranger in our home – even if the woman was trying to help. Breaching that topic would be a small war. I'd have to choose the moment carefully.

Tíwé accepted my judgment and told me to reach out to Angela as soon as I got clearance from Faye. He bade me farewell, and reminded me again to never waver in my devotion to my fiancée. His last words to me were, "but don't get so caught up in protecting her that you forget – she's protecting you too."

Chapter 16

Saturday finally rolled around. In the days since Faye had returned to a semi-normal state of mind, I was able to catch up on a ton of work. Now, I planned to spend today completely severed from the mountains of books and research articles that cramped my office up on campus. I even closed the door to the guest room, blocking the view of my desk and all the grueling work I'd come to associate with it.

Faye and I spent the afternoon in pajamas, lying all over each other on the couch and watching *The X-Files*. We'd made it up to season six before our visit to the cabin, but today was the first day she'd felt like resuming.

In one episode we watched, a strange creature made of soil roams a quiet neighborhood, brutally murdering anyone who disobeys the rules of the Homeowners' Association. When I was a kid, my stepfather was an *X-Files* fanatic, and he would let me watch the show with him after my mom went to sleep. I don't remember much of the storyline, but this particular monster terrified me and plagued my dreams for years afterward. Because of its composition it was nearly impossible to see – it only seemed to have any substance at all when it moved, as its wet body glistened under the street lights. The monster could travel any distance at will, collapsing into a heap of dirt and popping out of the ground somewhere else. But the thing that scared me the most was that it always knew where to find its victims, and never stopped hunting them. Watching the episode now sent chills up my body, so I abruptly turned it off.

"What'd you do that for?" Faye protested.

I sat up so that I could look into her eyes. She burrowed her feet beneath my thigh to keep her toes warm.

"How about something happy?" I said.

She flashed a coy smile.

"You've got *me! I'm* your happy."

"Oh yeah," I said, rolling my eyes. "You're a frickin' barrel of fun."

"What about a happy memory?" she said, prodding my knee with her foot.

"You mean like the time in college when you went to visit Becca and I had our apartment to myself for eight days?"

Faye drove the heel of her foot at my crotch. I blocked it just in time.

"*Even happier,*" she threatened.

I laid my head back on the couch and gazed up at the ceiling, trying to think.

"Milkshakes," I finally said. "In senior year, when we'd get all dressed up and go downtown to the burger place."

Faye smiled. She withdrew her foot from its attack position.

"I remember how cold it was on those nights," I added. "I always wanted you to eat cold stuff so that you'd want me to put my arm around you on the walk back to campus. Worked every time."

"Sly dog," Faye said. She blew me a kiss. I pretended to dodge it and then watched in relief as it drifted past.

115

"What about you? A memory, I mean."

"When we went out to the stoner meadow one night," she replied. "Back when we were just getting to know each other."

"Porter Meadow," I said, cracking up. A bunch of goofy memories from junior year flooded my mind. I'd never shared them with Faye.

"We broke off from the group and just looked at the stars," she said.

"I recall a rather spirited exchange of creepy stories."

"I wanted to kiss you that night. That was the first time I thought about it."

"Why didn't you?"

Faye ran her foot up my chest and poked my chin with her toe.

"Because your face looks like that."

I pretended to wipe a tear from my eye. She was delighted with herself. Just seeing Faye's smile lit me up inside. It gave me hope that no matter what terrible or tragic things befell us in life, we'd always weather them together.

"I still dream of you," she added.

"Oh yeah?"

"Oh yeah. Sometimes they're about when we first met. Sometimes about the future. I see us with a little boy."

"You know," I replied, "I actually think I'd like to have a little tiny Faye running around here someday."

She laughed. Her hand found mine.

"Then again, I can barely handle you," I said. "Don't know how I'd manage."

She gazed up at me for a long moment. Her big green eyes moved over me, like she was trying to take in my memory before leaving on a trip.

"I still dream of you," she said again.

For four days, Faye had slept soundly all through the night. She didn't report a single nightmare, and I hadn't heard any strange noises outside (or inside, for that matter). Privately, I feared that whatever – or whoever – was tormenting Faye had not given up. Instead I worried that this was a mere interlude before the onslaught of new horrors, and in the wee hours of the fourth night, my suspicions were realized.

I was awoken by the feeling of someone sitting down on the far end of the bed. The mattress sank and pulled my foot with it, instantly setting off the siren in my head that wailed, *"Faye's up. Grab her before she falls down the stairs!"* But when I opened my eyes, I noticed the tangled mess of blankets and limbs that was Faye, fast asleep beside me. Someone else was sitting on the bed.

It took me a second to make out the pale, withered hand that clutched her wrist. My eyes moved up the long arm and perceived the shape of a bony man, sitting with his back turned to me. His shoulder blades and ribs jutted painfully from his body, and the skin looked stretched over him like dried leather. A black and shaggy mane of hair dangled from his head and obscured his face, but I could see that he was leaned over Faye, examining her with predatory intent. He whispered long strings of words I could not fully hear, but the hateful way they were enunciated told me enough. He seemed to be giving her a vile command. She lay there motionless, smiling every few seconds as if listening to a slew of comforting promises.

I bolted upright, ready to tackle the man, but the second I moved he issued a slow growl. It rolled up from deep inside him like the warning snarl of a tiger and sapped the courage right out of me. He dove to the floor and wriggled his way underneath the bed. I screamed for Faye to wake up and threw the sheets from my body, trying to get to the light switch near the bedroom door. Before I could reach it, the impact of something heavy against my shoulder blinded me with pain.

I rubbed my face and looked around.

Bright light stung my eyes. The sun burned through the curtains and lit up the whole room. Everything was sideways. I was twisted up in the bedsheet, lying in a heap on the floor. Faye looked down at me from the bed, shocked at my appearance.

"I sleepwalk, dude," she said, lips curling into a smile. "Even when my eyes are closed, I know how to get out of a friggin' bed."

"He was here," I said, shrugging off her jab. "I saw him."

"Who?"

"Him," I said, scowling at her. "He went under there." I reached a tingling hand toward the bed skirt and yanked it up. There was nothing but a few pairs of shoes.

"I guess bad dreams are contagious," she replied, half-joking.

Faye sighed. She knew, just as I did, that we weren't through the hurricane yet. We had simply been drifting through the lull of its eye.

I hoisted myself from the ground and plopped onto the bed. My side of it was drenched in sweat.

"Tell me who he is, Faye," I said with defeat. "Please."

Her eyes narrowed in offense.

"If I knew," she said, slapping a lock of hair away from her face, "why the hell would I hide it from you?"

"Then tell me what he wants. You must know. Every time you go to sleep, he's right there talking to you. Just tell me what he says."

Faye leaned back on her pillow and gazed up at the ceiling. Her eyes sparkled like little green gems in the morning light.

"It's always hard to remember," she offered. "It's like

fog, or static. He wants to know things, but he wants me to forget that he asked."

"What does he ask?"

"Stuff about my family. My childhood. What I like...what I hate. What I want. He always asks weird things, like who I played with as a little girl, or which of my parents I like best." She looked up at me. "And he wants to know all about you. So many questions."

"What do you tell him?" I asked, combing her hair with my fingers. It covered the pillow in a fountain of golds and reds.

"I try not to say anything," Faye replied. She swallowed hard. "But sometimes he wears me down. Tricks me. Makes me think I'm having a conversation with my dad or with Becca. He knows your name now, and a little bit about us."

I shuddered. The thought of some intangible husk lurking around in the dark, trying to get to know us, profoundly creeped me out.

"Do you ask him anything? Does he tell you anything about himself?"

"Never."

I cupped her cheek, pulling her gaze toward me.

"Why does he want to know all this stuff, Faye? What does it matter to him?"

She got out of bed and wrapped a little robe around herself, then headed for the hallway.

"I think one of us has something he wants."

Chapter 17

Whatever it was that our uninvited guest desired, he was having a lot of trouble finding it. He seemed committed to darkening our home until he got what he came for.

Something struck me as I looked at Faye. When she tied her robe, I watched her hands, and realized that she hadn't been wearing her engagement ring for several days. Only now did I realize that she hadn't even worn it out to dinner last week. Faye never leaves our house without it. When I brought it up with her at breakfast, she dismissed the idea that it was lost and assured me that it was in a pocket of her suitcase. I reluctantly accepted this explanation; I couldn't remember the last time Faye had misplaced her car keys, let alone an expensive ring. She was also one of the slowest unpackers in the world, and I knew for a fact that the luggage in our hall closet was only half-empty.

During that conversation, I almost brought up Tíwé's request to have his friend Angela visit us. At the last moment I held my tongue, reasoning that there was probably a better time to bring it up. Faye was a very headstrong person, and although I admired her confidence, she was quick to interpret my concerns as accusations that she could not manage her own problems. Having someone come "check on her" would certainly injure her pride and cause a fight. It would have to wait. But I made a mental note to check her suitcase for the ring.

I barely had any friends, and as a graduate student I had virtually no time to spend with the ones I had. The only people I ever saw were the other students in my cohort, and aside from the shared misery of a Ph.D. program, we didn't have much in common. Whenever they weren't working, they were getting blind drunk at the bars downtown. Even when I showed up to their Pint Nights, I was always the sober introvert with the root beer, totally excluded from the festivities.

Tonight, however, they invited me out for pizza, and I desperately wanted to go. I needed to get away from the house, which was beginning to feel more and more like purgatory. Surprisingly, Faye encouraged me to get out of the house and unwind. I promised to be home before she fell asleep. It would be the first night since her sleeping pills ran out, so I privately worried that something might happen. In fact, I dreaded it. Faye could read me like an open book and knew what I was thinking, so she grabbed my face and promised she'd be fine, then kissed me and shoved me out the door.

It was great to see everyone. They were all in high spirits, celebrating the passage of another punishing week, and seemed glad to see me. I fought back my desire to tell them all about the awful things Faye and I had been through; they already thought I was a bit weird for being a teetotaler, and tales of shadow-men and dreamcatchers would surely make me look insane. That evening I pretended that my life was completely normal, and for the first time in a long while, it almost felt true.

I pulled into our neighborhood just before 11:30 P.M. The moment I pushed open the door, I knew something was wrong. Every light in the house was off, including the cable box. Someone had unplugged it. The air was cold, and the memory of the freezing wind on Pale Peak bolted through me. I scolded myself for having lost track of time.

"Babe?" I called out.

Maybe it's a power outage.

I looked over my shoulder at the rest of the housing complex. Several windows glowed and all the street lights were on.

I moved inside, cautious not to trip over anything. My hand ran along the wall until it found a light switch, and when I flicked it on, the empty living room appeared before me. A water glass lay on the floor, and a big pool of water soaked the carpet. Just beside it rested a large notebook, splayed open to a page filled with harsh scribblings.

I scooped it up. This was the dream journal that Dr. Farmer had encouraged Faye to keep. For a brief moment I hesitated, partly because I didn't want to invade her privacy, and partly because I feared what I'd find there – but a dark curiosity took hold.

The page looking up at me had two styles of handwriting. Near the top, a neat and methodical script ran across the lines in perfect order. A much stranger, more frantic scrawl crowded every inch of the bottom, written lighter and faster than before. Words and letters collided with each other; some sentences were written over others. It bore resemblance to Faye's handwriting, but seemed almost as though Faye were holding the pencil with a looser grip – the way a sleeping person might.

Most of the lines described dreams, and were dry observations in shorthand:

I'm on a beach in a place I don't recognize. The sand is white and there are rock formations jutting out of the water.

122

A storm approaches on the horizon. I'm alone.

It's night and I'm thirsty. I try to walk to the kitchen, but I trip and fall into a huge black hole in the floor. At the bottom, there's a pool of things that look like human-crocodile hybrids. The sounds of splashing and thrashing wake me up and end the dream.

I'm very young, maybe four or five. I'm with my mom at a restaurant. We're eating ice cream. When I look out the window, there is a giant obelisk sitting inexplicably in the parking lot. It's made from black stone, and there are strange carvings all over it. Everyone is afraid, but they're trying to ignore it. I've seen this statue in other dreams before.

The other handwriting was almost poetic, and reminded me a bit of the strange babble we'd heard at the cabin:

Child don't wander too far out, they'll get you once they know, they pray you'll every warning doubt, and meet them in the snow

One was old in soul and skin
Two was very small
Three was watching over them
And four was none at all

What is your name? Tell me yours first

What makes five
What makes five

Littered across the subsequent pages were disturbing

sketches, no doubt snapshots from Faye's dreams. I could barely make sense of them, but by their expert artistry I knew that she must have been awake when creating them. They were drawn in colored pencil, her favorite medium.

The first depicted a stormy bay with a half-dozen ships floating in it. The ships appeared ancient, with gigantic masts and wooden hulls. Every one of them was on fire. Tall creatures – maybe demons – were throwing themselves from the decks into the water.

On the next page, a little girl was standing on her bed. A grotesque monster was seated next to her with its mouth wide open. The girl was reaching her hand down its throat into a cross-section of its stomach, where a crucifix necklace rested. Sharp fangs lined the monster's mouth, ready to bite off the girl's arm.

The next picture showed a little boy walking toward the viewer. He held his arms open as if approaching for a hug, but his fingers were elongated and became razor wires that stretched across the breadth of the drawing. He had a cheery grin plastered on his face.

Next was a bird in a cage, looking up at an enormous shadow that loomed on a nearby wall. The shadow reached its featureless arms across the ceiling and down another wall toward a distant bed, where a man and a woman were sleeping.

Next was a snowy forest, not unlike the one visible from the cabin. A figure stood in the shadows. He appeared to be facing away, pointing up to something in the trees. The entire image was framed from a window, as though the viewer were inside a house, looking out.

The last image had the same window and forest as the one before, but this time, the figure was absent. Instead, a clawed hand was reaching up to the window from outside, scratching the number 5 into the glass.

There were more pages of writing beyond that, but a loud *bang* from upstairs tore my attention away from the journal. Something heavy had fallen up there. The entire ceiling above me rumbled and creaked. Then, the pitter-patter of quick footsteps resounded across the ceiling.

"Faye?" I called, heading up the stairs.

As I neared the top, she darted past me. Faye had been in the guest room and was now making her way toward our bedroom. The way she moved solicited a very loud "Jesus Christ!" right out of my mouth. She trotted high up on the balls of her feet as she had done once before, and staggered around awkwardly as though her legs and spine were made of cement. Her neck and arms, however, flopped around like noodles with every jerky movement. Faye stormed into the bedroom and stopped abruptly. Then, she drew in a raspy breath, whirled around, and peered at me. Her eyes were open and rolled up so that only the whites of them showed, but the subtle movements of her head told me she knew I was there, and somehow she was studying me. She flashed an eerie smile and sucked in another breath through gritted teeth, then charged down the hall, laughing as she went.

I watched this spectacle from the staircase, unable to command my legs to move. Faye ran past me four or five times before I could tear my eyes away from her. Eventually, my gaze moved from her to the hall window just in front of me. Something moved out there.

It was the man.

He flailed and jerked and staggered just at the edge of the tree line, moving parallel to it. This time, he was actually a few feet out of the woods. The moon was just a sliver now and barely illuminated him, but I could see how long and gangly his limbs were. What looked like a filthy dress shirt clung to his misshapen body, and the thick mane of hair that I'd seen in my dreams hung from his

125

head. He began singing – only the voice that came out of his mouth was that of a small child.

Faye ran past me again. The person outside moved with her.

Their movements were synchronized.

I gasped and stumbled backward. I'd have plummeted down the stairs and snapped my neck, but Faye's hand shot out and caught me by the shirt. She pulled me toward her with inhuman strength and held me tightly as I regained my balance. Her hands ran up my chest and neck, onto my cheeks. They moved across my features, poking and cupping, and the ominous whites of her eyes drilled into me curiously. The smile fell off her face.

"Faye," I said, grabbing her by the shoulders, "it's me. It's me. Wake up."

But she didn't wake up. Her breathing became more rapid and heavy, until the air wheezed in and out of her between gnashing teeth. As her fingers painted a picture of my appearance in her mind, her expression changed from confused to terrified. She began shrieking at the top of her lungs, and her hands shook so violently that they rattled against my face.

"What the hell's the matter with you?!" I shouted. "Faye!"

She backed up against the window and held out her arms defensively, trying to protect herself from whoever she thought I was. As I moved to comfort her, she slipped past me and dashed away into the bedroom. The man outside darted off too, withdrawing into the forest.

I barreled down the stairs and practically broke down the front door. The complex was dead as usual, spare the few neighbors who peeked out their windows to see what all the commotion was about. I ignored them and sprinted across the meadow toward the woods. Tall blades of grass licked my skin. The sounds of frightened little critters scurrying away rang out all around me.

It was nearly impossible to see inside the grove. Whoever was in there could surely see me, though, and I felt naked just standing there looking in. Memories of the woman who tried to coax me into the woods at the cabin popped into my head, but I drowned them out with thoughts of Faye and stepped inside.

Darkness enveloped me. A branch cracked somewhere to my left. Leaves crunched. A billowing shadow ducked behind a nearby tree; I only recognized the shape after it moved.

"Hey!" I shouted, making my way toward it. "Get back here, you son of a bitch!"

I tried to pursue the dark form, but it deftly snaked between the trees. Branches battered my head and chest as I followed, and the hard roots that jutted from the earth caught my shoes. In mere moments the figure had vanished, and I found myself wandering around in the dark alone. The streetlamps of the neighborhoods surrounding the grove whirled around me.

I trudged through the woods in defeat, entertaining crazy thoughts of leaving Faye and moving somewhere else. My hope was nearly smashed, and my partner was not going to get better without a miracle or some serious medical intervention. Both possibilities seemed more and more distant with each passing day. Faye was going to end up in a filthy asylum, and I would too if I corroborated anything she said. This man – this *thing* – wasn't going to stop until one of us was dead.

In my mournful reveries, I had lost track of the way out of the grove. I looked up just in time to dodge a huge spider web that loomed right at face-level. I stood up to regard the thing – and realized it wasn't a web at all.

It was a dreamcatcher.

This one had no ragged twine in its center. The material was much finer, and glimmered in the twilight. For a long moment I stared into it, nearly hypnotized by the way it gently swayed and twirled in place.

Is that hair?

I finally reached out and plucked the thing from its branch. It was ice-cold to the touch. The second I removed it, a powerful gust of wind rushed through the grove and set all the trees shivering.

I carried the object back to the house. A terrible feeling grew in the pit of my stomach with each step, weighing me down as I moved. I had to know what this thing was made of. I examined the thing under a street light.

I instantly recognized the strawberry-gold color that wove a pattern at the dreamcatcher's center. It was Faye's. In silent rage, I tore the thing apart and heaved it into the bushes on our lawn. There was no will left inside of me to try to make sense of it anymore. I held back tears of frustration and returned to the bedroom. Faye was sleeping peacefully.

For hours, I lay motionless in bed, but no rest came to me. All of the terrible things I'd seen haunted my mind: the images from Faye's dream journal, the wicked way she moved, the terrible man who shrouded our every step. Something about that drawing of the window kept popping into my head, over and over. It showed the view of the woods outside the cabin, but the window frame itself was the wrong color. I recognized it from somewhere else.

Then I remembered Faye running in and out of the guest room. She almost never went in there, for fear of messing up my workspace. All of my research materials were scattered across that room in an organized chaos that only I could navigate. Faye didn't even bother going in there during her compulsive cleaning projects.

But the window in that room – it had a perfect view of the grove across the street, where the man always stood.

I got out of bed and walked down the dreary hall.

There was nothing to see outside. The woods I'd just stumbled through were faintly visible in the gloom, but if a strange figure lurked within them, I could not tell. The breeze had died down, and nothing moved at all. The neighbors I'd disturbed had long since gone to bed. No lights glowed in any of their windows.

I moved my face closer to the glass. My breath fogged it and obscured the view.

A finger-drawn line appeared in the wispy condensation.

Puzzled, I breathed again on the glass, illuminating more of the line.

It was the number 5, drawn backwards.

I traced over it with my finger, trying to understand what it meant. And then I realized – Faye had written a message that could be read by someone standing outside.

"What makes five?" I muttered, recalling Faye's dream journal.

In the distance, a child began to sing.

Chapter 18

"I'm not a fucking science project, Felix."

Faye was pissed, as I had anticipated. She threw the couch pillow to the floor and put the TV on mute. It was morning, and she was already in a bad mood because earlier I had made the mistake of trying to explain last night's events. The words tore her up, so I stopped halfway through.

"I figured you might be, you know, open to the idea." I pointed to the screen. Mulder and Scully were engaged in a heated argument. I was surprised to see her watching *The X-Files*, given our current situation.

"Why has nobody asked me what *I* want to do?" she said, staring daggers at me.

"Because you don't want to do anything," I snapped. "You want to pretend none of this shit ever happened. And each day, you get worse. You vanish, Faye. It's like you just disappear. For hours at a time you're gone. Do you even know where you go?"

I expected Faye to really let me have it, but she gazed up at me with a mixture of hurt and acknowledgment.

"I just want to go back to the way things were," I said, softening my voice. "I want you to be okay. It's like I'm slowly losing you to some other guy. But this guy wants to wear you as a fuckin' suit."

Faye cracked up. She flashed a glittering smile at me, then quickly buried it under a blank expression. For a moment we just looked at each other, but then she reached her arms out for me. I dropped into her and got swallowed up in a tight hug.

"I miss you," I said, breathing her in. "What else can we do? If we go back to the hospital, this time they'll lock you up. They'll hook you up to a bunch of machines and diodes. Stick needles in you. Take more blood. Lots more. You're gonna get committed. I'd rather try this first. Please work with me on this, Faye."

She kissed me and ran her fingers through my hair. Her eyes moved over mine, studying me, seeing within me the honest desire to pull her back from the brink of whatever darkness she was slipping into.

"Come back to me, Monkeytoes," I said. "Please. I need you back."

Faye wiped a tear from her eye before it could fall.

"Okay," she said. "I'll talk to her. For you."

Angela arrived at our home by late afternoon, and was just as warm and friendly as Tíwé. Her hair was straight and black with a sprinkling of gray. It framed a lean face with two green eyes, just like Faye's. And although she can be reserved around new people, Faye instantly took a liking to our guest. Within minutes they were complimenting each other's hair.

"So how do you know Tíwé?" Faye asked. I dragged a chair into the living room while the two sat next to each other on the couch.

"He and I go way back," Angela said with an ill-concealed grin. I suspected that they were more than friends, once upon a time. "When we were kids, we lived

131

next to each other on the reservation. His grandfather was a tribal elder, and he gave lessons on our people's language to me and my mother. There's a big effort to preserve Native languages now, you know."

"That's amazing," Faye said. "Can you speak it?"

Angela hesitated.

"It's been years since I've practiced," she replied. "After my mom passed, I came out to California. Some members of my family are still upset with my decision, so I never had anyone to speak it with."

"Faye left Colorado to come here as well," I offered. "You've got something in common, then."

Angela put her hand on Faye's and smiled.

"*Na'hepa*," she said. "It can mean friend, or sister, depending on how you use it."

"When we visited Pale Peak, we bought a magazine at the airport," I said. "It mentioned something about how Indian – er, uh, Native – languages are dying."

Faye glared at me. Angela noticed and laughed.

"It's alright," she said, patting Faye's hand. "Most people don't read a damn thing about us. There's been some debate over how we should identify ourselves. Until recently it was considered taboo to call us 'Indians,' since the Europeans who called us that thought they were in India. But some communities embrace this name. Others prefer the term 'Native,' for obvious reasons. I'm fine with either. The term 'Indigenous' is used in universities because it describes people who first inhabited the land in any place, not just the United States. Heck, the Natives of Canada are sometimes called 'First People.'

"And yes – my ancestral language is spoken by fewer and fewer people. This has been happening for hundreds of years. For a long time, people like me were taken from our nations and forced into schools where we'd learn English or Spanish and adopt European ways of life. The
132

settlers wanted us to forget our cultures and spiritual traditions. Wanted us to be more like them, you see. So whole generations of Natives grew up without ever hearing their own languages, and now very few of us speak them anymore. In fact, there are many languages that have been totally lost."

Faye and I exchanged sad looks. The words "I'm sorry" welled up in my mouth, but it would have been a paltry thing to say. I regretted bringing up the subject. Angela noted our silence and rescued us.

"I came out here to study these issues at the university, rather than remain with my community. And that's why I'm at odds with some members of my family. Thankfully, Tíwé has always been there for me, that old goat."

"He's quite a guy," I said. "I didn't mean to make you sit here and explain all this to us. I hope—"

"Don't even," she replied, silencing me with a hand. "Some don't like talking about it. I do. That's my choice."

We nodded.

"But here I am droning on," she continued, "when really I came to listen. Faye, do you mind telling me a little about yourself?"

Faye glanced at me again, then cleared her throat. She likely wanted to gauge how honest she should be about our situation.

"Well," she said, taking a nervous breath, "I'm twenty-six, I've got a degree in biology, and uh…I've got one sister."

Angela seemed disappointed with Faye's response. She turned to me. Faye flashed me an *I don't know* shrug.

"Felix, tell me about her."

I figured Angela wanted to learn about who my fiancée was beneath the surface. Faye was a complicated universe of great and terrible wonders, and always tried to hide her real personality from the world.

"She's a remorseless chocolate addict," I said, scowling

133

playfully at Faye. "Stubborn as a damn mule. Occasionally homicidal. Especially when she sleepwalks. But she's hilarious. Always knows how to cheer me up. She's the only person who's ever really appreciated me, so I keep her around."

Both of them laughed and glanced at each other. Faye rolled her eyes.

"She doesn't forgive easily," I added. "Especially when it comes to forgiving herself. She pushes herself in everything she does. Such a perfectionist. She doesn't even realize that she's already perfect."

Angela smiled a knowing smile, and nodded.

"Guess I should have asked you first," she said.

We talked for an hour or so. The conversation meandered around our relationship, but eventually it focused on Faye's tendency to sleepwalk in times of stress. Angela was fascinated, so we gave her the rundown of all the funny things Faye did at night when we first started dating.

Finally, we arrived at the story of our vacation to Pale Peak. Faye hesitated. Angela sensed that we were reluctant to talk, for fear that she'd not believe us.

"Look," she said, "Tíwé already told me a little bit about this. You can share whatever you're comfortable sharing, and I promise to keep an open mind. Sometimes I come off as a bit stuffy, but that's just from years of teaching." She patted Faye's hand again. "I have a spiritual side too, you know."

"He doesn't," Faye said, motioning at me.

"He will," Angela replied. I took it as a light-hearted joke, but her voice was so flat it almost sounded like a threat.

Faye remained silent a few moments, no doubt collecting all the fragments of our trip that she'd scattered and buried in her memory. She told the story in its entirety, from our arrival at the cabin all the way up until this very moment. I jumped in occasionally to corroborate her claims or to offer my own interpretation of an event, and I filled in the gaps of what happened when she was sleepwalking. The one element I left out was the new dreamcatcher just outside our home. I just couldn't burden Faye with any more bad news. But I did admit that I'd rummaged through her dream journal, and that she had drawn a backwards '5' on the window.

Angela's expression grew more and more horrified as we proceeded down the list of terrible things we'd suffered. Her questions became fewer and farther between, until she was utterly silent, staring back at us with a colorless face.

"Faye," she said at last, leaning back against the couch and taking a measured breath, "this man who visits you. Has he told you his name?"

"No. I've asked."

Angela stood up. Her eyes moved all around the room, searching for something.

"May I have a look around upstairs?"

The three of us headed to the second floor hall.

"That's our bedroom down there," I said, pointing to the left, "and the guest room's over here."

Angela seemed more interested in the windows than the rooms. She wandered around the top floor of the house, gazing out each window for several seconds. Her eyes always moved to the grove across the street.

"His voice," she said, fixated on the trees, "does it sound like wind?"

Faye crossed her arms and shuddered.

"Yes," Faye said, nodding at the window. "He waits until I fall asleep. Waits until I'm dreaming."

"Is this where he stands?" Angela asked.

"We've both seen him," I said, putting my arm around

135

Faye. "At the cabin, out the kitchen window. And I've seen him out here too. I think he even came to the door one night."

Faye looked up at me with fear in her eyes. Up until this point, she probably thought the figure outside was only visible to her, in her dreams.

"Oh yes," Angela replied, voice low and dreary, "he'd wait right down there by the front door. Whisper to your fiancée for hours and hours."

Faye pushed herself away from me and left the bedroom.

"What does he want?" I asked. "Faye says he just asks about all kinds of random stuff. It doesn't make any sense."

Angela traced something on the window with her finger, then took a step back and regarded it.

"Did she say if she talks to him? If she told him anything?"

"A little," I replied. "What does it matter? Who is he?"

Angela turned and walked back into the hall, looking at the window out there. Still trying to retain some level of skepticism about all this, I mentioned that Faye had drawn a '5' on the glass here, and I believed it was a signal to the man outside. What I said was true, except for the fact that I'd intentionally chosen the wrong window. Angela studied it for a few moments and then walked toward the staircase. As she passed by the guest room, she said,

"Something about that room feels really off. I think that's where she lets him in."

Faye was downstairs on the couch, wrapped up in a blanket. She looked pale and exhausted, as if ready to disappear again for another few hours. I moved the chair closer to her and put my hand on her forehead.

"You have to take this with a grain of salt, you guys," Angela said, sitting back down on the couch. "I'm not really
136

sure what I think of this stuff. I go back and forth every day. On the drive here I was a skeptic, but I'm leaving as one of the devout. Who knows what I'll be tomorrow? School and life in California have turned me to stone, but I still get those old feelings. I got them here, in your home. They're not quite visions, but they're something. Tíwé makes fun of me when I get them. He calls me a 'daytime atheist.'"

I laughed. This whole experience had certainly made me into a believer, if only late at night.

"He won't tell us anything," I said. "I've tried asking."

"Our beliefs are a very private thing," she replied, "but given your circumstances, I think Tíwé wants to make an exception – and I agree with him. Faye, your family has visited Pale Peak over the years, right?"

Faye nodded.

"My people tell a lot of stories about the mountain," Angela went on. "Like any old place, there are legends and folktales about things that happened long ago. Unfortunately, Pale Peak has a terrible history, so most of our stories are sad. Or scary. It would take a long time to explain how the Creator and the soul work in my culture, so I'll try to say it like this.

"There are a lot of magical beings in our oldest stories. Most are manifestations of the Earth, or the spirits of ancestors and those who have passed on before us. But what you both are telling me reminds me of another creature. This one doesn't come from the world of the dead, but somewhere else, farther beyond it. I don't exactly know how to translate his name for you. You could call these creatures the *hollow ones*. They're jealous of living things, and the joy of this world. Jealous of its sunlight. They have none of it."

Faye shifted in her seat. Sweat glistened on her brow. "Why us?" she asked. "Why me?"

"I don't know," Angela replied. "The legend says they try to

137

coax children and gullible people into the dark with them. Take them away. I don't know much more than that."

I tried not to scoff at the exchange. It was still light enough outside that the analytical part of my brain hadn't surrendered yet.

"Okay, okay," I interjected, "let's just say this thing is real. What do we do now? How do we get rid of it?"

"I don't know."

"But Tíwé said you know this stuff better than he does."

"I know frauds better than he does," Angela corrected.

Another awkward silence fell. Angela looked down at her lap, deep in thought.

"Have you lost anything important?"

Faye burrowed her hands under the blanket.

"Like what?" she asked.

"The story I remember tells of a boy who goes into the woods looking for pine nuts. He carries a pouch, one that his grandmother made for him. The boy hears strange noises all around him and gets scared. As he runs back home, he trips and drops the pouch. When he and his father go to retrieve it that evening, they see a man squatting on the ground, sniffing the pouch. The man then turns around and speaks to the boy in his grandmother's voice. The boy and his father escape, but the man stands outside their home every night, calling out to the boy in familiar voices, begging for him to come outside."

"What happened to him?" Faye asked.

"The rest isn't important," Angela said, wearing a warm smile. "It's just a scary story, that's all."

"But come on, do you really believe in this stuff?" I asked. "I mean for God's sake, Faye's Catholic. This isn't the kind of thing we can talk to her priest about."

Angela sighed. I instantly knew I'd hit a sore spot.

Just stop talking, I thought to myself.

"Like I said," she responded, "There are two halves that make me whole. One is the girl who grew up practicing our spiritual tradition, and who still feels a duty to uphold those beliefs. The other is the adult who experiences the world on its surface, who hasn't had a sense for the 'supernatural' in decades. The believer and the atheist live inside of me together."

"I think it's like that for a lot of people," Faye offered.

Angela spoke with us for a few more minutes and then we parted ways. As I walked her to her car, she looked again to the tree line across the street and back at me.

"There's a dark cloud hanging over both of you, especially Faye," she said. "If this truly is a hollow one, I don't know what he wants. But he's not here to make friends."

Her words filled me with dread. I just stared back at her.

"Don't listen to it. Don't talk to it. And don't leave her alone with it. I'm sorry, Felix. I wish I knew how to help."

As soon as Faye went to bed, I headed straight for the closet with our luggage. As I had suspected, her engagement ring was nowhere to be found. There was little doubt in my mind that she had left it at the cabin – or worse, lost it in the snow. The likelihood of never getting it back crushed me, but the feeling was swiftly replaced with the mental image of that creature wandering around with it in the forest, sniffing it with glee.

That night, Faye sat up in bed, waking me in the process. As she tried to stand, I grabbed her by the arm and yanked her right back down.

"Nope," I said, pulling her close and wrapping her up in a tight hug from behind. "Sleep. Now."

Faye rolled toward me so that our noses touched. Her eyes were open and rolled far back in her head. She smiled

139

and ran a fingernail across my cheek, pretending to carve ribbons of flesh. She reminded me of a butcher delicately assessing a filet.

"They're gonna kill you," she whispered – then licked my face.

PART III

Chapter 19

"I think that's where she lets him in."

Angela's words ran through my head on repeat the entire night. The rational and superstitious parts of me offered dueling explanations for our predicament: some backwoods creep stalking my partner after spotting her at the cabin, or a demonic entity from some distant dimension preying upon her soul. I even imagined the creatures from Faye's drawings manifesting themselves in reality by the power of her own dreams. It was madness, and it pulled me ever downward to a place where I couldn't trust my own reason anymore.

By the time the sun rose, I had already emailed my boss, booked a flight back to Colorado, and left a voicemail on Lynn's phone. I knew there was something going on at the cabin that she and Greg didn't want me to find, but neither of them seemed the type to try and stop me. I told her that I'd already spoken to the ranger and his friends, and that I was beyond any capacity to tolerate one more lie. I ended the voicemail with, "This is an emergency. I'm doing this for your daughter, and I need your help."

I also texted my closest friends, Colin and Tyler, and

asked if they'd be willing to check in on Faye while I was gone. By 11 A.M., I'd heard back from both of them, each offering to put her up in his home while I was away. I knew that Faye would never return to Colin's house after the creepy incident with the bird all those years ago, but Tyler lived nearby, and his girlfriend got along with Faye pretty well.

Faye's reaction to all this was nothing short of breathtaking. She simply nodded in agreement, and thanked me for doing what I thought was best for her. I had expected a verbal mauling for making such a serious decision without consulting her, but her expression made it clear that she was even more fed up with this chaos than I was. I understood why.

I slept peacefully that night. Tyler and Colin had been in my life since we were kids, and they treated Faye like family. They'd guard her with their lives. I privately informed them of most of the things she'd been through, and why I was heading back to Colorado – but I spun it all in such a way that made our house seem haunted. Colin had always been a stone-cold atheist and didn't buy a word of what I said, but Tyler believed in all sorts of hocus pocus, thanks to his fervently religious mother and conspiracy-theorist father. Together, I hoped they would make a well-rounded team. Maybe they would see something I hadn't. Maybe they'd figure something out that I couldn't. The idea of Faye getting out of the house and being around other people gave me a glimmer of hope.

The morning was frantic. I parried a dozen of Lynn's attempts to dissuade me over the phone, threw some clothes in a suitcase, dropped Faye off at Tyler's apartment, rushed to the airport, and just barely caught the noon flight out to Denver. There was nobody around to hold my hand during takeoff this time, and that dreadful cabin loomed at the forefront of my thoughts. I loathed every moment of the journey.

One thing did bolster my resolve: Tíwé and I spoke briefly as I waited for the plane. He called just to check in, and was delighted to hear that I was on my way out to meet him. In the dizzying whirl of plans and plots, I'd forgotten entirely to warn him of my coming. On the plane, I wondered what else might have slipped my scattered mind.

Find the ring. Get the ring.

The reminder became a mantra to keep me focused. And if I ever pondered too deeply upon the what-ifs, I simply conjured the image of Faye, laughing and smiling. I tried to imagine her as she was before all this misery. I longed to see *that* Faye again, the wild-eyed lioness with a mane of fire. If I could get the ring back, maybe I could get my fiancée back too.

I arrived in Avonwood after dark. My cheap rental car stood out in the fleet of Mercedes and BMWs that sat in every driveway. Lynn answered the door with her trademark plastic-but-well-meaning smile. Greg was presumably so furious at my intrusion that he remained sequestered upstairs for the whole evening.

Faye's mother and I sat at the enormous glass dining room table, sipping hot chocolate and working our way through the miserable pleasantries of in-law conversation. It didn't take much to get her to hand over the cabin key. She burst into tears the moment I asked her, "Would you like to hear what your daughter has been through?"

"I'm so sorry I lied to you," she mumbled between sobs, "to both of you."

I was thrown off guard by the abruptness of her honesty. But I also recognized it as a rare moment that could vanish as quickly as it had appeared.

"Don't worry, Lynn," I said, trying to sound reassuring. "It's okay. Faye loves you, and I'm sure she forgives you. But you can make it up to us right now just by telling me what the hell is going on. What have you been lying about? I can't help her if you don't tell me everything."

Lynn looked up at me with an expression I'd never seen her wear before. It seemed devoid of any performance. What hung there on her face was a look of terror and sorrow, unleashed after weeks of denial. She gazed through me with bloodshot eyes, and fingered at the tiny gold crucifix that dangled from her neck.

"That cabin..." she said, taking a deep breath, "Faye's been there before. Only once. It's where her night terrors started. Something happened up there, Felix."

"Tell me," I implored. I reached over and held her freezing hand. It trembled.

"She was just a little girl," Lynn whispered, new tears rolling down her face. "She was only five years old."

Chapter 20

"When we first got the place, Greg used to stay there on fishing trips with his buddies," Lynn said, regaining some of her composure. She wiped her face and looked over her shoulder to make sure her husband wasn't around. "Mirror Lake's on the other side of the mountain, so they'd go up there for some competition every spring.

"One year was especially tough on us, emotionally. So we planned a little getaway for a weekend. Greg always loved the outdoors, and he wanted the kids to love it too. To be honest, I think he always wanted a boy, and he ended up trapped in a house with three ladies."

I chuckled. The image of Faye cleaning a rifle, or wrestling a bear for that matter, wasn't too hard to imagine. She was as tough as any boy Greg might have had.

"Faye's sister was around ten at the time, and she didn't come with us," Lynn continued. "There was some kind of retreat with her Girl Scout troop that weekend, so she went with them instead."

"Has Becca ever been to the cabin?" I asked.

"No. She's never been interested. Not much of a mountain girl. In fact, she lives in Phoenix now."

The sound of a toilet flushing came from upstairs, followed by footsteps across the hall. We both went silent for a moment. A door closed.

"They were outside the cabin," Lynn said, voice barely above a whisper. "Greg and Faye. Building snowmen in the field next to the driveway. I could see them from the kitchen window. I had the news on, and I remember looking over at the TV for a few minutes. When I looked back, I couldn't see Faye anymore. Greg was still rolling a big ball of snow.

"Faye had walked over to the edge of the meadow to look into the forest. Greg said he heard her talking, but thought she was just singing to herself. Eventually he realized that she was answering questions, like there was someone in the woods. Faye was trying to follow a voice. As Greg walked over there, he heard Faye saying things like 'just Mommy and Daddy' and 'she's not here' and 'I can't see you. What's your name?'"

Those phrases struck a nerve in me. They were just like Faye's sleep talk now. Whoever was interrogating her had been doing it on and off for *decades*. But what was he looking for? The question was like fire on my brain.

"All of a sudden, she started screaming," Lynn continued. "It was like she saw something terrifying. I heard it and came running outside into the snow. I didn't even have shoes on. Greg was already rushing over there, and he caught Faye just as she fell. She went rigid and her eyes rolled back in her head. Just seeing my daughter like that...I've never been so scared in my life."

Everything Lynn said resonated with me in a dreadful way. I glanced around the dark living room, sifting through the hundred questions that brimmed at the edge of my lips.

"Do you think she fell asleep?" I asked. "I've read about soldiers falling asleep in the middle of a battle. It's some kind of defense mechanism the brain uses to protect you from trauma."

"No," Lynn replied. "She was definitely awake. We hauled her back inside, and for a few hours, she would either cry hysterically, or just sit there in silence. She couldn't speak at all. We eventually decided to take her back down the mountain to a hospital, but when we got into town, she got better all of a sudden. Just went right back to normal, like turning on a light. The doctors thought she had some kind of seizure, but couldn't find anything wrong with her.

"To this day, Greg swears he never heard any other voices or saw anyone in those woods. We only stayed there one more time, about a year later – just the two of us, for our anniversary. And that's when Greg's night terrors came back. He never slept there again."

"And Faye? When did she start up with the nightmares and sleepwalking?"

Lynn picked at her fingernails.

"A few days after her incident. They've come and gone ever since."

A mixture of rage and fright churned in my gut, pushing the hot chocolate up to the back of my throat.

"And you thought sending us back up there was a good idea?" I demanded.

"I didn't know!" Lynn said, a bit too loud. More tears welled up in her eyes. "I honestly didn't think that trauma would resurface after all these years! What do you expect me to believe, that there's some phantom up on Pale Peak that likes to talk to kids?"

Lynn abruptly left the table and headed upstairs, apologizing as she went. I couldn't tell if she was more embarrassed by the fact that she'd doomed her daughter in sending her back to the cabin, or simply that she was crying in front of her future son-in-law. I threw my hands into the air and retired to Faye's old bedroom for the night.

I'd seen the home videos. Little Faye was adorable and curious. A kid like that would certainly hold a conversation with a stranger, maybe even one from another dimension, if he interested her enough. Whoever it was that called out to her from those woods, he was delighted that she spoke back. Perhaps he became fascinated with her, or something he thought she knew, and had been digging through her mind for years trying to unearth it. Faye's strong personality might have prevented him from fooling her while she was awake, but while asleep, she is as gentle as a lamb, and naïve. Almost like a child.

I believed that if Faye had remembered what had happened to her at the cabin, she'd never have agreed to go back – not even with me. It made sense then that she had probably repressed that experience or forgotten it entirely. What few physical details about the cabin she remembered were probably repackaged by her brain as dim flashes from an uneventful trip.

I was awoken the next morning by a text message from Tyler. He told me that Faye had slept through the night without incident, and that his fiancée Allison had been cheering her up. Colin and Gabriella were planning on making the drive to our town, so Faye would have plenty of company for the weekend. Knowing that our friends were rallying to her side made me smile.

As usual, Greg was up early, tinkering in the kitchen and grumbling to himself. As I made my way down there, he stopped what he was doing and watched me approach. For a moment, it almost looked as if he didn't know I had even come to visit – but then I realized he was simply unable to bring himself to speak to me. Maybe Lynn told him that we'd talked. Maybe he'd heard everything from the top of the stairs.

"Be careful with her," he said, tossing a ring of keys on the bar counter that separated us. "Weather's warming up but the roads are still icy up there, I'm sure." He brushed past me and headed out to the patio for his morning cigarette.

I examined the keys. That truck was Greg's favorite child. It had belonged to his father Alfred, and when he died, Greg had rebuilt the engine and restored the interior. He worked on it every week, rain or shine, always finding new problems to solve. Faye maintained that this was his way of managing the pain of Alfred's death; the ability to fix one thing balanced the inability to fix another. I couldn't help but wonder if Greg's gesture meant that he trusted me.

"Look," he said, holding the patio door open with his foot, "I didn't say anything, and I should have."

Of course you fucking should have, I wanted to snap at him. If it wasn't for Lynn and Greg's horrible negligence, none of this would have happened. Faye and I would be living normal lives like regular people, and I wouldn't be missing work and pissing off my advisor and colleagues. I wouldn't be heading back up to that god-forsaken place all alone. I swallowed the urge to bite back and nodded instead.

"We honestly wanted to believe there was nothing wrong with the place," he said. He forced the last words up with considerable effort: "I'm sorry."

Chapter 21

No matter how bad my mood was, the drive was undeniably beautiful. Seas of emerald grass washed over the landscape, frosted with big clumps of snow and perforated by jutting rock formations. In the distance, icy mountains glimmered under a sapphire sky. A blood red ring would ignite the Rockies by sunset.

The cold still clung to the earth out here, but thankfully the snow had diminished a bit. Big patches of it caked the trees, occasionally sloughing off and battering the truck or the road as I drove past. The trees thickened to forests, mountains erupted from the earth, and then the shadow of Pale Peak fell over my path. The massive thing loomed over the highway, darkening it in broad daylight, and almost seemed to taunt me. My resolve wavered, and doubt plagued my mind. A cruel voice in my head whispered, *"You'll die up here. There's no hope for Faye."*

Greg must have called ahead, because the ranger was parked in the driveway by the time I pulled up. He stepped out of his SUV as I fumbled with the shifter.

"Can't believe the old coot's lettin' you use it," he said,

thumping the side of Greg's truck.

I finally jammed the thing into Park and got out. The air bit my face, reminding me of just how unwelcome I was up here.

"Mr. Blackwell," William said, giving my hand a firm shake.

"Ranger Pike," I replied.

"Thought I'd have a look around the place again once y'all got here, make sure everything's in order."

We stepped up onto the porch. As I sifted through Greg's keyring, my eyes kept darting to the forest's edge.

"Ain't nothin' out there," William said, patting my back. It felt good having someone there with me, especially someone bigger than me, but I knew that eventually I'd have to sleep. The ranger would go home to his family somewhere far away, and I'd be all alone out here.

"You guys never found the dreamcatcher?" I asked, stepping inside the cabin.

"Nope. Damn sure weren't a thing out of place outside. In here's a different story." William casually rested his hand on his gun and swept his gaze over the living room and kitchen. "We cleaned it up real nice," he added.

Everything looked in order, save one little thing I hadn't noticed until William flipped the light switch. The standing lamp next to the television was missing its lampshade. The bulb glowed fiercely, casting hard shadows across the room.

"What's the deal?" I asked, pointing at the light.

William paused for a moment and replied, "Been like that since y'all left."

He poked around for a bit, making sure that no points of entry had been breached, and tried to avoid any conversation about the fact that someone had definitely been inside. He informed me that Tíwé was dealing with a family emergency and would drop by in the morning

153

instead of tonight. My heart nearly died in my chest. I had expected to be alone at the cabin, but not before getting some kind of counsel from Tíwé.

"You just make sure you call me at this number if anything goes wrong," William said, handing me a card. "That's my cell. It's on 24-7, just in case."

With that, Ranger Pike dropped a heavy hand on my shoulder and turned to leave.

"Hey, uh...you guys find a ring in here by any chance?" I asked. I already knew the answer, but I really didn't want him to leave.

William looked back at me from the doorway. Cold air rushed in all around his bulky form.

"I'd have pawned it if I did."

We both hesitated.

"You know," he said, clutching the doorknob, "you ain't gotta be up here. Plenty motels at the base."

"You really think I'm in danger?" I asked, almost pleading for reassurance.

"Naw," he replied. "Maybe it's just one a' them things where if you stop believin', it'll just go away. But uh, you call me and I'll come."

Darkness ate away at the sky. I rushed around the place, dragging my bags in from the truck and ensuring that the windows were locked and curtains drawn. The old CD player helped with the loneliness, but I still couldn't relax. The dreamcatcher kept appearing in my mind. I had to know if it was still there.

Against my better judgment, I bundled up and trekked across the open field behind the cabin. The last light of day rapidly withdrew across the mountains in the distance, and in that moment I wished Faye were there to see it with me. We hadn't been this far apart in years, and the ache reminded me that I didn't want to know what life might be like without her. I had to find the ring, even if I had to pry it from the putrid fingers of this thing Angela called "the hollow one."

The snow felt thin and crunchy beneath my shoes. Each footfall sent a message throughout the surrounding area that I was here – and alone. It took every drop of my courage to move into the abyssal gloom of the woods.

I circled a few trees, trying to remember which one had the dreamcatcher. Greg's flashlight rattled in my hand, its beam moving over branches and rocks and trunks. Something gently brushed against my neck. It felt like a cold finger. I yelped in surprise and whirled around.

And there it was – a long feather, fluttering softly in the breeze, attached to a string that dangled from a huge circular object.

Not string, I realized. *Sinew. And blood.*

"Ugly son of a bitch," I mumbled, rubbing my neck.

White bones gleamed in the flashlight's glare. They looked slick, almost wet, as though someone had replaced the old ones with fresh pieces. The urge to tear it down surged through me, but I wanted to show it to Tíwé.

As I gazed upon the strange thing, a chorus of wicked voices erupted from deeper in the woods. One was an older man, and the other a boy. They shouted to each other, back and forth, but none of it made any sense.

"What'd you put up there? What the hell is that?!"

"Weeeee foouuuund 'em, found 'em down in the hole, daddy-o!"

"Put us back. Put us back. God, please hear me."

I broke into a full sprint through the meadow, blazing toward the cabin like a meteor. Otherworldly terror fueled me, and the image of psychotic cannibals jabbering with their tongues hanging out of their mouths swirled in my mind. I flew inside and slammed the door shut, holding back tears. There in the stillness, I listened to the screams

155

of the wind and the hellish beings that chattered over it. The light vanished. Darkness conquered the landscape and imprisoned me in the cabin.

Chapter 22

The relative safety of the cabin brought me no solace. I barricaded the door with furniture, set the gun on the counter, and blared the cheeriest music I could find in Lynn's CD collection, but the primal dread of death never lifted. I tried to reach out to Faye, but my phone's reception was so spotty that I couldn't get more than a single text message out.

The wind howled for my blood all night. Every noise it produced caught my ear, and I imagined unspeakable creatures slinking and slithering around in the dark outside. And whenever the wind died down, the voices returned, sometimes in the distance and sometimes close by. To busy myself, I searched every inch of the place, room by room, for Faye's engagement ring, hoping that it had simply fallen behind the bed or under the couch. Deep down I suspected that it was far away in the woods, clutched in the gnarled hands of some ghastly creature that desired Faye as strongly as I did.

After an hour of hunting, I found nothing, and retreated to the bedroom with Greg's gun. The bed felt bigger and colder without Faye here, and instead of dozing off to the sounds of her breathing, I listened with morbid fascination to the yammering of the madmen outside.

"It's so deep, deep down," a child cried. "So deep you could crawl forever." As he spoke, his voice occasionally splinter, becoming deeper and raspier – like a grown man impersonating a boy. He hacked and wept and choked. He begged for help. But I didn't fall for a single word of it. Somewhere farther out, another voice shrieked, "They're lying, they're lying, the ones out there! *La la la la la la*."

I somehow managed to drift into a fitful sleep, but was awoken a little before midnight by a new sound. Someone tapped on the window in the living room. It was soft, like a neighbor who was reluctant to bother me. I stood there in the bedroom with the door open, holding my breath, trying to figure out if I'd imagined it. Then it happened again, so I crept down the short hall and peeked around the corner – just in time to see a figure walking past the window near the TV, heading toward the front door. With the curtains drawn, I only saw a lumbering shadow, but it was so huge it blocked out the moonlight and threw pitch blackness over the entire room.

Then, it knocked gently on the door. A man's voice called out softly,

"Hello?"

I remained still as death, listening to every noise he made. Eventually he knocked again, and said,

"Hello? I...I need to speak with you."

The man spoke through clenched teeth. He sounded either very cold, or full of rage, but his words were frighteningly restrained.

I tried to sneak back to the bedroom where I'd left the gun, but the old place betrayed me. As I moved I nudged the bedroom door, and it squealed like a dying pig. The man outside whispered, "I know you're in there."

158

For just a moment, in my lethargy, I considered the possibility that this was Tíwé, or maybe somebody else who lived on the mountain. There was no way I'd open the door, but I stupidly figured that responding was a good idea.

"Who the fuck is it?" I said as forcefully as I could. I grabbed the gun and marched to the front door.

Whoever was out there repeated my question – while accurately mimicking me. It almost sounded like an echo. Then he said,

"May I come in? Please?"

It was my voice, filtered through gritted teeth. The words seemed shaky and uncertain, but it was an impressive mockery of the way I spoke. Icy terror swept over my body and every muscle in my back knotted up. I planted the barrel of the gun against the door.

"You hear that?" I said, tapping it on the wood. "That's a .357. If you don't get outta here, I'll turn you into a fucking milkshake."

We both stood there for a dreadfully long minute. The person outside began testing my voice, groaning and whispering and muttering. He spoke a few discernable phrases and a lot of gibberish, seemingly unconcerned that I was listening:

"What's your name? What's your name?"

"A sssssuper...Nin...Nintenun...Nintendo..."

"What did you dream?"

His voice wavered, cycling through other accents and cadences. The words seemed stitched together from different mouths, cobbled into phrases he strained to get out. At that point I immediately stopped believing there was a human being on the other side of the door.

"Stop it!" I shouted. "Whatever you want, I don't have it!" It took all my strength not to open fire. I was terrified that shooting him would only piss him off.

"You go up in the trees...or down in the hole," he replied, nearly perfecting my voice. "That's where you go. Oh they'll find you. Either way...either way...either way..."

The wind picked up, rattling the windows. The man knocked again, gentle and polite.

"You aren't alone in there. I'm not alone out here. What's your name?"

"Leave now, or I *will* shoot you!" I screamed. I fumbled with the gun, uncertain of whether the bullet would travel through the door if I opened fire.

"A little cabin for the weekend, for the weekend, *shhhhhh-k-k-k-k*," he replied, making a slew of lip-smacking and chewing noises.

I had never felt so terrified in my twenty-eight years of life, even after witnessing my own fiancée creeping around the house like a fleshy marionette. The experience of my own voice making those horrific sounds and phrases set every inch of my skin on fire. My body felt hot and cold and wet and sticky all at the same time, like waking up with a bad fever. I smashed the butt of the gun into the door in an attempt to ward off the terrible visitor, and screamed at the top of my lungs,

"I will *fucking kill you!*"

The man – the *thing* – outside fell silent. I stood there clutching the revolver, waiting for a response. Finally, there was a *knock-knock-knock*, this time a bit harder than before, followed by,

"I...will fucking...kill you."

Before I could respond, he shouted, "I see her! I know where she is!" and bashed the door with a powerful kick. It sounded like two hooves striking against it; the impact threw me backward and shook the entire cabin. He barreled across the porch on what sounded like four legs and bounded off into the woods, laughing in the voice of a child as he did.

An eerie silence fell. The wind and wretched voices died away, leaving me with only the throb of my temples and the labor of my breathing.

I remained in a state of extreme paranoia for the rest of the night. The delirium of terror and insomnia stole my balance and blurred my vision. I stumbled around like a drunk and cowered between the bed and the wall, fantasizing about putting a bullet in my head and ending this nightmare once and for all. But thoughts of Faye anchored me to my sanity. The desire to protect her gave me strength. Still, the encounter haunted my thoughts, and I realized that this entity was intelligent and had a plan. When he spoke, he chose his words carefully, knowing that the right combination could weaken my resolve. He knew exactly what to say. If he couldn't coax me outside, he would whittle me down until I let him in. And then he would drag me off into the forest, where the voices cry.

Chapter 23

We do idiotic things for love. It was a foolish decision to risk my life staying alone at the cabin, but I truly believed that if there was any way to stop this entity from harming us any further, I would find it here. Maybe he would lose interest in Faye if I could get the ring back. Maybe I could find a way to undo whatever we had done to attract his attention in the first place. As far as I knew, this "hollow one" had first discovered Faye here on Pale Peak, and thus it made sense to me that the solution too lay on the mountain. At least, that is what Tíwé seemed to believe, and at this point I had little choice but to trust him.

Many possibilities ran through my faltering mind between midnight and sunrise. I considered the idea that the Faye who had returned home to California was not the same one who'd come to Pale Peak. What if the nude woman on my car was the real Faye, and she'd been out in the forest all along? What if she had died out there weeks ago, and the woman sleepwalking around my house was some wicked simulacrum?

Just before dawn, I went to the kitchen for a glass of water. As I drank, I peered out the window and saw the familiar dark figure at the edge of the woods. He remained there, completely motionless, staring up at the trees with his back to the cabin. I checked on him every twenty minutes until daybreak, and only then, when the sunlight touched the tops of the trees, did he leave. I still couldn't get a look at his face.

The sun became my guardian. It made me feel safe enough to risk sleeping, so I dropped onto the bed like a corpse into a grave. Sleep washed over me and dragged me down into a darkness beneath the dream world, where not even the creature outside could follow.

A loud knock at the door roused me. I instinctively grabbed the gun, dreading that the entity had come for another visit. Cheerful birdsongs and mumbling voices wafted through the cabin. I glanced at my phone.

10:49 A.M.

At least I got a few hours.

Lively chatter and the sounds of laughter eased my fears as I approached the door. The sight of Ranger Pike and two other men overjoyed me. I wasn't alone anymore.

"Mr. Blackwell," William said, tipping a cowboy hat, "like you to meet Tíwé Lopez and his son Nathan."

The older of the two men approached me with a big smile on his face. His graying hair was pulled back in a short pony-tail, and his brown eyes glinted with an energetic youthfulness that seemed out of place on such a weathered face.

"Felix," he said, shaking my hand and squeezing my shoulder. "A pleasure, finally!"

Nathan followed suit. He was probably a year or two older than me, and unlike his father, he had green eyes.

"You've come a long way," Tíwé said, "been through a lot, from what I hear. It's about time we talk."

I welcomed all three of them into the cabin, but the

ranger declined and said he needed to do a few house calls and map road conditions. He handed me a satellite phone and told me that he couldn't reach me on my cell. I told him I'd return his phone on my way down the mountain the day after tomorrow. We watched him back out of the driveway and head further up the winding road.

"How's Angela look these days?" Tíwé asked, taking a seat on the couch. "Been nearly ten years since she's come back to visit."

I dragged a chair into the living room and offered the guys some water. Nathan made a counter-offer of hot tea instead, and busied himself in the kitchen while his father and I spoke.

"She seems great," I replied, still unsure of the nature of their relationship. "Very nice lady."

"She bore you with her academic spiels?" he laughed. "Some things you cannot learn from books!"

"I'm actually an academic myself," I admitted. Tíwé's expression changed.

"My apologies," he said. "They come out here for their research trips all the time, organized by the universities. We can tell they mean well, but they sometimes treat us like...like..."

"Lab rats," Nathan interjected, carrying mugs of tea into the room. He sat down next to his father and studied me.

"I was thinking of Jane Goodall, living among the chimps!" Tíwé said, cracking up.

"Angela mentioned that, uh, Natives are sometimes hesitant to share information with outsiders," I said, trying to remember her exact words.

"It's true," Tíwé replied. "At least for my people. We aren't so cavalier in sharing our history. It's a very personal thing. You can't just tell the stories like a history teacher in

164

a classroom. The setting matters. The audience matters. How you tell the story, and where you tell it – why you tell it – it all matters! The wisdom of our fathers was spoken for generations, not written down and revised and published. Not sold and archived. The Europeans thought we were backward for this! And the anthropologists who visit us, they call this 'oral tradition.' I guess it's fitting."

"So it's like a performance," I said, trying to demonstrate that I understood.

"But not for entertainment!" Tíwé bellowed. He immediately regretted the outburst and lowered his voice. "Not always. This is how we keep our mothers' and fathers' teachings alive in the minds of our children."

"My father's crazy, by the way," Nathan added.

"*Te'anoi nakhan*," Tíwé said, tapping his head. "Too much snowboarding and Red Bull. Rots his brains." This time, we all laughed.

"Just let me know if I ask something I shouldn't," I said. "There's so much I want to ask."

Tíwé gave me a comforting smile and nodded.

"I wish we had all the answers you're looking for," he said. "But all we know are some of the stories. My great grandmother might have been able to help. My dad always said she had vast knowledge, and could even see into the spirit world. If you buy that sort of thing."

"Is that what we're dealing with?" I asked, daring to draw upon my extensive memories of *The X-Files*. "Some kind of demon? Like a...skin-walker?"

"Older than the skin-walkers," Nathan offered.

"This creature is one of the first beings, is what he means," Tíwé pushed back. "Not many of our people believe in the skin-walkers. Those come from the Navajo, and we don't know much of anything about them."

I fidgeted in my chair. Despite the warmth of my drink, my body felt colder.

"Angela called him a hollow man," I said, "or something like that."

"There is a power in words and names, Felix," Nathan responded. "We don't speak the names of the dead for some time after they've passed. And we don't repeat curses that were uttered long ago."

"Now who sounds crazy?" Tíwé said with a big grin on his face. Nathan rolled his eyes and dismissed his father's playfulness.

"It's a bit like the Christians and the devil," Nathan continued. "They don't say his name often and they don't use spirit boards to consult the dead. You don't want to call out to him."

"I won't repeat it," I promised. "I probably can't even pronounce it."

They both laughed. Tíwé got up to refill his tea. He returned with a glum expression.

"My people gave him the name *At'an-A'anotogkua*," he said quietly. "The term refers to water, and how it is formless until it fills a vessel. Angela wasn't wrong when she called him the 'hollow one,' because there is no direct translation, really. Maybe it is more accurate to call him 'the Impostor,' because this being fills himself with the life force of his prey."

"The Impostor," I echoed. I imagined a grotesque monster deep in the woods outside, suddenly opening his eyes at the sound of his own name.

"Felix," Tíwé said, leaning toward me, "a lot of people in my community would be reluctant to share much of our heritage with you. So I'm going to tell you just a little piece. Only the stuff that I think pertains directly to you and your fiancée. Is that alright with you?"

I nodded, eager to hear anything that could possibly help Faye.

"And I must stress," he continued, "we don't have any

166

experience with this sort of thing. No one in our community does, really. Some of the tribal elders recall the stories, and a few actually believe the Impostors are real. But Nathan and I don't go around purging evil spirits, you know. By God, this kid can't even purge a drain clog."

Nathan scowled.

"Thanks, Dad."

Chapter 24

Tíwé took a sip of his tea, then sat up straight as if to make a formal announcement. He searched the room with his eyes, carefully choosing his words. Nathan sat quietly and looked down at his hands. I wasn't sure if this was a display of respect, or if he was simply concentrating, so I turned my gaze to the floor and fell silent as Tíwé cleared his throat.

"Colorado has been home to many groups," he began. "The Ute, Cheyenne, Arapaho, Pueblo, and Anasazi people have all called it home at one point or another. There are many more who came and left. War and famine and weather always shifted people around, but the big movements came when the Gold Rush spread here. Thousands and thousands of Natives were displaced – or killed. Mining operations forced people out of their ancestral homelands.

"There's something you have to understand about land, Felix. How we think of it. The settlers thought of land as a possession. You claim it and put a fence around it. You sign a piece of paper, and it belongs to you. You sign another piece of paper, and now it belongs to someone else.

Doesn't matter where it is; land is all the same. You can even purchase land you've never seen before, never visited, a thousand miles away – and now it belongs to you!

"This is not how many Natives understood the earth when the settlers came. The land doesn't just belong to us. We belong to the land. We were given to it, just as much as it was given to us. Some even believe we are *of* it, that we came from it.

"Our history is embedded in the physical landscape, anchored there by stories that convey our ancestral knowledge. A Native is reminded of specific lessons when he sees a particular landmark: the mouth of this river has an important story attached to it. That fallen tree has one too. A battle was won here. An elder died there. Peace was made between warring tribes with a ceremony here. And so, when a Native group is forced out of its homeland, the people sometimes forget their stories. History itself is lost.

"What's worse, they leave behind the places where their dead are buried – their mothers and fathers. The dead are bound to that place, and have returned to the land there. Because of this, Natives who are forced out of their homelands no longer have connections to their ancestors, and thus, to the spirit world. Their medicines no longer work. Their prayers are no longer heard.

"Eventually, the younger generations forget the names of sacred places. And as the names and history and wisdom are forgotten, the peoples' spiritual power diminishes. The culture collapses. How they perceive this change affects their whole way of life."

Tíwé paused for my response, but I had no idea what to say. Nathan sensed my confusion and elaborated on his father's words:

"Think of Christianity and Judaism and Hinduism," he said. "Those are universal religions. The Jews were scattered all across Europe and the Middle East, exiled from their homelands – and yet they remained Jews. Muslims and Hindus emigrate from the other side of the world to live here in the United States, and they bring their religions with them. You could move to New York tomorrow and still keep your religion. Your god can still hear your prayers. He can still intervene in your life."

"It is not so with the Native!" Tíwé exclaimed. "It is much more difficult to recover those things when his land is stolen. This is why the anthropologists come to us. They want to ask us about our 'land-based religions.' We're telling you this, Felix, because you cannot understand the supernatural presence on this mountain without understanding the mountain itself."

I nodded, trying to digest his words as quickly as he spoke them. Tíwé took another long draw of his tea, probably to give me a moment to process everything.

"When the settlers arrived," he continued, "they forced my people and a few other tribes out of the valleys, where all the food grew. Some of us came to the mountain, and some went far away, never to return. When the settlers moved their mining operations farther up the mountain, they battled with our old neighbors, the Pozi. Many died on both sides. The remaining Pozi allied with the Ineho, the people from the mountains to the North, and together they slaughtered dozens of the miners.

"The settlers mounted a counter-attack, and murdered hundreds in retaliation. This went on and on, back and forth for a long time, until the alliance collapsed and the Natives turned against each other."

"Why did they do that?" I asked. Tíwé nodded at his son.

"No one knows," Nathan said. "Some believe the settlers bribed the Pozi. Colonists have always used bribery to turn Natives against each other. Made them fight in their wars. It is said that the Ineho found out about these bribes and killed many of the Pozi, then dug holes and buried them with their feet sticking out of the ground. Legend says they wanted the wolves to eat the meat on their legs, so that the Pozi could never make the journey back to their homeland – even in death."

"This is dark," I said, glancing at the pristine snow through the window. I imagined it
soaked red with blood.

"Try getting those anthropologists to publish that!" Tíwé boomed, laughing hysterically. "They want you to think we sit around campfires singing about world peace and Mother Earth. We're human, aren't we? We make war and peace like anybody else – blood feuds aren't just a European thing!"

"Try to keep in mind," Nathan added, "that story is a brief moment in the long history of this mountain. Perhaps my father might have told you about the times of great peace instead, if he knew you wouldn't fall asleep."

I nodded my acceptance of the rebuttal.

"But what's this got to do with the Impostor?" I asked, pointing to the window. "Did the Pozi summon him for revenge or something?"

Nathan laughed, but Tíwé did not.

"There are fewer believers among us these days," Tíwé replied. "But once, many of our people thought that the Impostors snuck into our world from time to time, looking for things they coveted. We believed that they are sometimes drawn to the sites of terrible suffering – like here on Pale Peak.

"Shortly after the Pozi slaughter, the Ineho suffered a tragedy of their own. Every child in one of their villages disappeared. Some Ineho believed that the slaughtered Pozi rose up from their graves and stole the children away.

"But my people told a different story. They believed the *At'an-A'anotogkua* had come to the mountain, and

171

called out to the children in the night. He killed a few of them and stole their skin and hair, and hung them up in the trees for the villagers to find. Then, posing as a child, he led the rest deep down into the mines. They were never seen again, but their voices still echo on the mountain."

My breath froze in my chest. The laughter and crying of little kids ran through my imagination, sounds that were all too familiar to me in this cabin.

"Did he lure them with a song, by any chance?" I asked. "Did he stand at the edge of the woods?"

"You've actually seen this being?" Nathan asked. He looked at his father with grave concern.

"I think I've met him," I said, and explained at length the encounters I'd had with the strange man.

Tíwé studied me carefully, and Nathan looked upon me with disbelief.

"I've heard it said that the Impostor cannot pass for a man," Tíwé replied, "no matter how hard he tries. That is why he appears only at night, and why he always faces away from his victim – even when he is watching."

"You're the first person we've ever met to describe such things," Nathan added. "Tourists that visit the mountain sometimes report strange noises at night, or someone peeping into their windows. But no one has ever told us something like this."

"One family did," Tíwe corrected. "A long time ago. And they lived in this very cabin."

"Do you believe me then?" I asked, point-blank.

Both men hesitated.

"We need time to think about all this," Tíwé said with a sigh. "This is very serious. I have no idea how the leaders of my community will react, but I need to speak with them about it."

"I believe you," Nathan offered. He smiled and dropped a fist onto his palm in a gesture of camaraderie.

Chapter 25

After our conversation, Tíwé asked me to lead them to the dreamcatcher I'd described to William. When they had first investigated the cabin, they couldn't find it, but it took me less than a minute to locate it. We romped through the shallow snow and made our way into the trees. Tíwé seemed reasonably certain that he had checked this location, but blamed the oversight on his old age, rather than some strange magic. I was unsettled by the idea that the object had been hidden during their last visit.

"I don't think this is really a dreamcatcher," he said, examining it closely. He manipulated it with a stick, rather than touching it with his hands.

"Why's that?" I asked.

"Well, I don't know for sure. My people don't make these. In fact, very few Native tribes do. They've sort of come to represent all Indians, but they're not some universal thing we all use. The reason I think it's something else is because dreamcatchers were made for protection and balance. This one was made using symbols of death." Tíwé pointed at the jagged bones and bloodied feathers. "And the woven pattern here is a disaster. It could be sloppy craftsmanship, but it could also be intentional – to represent chaos."

"Looks like it was done by someone with claws instead of hands," Nathan said, half-joking.

"Or a drunk-ass redneck," Tíwé mused. "But honestly, it could be some other kind of totem. Who knows."

I shrugged at the term.

"It's like a crafted object with a link to the spirit world," Tíwé explained. "Or at least some kind of spiritual meaning. Ever worn a crucifix?"

"Sure," I replied. "Long time ago. Faye's got one."

"There you go," Tíwé said, taking one last look at the strange object. "I recommend you don't touch this thing, Felix. Someone put this here on purpose, and we have no idea what it means to them."

"I need you to be honest with me," I said, looking off to the woods, then back to Tíwé. "You wouldn't have told me all this stuff if you didn't believe the Impostor might be real. I need to know if you think Faye and I are in danger. Something evil has been visiting us every night, and so far we still don't know what he wants."

"Not evil," Tíwé replied. "Not good, either. At least not in our stories."

"How could he not be evil?" I argued, baffled by his response. "You said it yourself. He kills people. *Children!*"

"Is the wolf not evil in the eyes of the deer?" he asked. "or the hawk, in the ears of the rabbit? We don't believe in good and evil spirits. At least not like the big religions do. In our tradition, there is no Heaven or Hell, no duality. It's more complicated."

"So we're just dinner," I said, perhaps a bit too harsh. Tíwé didn't acknowledge the statement. Instead he grabbed my shoulder with a gentle hand.

"How long will you be here?" he asked me.

I shrugged.

"One more night. Maybe two, tops. I need to find Faye's ring. Then I'm gone."

"I do think you're in danger," Tíwé replied, "Both of you. I'd tell you to come with us, but it doesn't seem to matter where you go."

I nodded. If the creature could follow us back to California, he certainly could track me a few miles away to Tíwé's community.

"Nathan and I need to ask for help," he continued, "because there's little we can do on our own. But we will come back tomorrow. I promise."

I was surprised to learn that the ranger wasn't going to pick Tíwé and Nathan up. They had apparently hiked to the cabin and met him here, and now planned to hike back down the mountain. Nathan dismissed my concerns about the dropping temperature, insisting that they walked this road almost every day. "Keeps his veins clear," he said about his father. They zipped up their coats and bade me farewell. As I saw them off, Tíwé whirled around and tossed me a small neck pouch he'd produced from beneath his shirt.

"My dad made it," he said, smiling. "Always makes me feel safer. I'll pick it up when I get back."

"What is it?" I asked.

"Just a bit of sage. I change it out every so often. Might not ward off the devil, but it'll protect you from the smell of your bad cooking."

"You really crack yourself up, eh?" I shot back. Tíwé's ill-concealed snickers broke to open laughter.

I waved goodbye to my new friends and retreated into the cabin. The sun edged closer to the distant mountains, and a bitter wind whipped across the field. Thick clouds approached from the East and collected above my tiny prison, promising a new blanket of snow in the morning. I had flown to Colorado and spent half a day with the only

175

person I believed could help my family, and yet I had little to show for it. I didn't feel any closer to ridding us of the malevolent presence that hungered for Faye.

The dues of sleep deprivation caught up with me just after sundown. Too exhausted to stay up any longer, I crawled into bed and vanished into a near-coma. I woke before midnight to the nagging of a full bladder, and dragged myself to the bathroom. The entire cabin was freezing; I must have forgotten to set the thermostat. Instead of waiting for the heater to slowly warm the place up, I drew a boiling hot bath and slid into it like a sedated eel. As I lay there, floating at the precipice of sleep, Faye's voice drifted into my mind – her laughter, her jabs, her flirtatious coos. I hoped Tyler and Colin were keeping her happy and distracted. I missed her.

My eyes rolled around in my head, dragging my blurry gaze across the room. They landed on the steamy window just above the tub. There was something on it, something written. I stood up, splashing water all over the floor.

It was another '5', written backwards on the glass from inside. The writing didn't look fresh; it seemed faded and poorly defined compared to the reference '5' I drew beside it with my own finger. Faye must have done this when we visited.

And then it hit me: she was signaling the Impostor long before we returned to California. How long had she been communicating with him?

I leaped out of the tub and wrapped a towel around myself, ignoring the sting of my freezing feet and the pools of water they tracked everywhere. I marched around, fogging every window in the cabin with a few breaths, searching for more hidden messages. Each breath revealed the number five, always written backwards so that a person outside could read it. They varied in size, and the
176

bedroom window had ten or eleven of them scribbled all over it.

As I examined this window, there came a knock at the front door.

My breath caught in my throat. I poked my head out into the hall, gazing down the long darkness of it.

Knock-knock-knock.

"Hello?" my voice called out. It came not from my own mouth, but from outside. "Hello? Are you there?"

I held still, considering whether it was smarter to pretend I wasn't home, or to argue with the dreadful visitor as I had the night before. Would he come inside if he thought I wasn't here? Then, I remembered the missing lampshade, and the ranger's observation that someone had searched the cabin and rifled through our clothes. The thought of this creature climbing in through a window raised every hair on my neck.

Knock-knock-knock-knock-knock-knock-knock-knock.

"This is dark," he mumbled. "Dark, dark. Acada...acadack...acaddada...emic...aca...demic."

Please go away, I prayed. In that moment I had never so dearly missed Faye. Her image swirled in my mind; my brain conjured her because it believed I was about to die. I was going to die a thousand miles away from the only person who loved me.

The creature outside suddenly drew fast, raspy breaths. It was as if the very thought of her innervated him.

"Is that...is that a fucking dreamcatcher?" he said. He tapped something against the door, maybe a claw, then walked slowly across the porch. The tapping became a scraping sound, and it grew louder as the creature made his way around the house toward the bedroom. Toward me.

I flicked off the light and darted over to the window,

yanking the curtain shut just before a large form moved behind it.

Tic-tic-tic-tic-tic.

The figure tapped on the glass and issued a deep gurgling sound from his throat. The guttural noises took shape and became my voice once again, and out came sentences he must have overheard me saying weeks ago. He had been here all along. He was listening to us all the time, crouching beneath the windows and memorizing how we spoke.

"What is your name?" he asked.

My stomach leaped into my throat. I couldn't risk letting him think I wasn't around.

"M...my name is David," I muttered.

The Impostor hesitated, as if surprised to hear me respond at all.

"What is your name?" he asked again, making wet smacking noises. I imagined a gruesome being sliding its tongue all over its lips and jagged teeth. "Feeeelix...Fffffffeeelissssk..."

"My name is *David*," I said, raising my voice to nearly a yell.

He hesitated once more, then tapped the glass again.

Tic-tic-tic.

"Felix..." he said, then drew another raspy breath. "Faye. Faye."

Hearing her name spoken by the very thing that wanted to harm her filled me with rage. The fire inside me burned away my fear. It scorched my reason, and ignited in me fantasies of leaping through the window and beating the son of a bitch to death with my bare hands. It became a death wish that I could barely control.

"Monkeytoes," he taunted.

A strange thought occurred to me, momentarily decoupling my mind from the hatred that plagued it. If this

178

thing was learning to communicate by parroting me, perhaps I could confuse him. I began to recite a poem I'd memorized for German class in high school: *Die Frauen von Ravenna Tragen.*

The creature paused to consider the noises I made. He had probably never heard them before. I listened as he tried to mouth the syllables. He failed to reproduce much of what he heard.

"May I come in?" he said, speaking through gnashing teeth. He was frustrated.

"Ich heiße Hermann," I continued, trying to recall other German phrases I'd learned. "Ich komme aus Kalifornien. Ich schreibe gern. Mein Klavierspiel ist schrecklich. Ich möchte ein Lehrer werden."

Tic-tic-tic-tic-tic-tic. The creature rolled his nails across the glass. I couldn't understand why he didn't punch through it and drag me off into the woods. I still couldn't understand what he wanted, or why he didn't just kill me.

The figure lurched over to the back door, a few feet away from where I stood. The knob rattled. I carried on with my silly recitations, and he became more and more upset. He growled and rasped and wheezed and tapped on the door, until finally he let loose an ear-splitting howl and stomped away from the cabin. I threw the curtain open and caught sight of a dark shape moving toward the woods. It looked like a man, except all the limbs were slightly elongated. No two of them were the same length, and so his movements were eerily off-balance. He howled one last time, provoking a thousand mournful voices to cry out in horror, and then silence washed over the snowy landscape. On the window before me was a '5', smudged across the glass with mud. The Impostor had written it backwards, so that I could read it from inside.

That night, I lay in bed with the gun, reflecting upon the encounter. I did not feel safe. I did not feel free of the

179

monster that haunted my life. But for the first time in weeks, I felt something other than hopelessness in the wake of the monster's presence. After pondering everything that had transpired over the past few weeks, I concluded that the Impostor was stuck. He desperately wanted something from Faye, something only she knew, perhaps something secret. He tried to ask her directly – and she refused. He tried to trick her into following him into the woods, and failed.

I now believed that the Impostor was rehearsing my voice with the intention of convincing Faye that he was *me*. Perhaps this wouldn't work on a normal person, but Faye is highly suggestible when she is unconscious. The creature whispered to her at night, speaking to her through dreams. He wanted entry not only to our home, but to Faye's soul – and yet he seemed to need her permission.

Chapter 26

A brilliant glow enveloped me as I awoke. The sun blazed against a blanket of new-fallen snow, and the forest shivered at the rush of a strong breeze. I'd forgotten to shut the curtain last night, and so the morning light dragged me to consciousness far earlier than I'd planned.

My head throbbed. I'd gotten half my average amount of sleep in the past several days, and now a faint dizziness always clung to me. I used the satellite phone to call Faye, and as it rang, I sat there on the bed, staring at the ugly '5' scraped across the window. The creature had probably taken the opportunity to stand there all night, gazing down at me as I slept with a grin smeared across his face.

"Hello?" a meek voice answered, snapping my attention away from the muddy inscription.

"Hey you!" I said. It felt so good to hear her voice.

"Hi."

"How are you? How's Colin and everybody?"

"Fine."

Her voice was empty and distant. She must not have recovered as much as I'd hoped.

"You okay?" I asked.

"Didn't sleep too good," she replied, "but I'm alright. I

miss you."

The words tore at my soul.

"I miss you too, Monkeytoes. You have no idea."

"Did you find my ring?" Faye asked. "I had a dream you found it. Didn't make much sense though."

My heart sank at the reminder. I feared I'd never find it.

"Not yet," I said, trying to reassure her. "But I will. If I don't find it here, I'm going to ask your folks to look around their place. It's around here somewhere. Don't worry."

"It's not important," she replied. She paused for a long moment and then said, "Keep looking. Need more sleep. Keep looking."

The phone clicked and she was gone.

"Hello? Faye?"

Even in the serenity of daylight, I felt afraid. I reminded myself of why I had come to the mountain, and what I had to do: find the ring, and wait for Tíwé. I planned to search the driveway, the outside perimeter of the house, and the path we'd taken into the forest.

In an effort to feign some semblance of a normal life, I made myself breakfast and sat at the little table with my laptop. The WiFi slowed to a drip, but I was able to read a bit of the news and skim through emails from students demanding their midterm grades. As I scrolled through my inbox, my eyes stopped at a message sent at 11 P.M. last night. The subject line read: *FELIX, OPEN THIS NOW. RE FAYE.*

The message was from Tyler. It was long and frantic, obviously written in great haste, and detailed the events of the past few days of my absence. He explained that he'd left several voicemails, but knew that I was unlikely to get any reception to check them on the mountain.

Tyler described how Faye had been alert and cheerful

the day I dropped her off at his house, but the next morning, she had become more and more lethargic. At some point she told Allison, Tyler's fiancée, that she felt sick, and wanted to go home. Tyler resisted for a while but eventually caved, on the stipulation that he and Allison stay at our place with her. Faye obliged and set them up in the guest room.

Things seemed to be going well until Tyler got the bright idea to test his superstitions. Faye keeps a photograph of her grandfather Alfred on a shelf in the living room, with a little crucifix and some old rosaries. There is also a vial of holy water from her family's priest, which Tyler stole and dumped into Faye's shampoo bottle – "just to see what would happen."

That day after her shower, Faye inexplicably threw a tantrum and locked herself in the bathroom. She claimed she felt like "hurting someone" and wanted to be alone, and only came out after much prodding from Allison. Eventually she calmed down enough to rejoin everyone downstairs, but she refused to eat anything for the rest of the day. Instead she sat quietly, gnashing her teeth in rage. She seemed to return to normal after several hours.

Colin showed up that evening and camped out downstairs. Faye was kind enough to set him up on the couch, and they even had a brief conversation about Carrot, so he was under the impression that Tyler had been exaggerating her strange behavior. Colin is a web designer who tends to stay up late working on commissions, so at 2 A.M., he witnessed Faye rushing down the stairs. She dashed into the kitchen and started lapping water from the faucet like an animal. When Colin turned on the light, he saw that her eyes were closed, but she stood up and "stared" at him for a while without moving. Then she spoke the word "Felix," to which Colin answered, "He's in Colorado, remember?"

Faye's response to this was, "We sent him there to die." She resumed slurping water from the faucet.

In the middle of the night, Allison and Tyler had an argument, which ended with Allison storming out of the house. Allegedly, Faye had spent hours singing and talking to herself in our bedroom, which prompted Allison to investigate. Faye told her that she was afraid to be alone, and begged Allison to stay with her through the night. Allison slept on the floor, but woke up at one point to Faye leaning off the side of the bed, whispering that there was a man without a face wandering around in the dark downstairs. She said, "he keeps asking about you," then reached out and combed her fingers through Allison's hair.

Tyler spent the last paragraph of the email reassuring me that he was committed to protecting Faye no matter how weirdly she acted, and that he would call the police or take her to the hospital if she did anything dangerous. At the bottom, the final line read:

There's something else you need to know, but I'll let Colin tell you himself. Call us as soon as you can.

This new development crushed me. Not only had I failed to draw the creature away from her by returning to Pale Peak, I'd abandoned Faye, and put my friends in danger. The more I learned about the Impostor, the less he made sense. Could it be that more than one of these things was following us around? Or could one of them simply move across great distances at will?

Colin's phone was off, so I left a message requesting that he call me immediately. Then I headed outside with a paper towel to see if I could clean the muddy '5' off the window.

The moment I opened the front door, my eyes remained glued on the tree line in the distance. I half-expected a grotesque monster to come barreling out of it

184

on all fours, and in my dark reverie I missed a patch of ice on the porch and fell hard on my side. One of the steps bashed into my ribcage and knocked the wind out of me.

Cursing, I picked myself up and limped around the side of the cabin. As I rounded the corner, my breath rushed out of me again. The big stack of firewood that sat near the bedroom window was now a scattered mess. Snow had been scraped away from the place where it once stood. As I moved closer, a heavy cellar door came into view. Thick chains ran across its face, and two fist-sized padlocks joined them. All of it was conquered by years of rust, and it appeared that someone had tried frantically to get inside.

"The hell you got here?" I said aloud, kicking a log out of the way. Greg, or perhaps Tom before him, had a secret, and had hidden it well. By the looks of it, nobody had tried to open it in a decade. The place was long-forgotten by all but the Impostor himself.

An icy breeze kicked up and the bruise on my side gnawed at my ribs, both sensations working in concert to force me back into the cabin. As I limped back, the satellite phone rang in the kitchen. The sound of branches snapping in the woods behind me hastened my walk.

Chapter 27

"Where the hell have you been?" Colin demanded. His voice came through distorted, making him sound like an angry robot.

"Tell you when I get home," I replied, peering out the kitchen window. "What's the news out there?"

"Honestly, I thought Faye was mentally ill," he said. "My mom's sister developed schizophrenia in her twenties, and she started hearing voices. Talking to God and the devil and all that. Wandered around the house at night. I assumed that's what was happening to Faye when you told me all this...I had to see it for myself."

"What are you talking about?" I pressed. "See what?"

"Everything. The other stuff. The shit we don't believe."

I dropped into a chair at the kitchen table.

"I still have trouble with it," I said. "Like I'm gonna wake up and it was all just a dream. Ghosts don't exist. They can't."

Static hissed from the phone, then Colin's voice filtered through it.

"After last night, I think I'm willing to believe." He paused for a moment, trying to collect himself. "Allison left the day before yesterday. So it was just me and Tyler at your place. I stayed up late to get some work done – and maybe because I was a little afraid that Faye would stab us to death in our sleep and burn down the house."

"Dude."

"You weren't bullshitting, though. Around midnight I heard a little kid making noise outside, so I went out there to check. I circled the house before I realized the sounds were coming from your bedroom window. So I went up and woke Tyler, and we stood outside the bedroom door. I've never been so creeped out, dude. I swear there was a child in that bedroom, singing and talking real slow like she was drunk. I swear I heard it."

"What did she say?" I asked.

"Couldn't make out the words," Colin replied. "Sounded like gibberish. Maybe, 'saw me undo' or something. Sang it like a lullaby. So we knocked on the door and asked who was in there, and I distinctly heard the kid say 'shhhh' and then mumble something. Tyler pushed open the door, and there she was, standing in a corner facing the wall."

"Wait, there was a kid in there?"

"No," Colin said. "It was Faye. She was lifting up the framed photos, lookin' behind them. She said there were little windows back there, and that's where he gets in."

A faint nausea burbled within me. Years ago, Faye had moved paintings and portraits off the walls, claiming that there were things hidden behind them. It was as if the Impostor could read her memories and use them against her.

"She said something like, 'Oh, their skin is so perfect, which one, which one, put him down in the hole.' So I went over and gave her a little shake. She spun around and covered her mouth with her hands, and started talking in the voice of a little girl. Same one as before. Her eyes were open, man. Wide open. She looked at me like she *hated* me."

187

"What did she say?" I asked. The heater kicked on, causing me to jump.

"It's hard to explain," Colin replied. "She was makin' these whining and crying sounds, and cradling her arms like she was holding a baby. She turned around to hide it from us, and then said a bunch of weird shit. I dunno, man."

"Try to remember," I said.

"She wasn't talking to us, I don't think. But she said stuff like, 'It's Faye. I can't see you. Are you up in the trees or down in the hole?' So Tyler hit the light switch, and as soon as he did, I saw a little kid through the window outside. He was down below, right where I was standing a few minutes before, and he was walking around on his tippy-toes and flailing his arms around. You know how when you're a kid, you pretend the ground is hot lava? It looked like that. When he noticed I was watching, he took off."

"Did you see his face?"

"Nah," Colin said. Static invaded the phone line once more, garbling some of his words. "...too dark. But...went after him. Got outside and chased him all the way to that little belt of trees across the street. He was laughing and moving around in there, but then the laughter turned into an adult's. I was scared to go inside, man. Felt like I was...heart attack. I just went a few steps in, and as soon as I did, there was a really tall guy standing there in the shadows. He was naked and had his back to me. I sort of froze up, and he just stood there for a while, then started rolling his head around real slow. Made this disgusting cracking sound, like a hundred knuckles popping."

"You've seen him, then," I said, exhaling the mixture of relief and horror that swirled in me.

"You're not gonna believe this shit, dude," Colin said.

"Try me," I said, peeking out the living room window.

"I was so afraid I kind of stumbled backwards. I tried

188

to leave without taking my eyes off him. And as I did, he goes, '*Heeeeeellllllllooooo?*'" Colin imitated a croaking sound that might as well have come from a toad, but toward the end of the word, his voice returned to normal. "It was like an animal talking at first, but then it became a human voice. *Your* voice, Felix."

"I think he's mimicking me," I said. "He's trying to get Faye to think he's me." Something moved past the trees outside.

"Wait, wait," Colin said, "I'm not done yet. So as I turned to run back to the house, the guy starts begging for help in your voice, and then he goes, 'They're gonna kill me tonight.'"

Colin and I spoke for a few more minutes, but his story weighed down on me so much that I had to force myself to get off the phone. The terror that had kept me alert and on edge when we first visited Pale Peak had clung to me ever since. I'd brought it home with me to California, and back again to this awful mountain. But over time, it had morphed into a different set of sensations. Now, that terror oppressed me. It loomed over me and pressed ever downward, dulling my wits and exhausting my muscles. It hung on my eyelids. It made me wish for death. If the monster didn't kill me outright, the sleep deprivation probably would. I pictured myself driving Greg's truck right off the icy cliff nearby, and sighed in relief at the thought.

Get some rest, I reassured myself. *Find the ring. Get the ring.*

It was still daytime. I reasoned that if I had to stay on the mountain until Tíwé and Nathan returned, I might as well sleep while it was still light out. I nose-dived onto the couch and hoped that if the Impostor truly did plan to kill me tonight, he'd at least permit me one last dream of Faye.

189

Chapter 28

"Felix," a voice called out. It was close by.

A cold feeling strobed across my body, rolling up my back and down my arms.

"What do you see?" the voice asked. Warm air caressed my face as it spoke. Two hands found my shoulders and squeezed.

My eyes cracked open, then snapped shut as blinding light poured into them. A man's face took shape in the stars behind my eyelids. It was passingly familiar.

"Come on. Need to get you back, you crazy kid."

The voice matched the face, and my brain clicked on. My eyes popped open.

"Tíwé," I tried to say. My jaw would barely open to let the words out. Freezing wind stung my face.

"What are you doing out here?" he asked, still grasping me by the shoulders. He was a bit shorter than me, but his grip was impressive. He probably could have held me up if I collapsed. A feeling of safety washed over me, then passed as I glanced over his shoulder. A line of snowy trees towered above us not fifteen yards out, and the sun already balanced on their tips.

I looked behind me. The cabin rested in the distance. Its door sat wide open, and a meandering trail cut through the snow from the porch to where I now stood.

"I can't...can't feel my feet," I said, shivering harder as my senses returned.

"That's why we wear boots up here, my friend."

Tíwé led me back to the cabin and put a blanket around me. He turned the heater up high and made me some tea from the little bag Nathan had left behind. I laid myself across the sofa.

"You damn tourists forget," he said from the kitchen, "this mountain is a reaper of souls."

I stared out the window at the path I'd wandered.

"I've never sleepwalked in my life, Tíwé. Not once. I don't even talk. I sleep like a corpse."

"Well, you're under a lot of stress. Sleep-deprived. And this place makes people crazy."

He made his way over to me with a big steaming mug. I cupped it in my hands and reveled in the warmth.

"Just don't drop that thing in the snow," he said, nodding at the kitchen counter. I glanced over and noticed the neck pouch he'd loaned to me. It sat next to Greg's car keys. A hot flash of embarrassment chased away the last bit of numbness in my limbs. Tíwé read the apology in my eyes, and silenced me before I could speak it.

"Why were you out there?" he asked.

"Actually I was just about to ask you the same thing," I replied. "Did you come up here just to check on me?"

Tíwé knelt down and looked into my eyes. He nodded and put a rough hand on my forehead, checking my temperature.

"I think you saved my life," I said. A morbid chuckle escaped my lips.

"Well, I was a bit worried about you. Rightfully so, it seems." His eyes twinkled a bit as he smiled. "And I try to get a few miles in each day. Which reminds me, I've got to get going soon. Storm's comin' from the north, supposed to be a doozy."

"I'm leaving tonight," I said, "with or without that goddamn ring."

"It's very special," Tíwé said. He stood up and studied the window behind him. "And the Impostor knows it. It symbolizes your unity, your love for each other. It's a powerful object, a bit like a totem. Where'd you buy it?"

"I didn't," I said, sitting up on the couch. Dizziness tried to pull me back down. "It was my grandma's. I never met her, but it was really special to my mom. Old silver, I think. Real diamonds too. You really think he could use it against us somehow?"

Tíwé sighed as he stared out the window. His breath fogged the glass.

"The spirit world is a curious place," he said, hovering a finger before the window as if he were about to draw something. "The entities within it...their desires, their motives...few of us will ever know."

"I was an idiot to think it would be just sitting on a dresser up here," I said, gulping down some of the tea. "Faye might have dropped it on our hike. I don't think I'll ever get it back."

"What makes you think she lost it?" Tíwé replied, turning to face me. "What if she traded it for something else?" He scanned the room until his gaze fell on the front door. "What if she gave it to *him*?"

The possibility baffled me. Faye had been conversing with the creature for a while now, giving him little bits and pieces of information whenever he was able to fool her into it.

"I just wish I knew what to do," I said. "I feel like he's gotten stronger. Like he can just come in and out of our heads as he pleases. What if I—"

"Felix," he interrupted, "I believed that if you came

192

back to the mountain, we'd be able to find the answers you seek. But I was wrong. You seem to be getting worse, and you haven't found the ring. No one in my community is prepared to help with this. We need to get you back to Faye, and when you're both safe, we'll try another angle. I'm so sorry for all of this. I've wasted your time."

I stood up to protest, but Tíwé embraced me in a tight hug.

"Keep yourself safe," he said. "No more walkin' around. Put that couch in front of the door if you have to. As soon as I get to the station I'll tell them you need a lift in the morning."

"Fuck that," I said, heading for the closet to grab my jacket. "I'm going with you." Before my hand reached the knob, my head and limbs turned to thousand-pound stones. I sagged to the floor. The room spun like a top.

"You aren't going anywhere," Tíwé said, hoisting me back onto the couch. "You'll never make it out there tonight."

"Then we'll drive," I replied, pointing at the keys to Greg's truck.

"I've never driven a car in my life," Tíwé replied, "and there's no way in hell I'm gettin' in a car with you like this. The roads are gonna be iced over tonight. Zero visibility. You can't even open a door."

I sighed in defeat. I couldn't bear the thought of being alone again. He sensed my worry and smiled.

"You and Faye are very strong. Keep her in your heart. I'll see you tomorrow."

With that, Tíwé zipped up his jacket and pulled a flashlight from his pocket.

"You sure you'll be okay?" I asked.

He pulled the door open and pressed out against the frosty wind, retrieving a walking stick he'd left on the porch.

"Been walkin' this road for decades," he said. "It's more dangerous in there with you in the kitchen! I heard all about Faye's little tummy ache."

"In that case," I said, leaning over the arm of the couch, "can I offer you some tacos before you go? They're her favorite."

"I'm sure they are," he laughed.

I took one last look at the barren landscape as Tíwé closed the door. Golden light poured sideways through the windows. Within the hour it would fade, leaving me again in the horrid darkness of Pale Peak. A knot formed in my gut.

I lay back down, trying to let my body warm up and recuperate. I slept on and off, and after a few hours, strange images began to flash in my memory. They were scenes I recognized but could not place. The more I focused on them, the further into obscurity they withdrew – until one of Tíwé's stories drifted into my thoughts.

I'd had a dream.

Images of a huge hole carved into a mountain rushed to the forefront of my mind. Snow and branches were caked all around the mouth of the cave, and an impossible blackness yawned from within it. I stood there, gazing into the vacant face of the deep, listening to Faye's pitiful cries. When I tried to pursue them, her voice warped into a laughing child's, and the entrance collapsed into a wall of stone.

I sifted through the images and sounds, grasping for more. There were flashes of trees, of the cabin, of Faye, of Tíwé and Nathan.

Then, figments of a longer scene took form.

I could see myself from behind. I was walking. At first I couldn't see where I was going, but then the snow appeared, and a tree sprung out of it. Then another. And another. In the distance, a crop of branches and bones hung suspended in the air, bending and groaning and crackling as they inexplicably wove themselves together. It was the dreamcatcher. I was walking toward it. As I made my way across the field, something glimmered from the object's center – something that wasn't there before. Something I recognized. It was a tiny thing, laced into the twine spiral among little bits of bone and teeth.

The ring.

I crawled off the couch and staggered to the window. Little of my strength had returned.

The dream was probably a trick, seeded into my head by the malevolent whispers of the Impostor, but I had to know. I shoved my sockless feet into my boots and pulled on a jacket.

As I hobbled out onto the porch, the air held still and the mountain fell silent.

Chapter 29

Greg's truck still sat in the driveway, but it looked as if it had sunken into the ground. When I approached, I noticed that the tires had been slashed to ribbons. My face went red-hot against the frigid night air, but I swallowed back the outburst that came rushing up inside me.

I stopped halfway across the field, in the same exact place Tíwé had woken me. Twenty yards ahead, the woods began so abruptly that they seemed like the outer wall of some fortress. Darkness seeped from them. It felt thick with an otherworldly presence that loomed just out of sight.

Child don't wander too far out.

Lines from Faye's dream journal echoed in my head. I forced myself onward.

The dreamcatcher was just inside the rim of the tree line. I planned to sneak a quick glance and run back to the cabin. Anticipating that Faye's voice might call out from the shadows, I reminded myself to go back no matter what I heard.

Trees towered over my head. Branches snagged my jacket – final warnings to the foolhardy traveler. The air sat heavy and still, holding my frosty breath before me for several seconds before allowing it to dissipate.

I circled a large trunk –

– and there it was.

The sickening object hung a few feet in front of me. The branch it dangled from looked gnarled and dead, tainted by the presence of such a foul thing. I froze in my tracks, fearing to approach, until the object began to move. It twirled slowly as if it had heard my footsteps, creaking and clattering as it did. As soon as the intricate pattern at its center faced me, the dreamcatcher ceased its movement. An explosive mixture of shock and fear arced through my limbs.

Even in the poor light, the ring glimmered faintly. Someone had put it here. Someone had given it back.

A hundred thoughts and emotions stampeded through my mind: had some benevolent force taken pity on me? Or was this a final taunt before the creature took my life? Should I take back the ring? Should I abandon it and tell Faye it was lost forever? What if the totem was a trap? Or what if it was the only thing protecting me from the creature? Retrieving the ring would require me not only to touch, but to destroy, the dreamcatcher – something Faye, Tíwé, and my own gut had warned me against.

There was no time for debate. The last gasps of daylight had already come and gone, and the forest began to unleash its gloom across the landscape. I strode up to the object and yanked it down from the tree. It was even more brittle than it looked; pieces of it frayed and broke apart as I tugged on it. I ripped the thing to shreds, snapping the bones and twigs that comprised it until I clutched a tangled mass of sinew. The rage and despair and fear within me condensed at the back of my throat, bursting from my mouth in a series of frustrated cries. I hated this mountain, this forest, and this cabin, for what they had done to my family. I hated Faye's parents for lying to us. And I hated myself for leaving her to come back here.

Nothing remained of the dreamcatcher but the engagement ring and the strings of gore it once clung to. I tore it away and grasped the ring in my hands, turning it over a dozen times to make sure it was truly Faye's.

The sound of crunching snow came from my left. Something big moved into my peripheral vision. All of my muscles seized up into ice blocks as my brain processed the huge figure. Even without turning to look at him, I instantly recognized his asymmetrical posture and the repulsiveness of his jutting bones. He stood facing away from me, rhythmically clenching his shaking hands. His head moved back and forth, studying the treetops.

Still looking down at the ring, my brain screamed at me to not move or make a sound. I held perfectly still like a surprised rabbit as the figure rolled his arms and head around. His limbs were horribly mangled, as if he'd been dragged out of a car wreck and dangled from puppet strings.

"*Feeeeeeliiiiiiiix...*" he gurgled, tilting his head so far back that I could see his face upside-down. "*I knoooow youuuuuu...*"

My breath rushed in and out of me so fast I thought I'd pass out. In response, my brain scolded me with images of the creature flaying my body and hanging it up in the trees. A muddy cackle issued from his mouth, and then he quickly turned around so that his body faced me. I couldn't help but look.

I could not begin to process the abomination that stood before me. He held the rough shape of a person, but even in the gloom it was obvious that this thing was never human. His form looked composed of different body parts, a patchwork mockery of the species he so desperately wanted to resemble. The head snapped back to its upright

198

position, and a gray ponytail whipped through the air behind it. Deep in their sunken pits, a pair of black eyes widened in glee as they met with mine. He opened his hideous arms as if to embrace me, and took a heavy step forward.

"*Feeeeee-lik-k-k-k-k-ssssss...*"

A shotgun blast of panic exploded through me, propelling me into a full sprint. My screams echoed all across the mountain, summoning a choir of evil voices to join in. A thousand cries rang out all around me, stoked by my fiery terror. Their maddening gibberish and the Impostor's croaks compelled me to move faster than ever before in my life, and I was back at the cabin in a matter of seconds.

I slammed the door against the wails and wind and darkness outside. My tear ducts ruptured and a deluge of fright and sorrow poured down my face. I tried to recite a prayer I'd learned as a child, but all that came out of my mouth was "Oh Jesus, I don't wanna die, I don't wanna die."

I grabbed the satellite phone and held it to my ear, sobbing as I did. No one picked up at the ranger station. William didn't answer his cell. No one was coming to save me. My heart ached with the truth my brain dared not comprehend:

The face I just saw was Tíwé's.

Chapter 30

One night when I was a little boy, I had trouble falling asleep. Sensing that other people were awake in the house, I got out of bed and walked to my older brother's room. He and his friends were watching a horror movie and eating pizza. When I pushed the door open, the room was illuminated only by television's glare. On the screen was a teenager napping on his bed. Unbeknownst to him, a living skeleton crept in through the window and loomed over him. The scene horrified me so much that it short-circuited my brain. I blacked out right there in the hallway. My brother carried me back to my own room, where I had no further trouble sleeping. When presented with incomprehensible terror, the mind will defend itself in strange ways.

The same thing must have been happening to me now. My heart slowed to a hypnotic rhythm. My lungs didn't burn for air. My guts didn't churn and wrench inside me. My body was making peace with the reality of its imminent destruction. I struggled to maintain consciousness.

Satisfied with the barricade I'd hastily constructed out of furniture against the front door, I used my last ounce of strength to crawl to the bedroom. Halfway down the hall I blacked out, and the ancient memory of that skeleton on the TV was my last conscious thought.

I don't know how long I slept.

I woke up in bed. The sheets were tucked gingerly around my body, and a full glass of water rested just beside me on the night stand. I glanced around the dark room, supposing that I had climbed into bed and simply couldn't remember doing it. My wits slowly returned to me, but it took a long time to realize...there was an arm draped across my chest.

The physical sensation of it was natural; Faye almost always fell asleep against me, or at least kicked and elbowed me as she argued with her dreams. Confused, I tried to recall where exactly I had gone to sleep. Was I back home? Was I in Avonwood?

I gently rolled away from the person lying next to me and reached for the bedside lamp. It wouldn't give any light. I squinted through the darkness, trying to discern the black shape on the bed. It felt familiar — its warmth, its texture. I was fairly certain that this was Faye, but I still couldn't remember if she was really with me up here. I couldn't even remember the last time I'd talked to her.

Then she spoke.

"What's wrong, Poptart?"

A cold hand stroked my cheek.

It was not so much fear, but confusion, that overwhelmed me in that moment. Faye's voice and touch were familiar, but something about them didn't fit together with the bed I sat in. Or the layout of the room.

"Where are we?" I asked. "Why's the light off?"

Faye cleared her throat.

"Power's out," she said. "It's done this before."

I got up out of bed. As soon as the sheets came off my body, I felt a blistering cold – colder than it's ever been in our bedroom. The heat must have been off for hours. A feeling of dread came over me, growing heavier and heavier the more awake I became.

"Jesus," I said, "did you screw with the heat? It's fuckin' freezing in here!"

Faye tried to get me to come back to bed. Her voice was clear and lively, as it had been when we'd first arrived at Pale Peak.

Are we still here? I wondered.

A gust of frigid air nipped at me from behind. Perplexed, I left the bedroom and felt my way down the hall. A strong draft pushed against me as I did, and Faye's voice called out from behind me.

"Felix, where are you going?"

The kitchen window sat wide open. Snow blew in from outside. My jaw dropped. More of my senses returned. I spun around, saying "Faye? Why the hell did you—" but the words tangled in my mouth.

Faye stepped out of the bedroom and stood there in the hall. I recognized the outline of her figure, but her posture was different.

"You alright?" she asked. "Did you have a bad dream?"

The feeling that this was *not* Faye crept over me. I instantly regretted leaving the magnum somewhere in the bedroom.

"Who are you?" I whispered, taking a step back. The kitchen knives were a few yards behind me to the left. The front door was the same distance to the right. I couldn't remember where my shoes were.

Faye didn't move a muscle. Her hair glowed faintly in the starlight that came from the bathroom window behind her, but her face was entirely black. Even though I couldn't see them, I could feel her eyes burning into me – just as Tíwé's had when I'd found the ring. It felt like we stood in the eye of a hurricane; a calmness fell over the cabin, but it

202

portended certain doom. Not a single noise came from outside. No branches snapped, no snow crunched, no voices moaned. It was as if time had stopped.

Faye stood with inhuman stillness. Even when she spoke, she held herself perfectly still with the rigidity of death. She hissed my name.

"Felix."

It wasn't to get my attention. It wasn't to convince me that she was the woman I loved. It was a threat. She was reminding me that she *knew* my name. In that moment, I still didn't fully understand the power in names that Tíwé and Nathan had discussed. But when Faye said mine, I felt smaller than her – even though I stood almost a foot over her head.

"What makes five?" she whispered, cocking her head sideways. Her neck crackled as she did.

"Huh?"

"I can't remember," she said. "Not in this place."

She took a menacing step toward me. She cleared her throat again, and then her voice dropped lower than Faye's ever could.

"What makes five? Tell...me..."

And that's when I knew. I remembered where I was, what day it was, and exactly what had happened up until this moment. My dark visitor had finally come to call, and he no longer needed to be invited in. I deeply regretted breaking that dreamcatcher. Perhaps it was protecting me after all, and perhaps by destroying it I had unleashed him. My hand instinctively slid over my pocket, and to my relief, the little shape of Faye's engagement ring pushed back against my fingers.

A strange feeling came over me then. It was the knowledge that I was about to die. It felt different from all the times I feared I *might* die. In prior instances of mortal danger, terror completely overwhelmed my senses and

203

compelled me to flee. To fight. To save myself. But now I had passed the point where death becomes a certainty. I was convinced that my life was about to end, and so fear became useless. There was nothing left to do now. My time had come. I decided to throw down the gauntlet.

"You're not Faye," I said.

The creature twitched, tilting his head further. A slew of crackles issued from it. He took another step.

"Five," he gurgled, *"what makes. What makes."*

"I have no idea what it means," I continued. "No matter what you do to me, it won't change that."

The creature shook with rage. He reached a clawed finger to the wall beside him and dragged a talon across it. His breathing grew raspy and shallow.

A peculiar revelation struck me in that moment.

This being, whatever he was, had been invading Faye's sleeping mind for God knows how long, perhaps many years. Maybe even since she first visited the cabin as a child. He had asked her hundreds of questions. Watched her all night. Listened to her dreams. And in all that time, he still hadn't discovered what he sought from her. Faye kept some things buried so deep within herself that not even he could find them. Whatever the number five means to Faye, that deep place is where she hid the secret, and the creature seemed to have no power to access it.

"You're the one who followed us home," I said.

He nodded.

"You've asked her many times," I said. "Each time, she tells you nothing. I'm her future husband and she's never told me. You'll never get your answer. Not in a hundred years. And if you ever talk to her again, I'll beat your ugly ass to death with my bare hands."

I squared off with the creature, ready to get mauled. I was satisfied in the knowledge that I had not given him what he wanted, and had thereby blocked him from using

204

that information as a weapon against Faye. Whatever the number five meant, this thing seemed to need it to take full possession of her. And that wasn't going to happen – not even over my dead body.

The creature let out a growl so deep I felt it more than heard it. There in the dark hallway, he twitched violently, then began to change. The likeness of Faye stretched wider and higher. Limbs popped and bent into new positions. The neck rose. The head tilted up toward the ceiling, revealing a different face beneath the chin. The shoulders rolled backward and folded like a butterfly's wings, then returned, broader than before. The fingers uncurled into longer, clawed digits, and now my visitor towered over me by several inches.

He sucked in a huge, rasping breath, then mumbled through clenched teeth. The words all came from different voices; he didn't even try to mimic Faye this time.

"Then...we don't...need you...anymore."

My courage dissolved. The Impostor was on me like lightning. In a single lunge, he covered fifteen feet and knocked the wind right out of me with a brutal head-butt. I toppled backward and crash-landed on the floor near the front door, my neck and shoulders bearing most of the impact. He was on me in an instant, unleashing a barrage of blows to my head. He raked my chest with razor-like claws. I tried my best to defend myself, but it was so dark in the house that I couldn't see where the strikes came from.

As the shadowy figure beat down on me, I freed a hand and clawed at his face, searching for eyes to gouge out. A row of teeth caught my fingers and bit down hard on them, and then I felt a mixture of blood and saliva drip down my forearm. I screamed and threw a wild elbow, rallying my strength as it collided with a wet *smack* against the creature's jaw. He howled in pain and relented just long enough for me to get to my feet.

I hoisted myself up by grabbing the counter that separated the kitchen from the living room. As my hands moved over it, they brushed against a familiar object – Tíwé's neck pouch. I don't know what compelled me to do it, but I snatched up the pouch and ripped it open, palming a handful of the crunchy substance inside. The creature yanked me back by the neck with the strength of a linebacker. I whirled around and jammed my palm into his face, twisting the heel of my hand against his eyes and shouting "Leave my family alone, you son of a bitch!"

I wrapped my other arm around his head for leverage. Faye's curly locks tangled between my fingers. Hours before, I had seen the gruesome remnants of my friend, stretched over the creature like an ill-fitted Halloween mask. Now he donned human features I'd known far longer. I prayed that Faye was still alive, and that the Impostor had not taken this hair from *her* head. He shrieked and growled in some inhuman language, trying to push me away, but I held on as hard as I could and kept driving the sage into his eyes. As my hands slid over the misshapen lumps of his face, I felt his bones shift and slide. I felt a mouth too wide to be human, and wet, sticky lips that draped across a hundred jagged fangs.

And then it was over. The bastard had had enough. He took off on all fours, shrieking like a banshee in five different voices. He barreled up the kitchen wall and out the window, disappearing into the night.

Chapter 31

I cried long and hard in the empty living room. Never had I felt so utterly, miserably alone. I only managed to stop when the power came back on about twenty minutes later, and the sound of the heater kicking on felt like the greeting of an old friend. The entryway was decorated in my own blood. The satellite phone was gone. The gun was gone. My shoes were gone. Everything was probably outside in the snow, or up in a tree. Or down in the hole. But at least I still had the ring. The Impostor could have taken it while I slept, but for some reason, he did not.

I vowed to myself that at daybreak, no matter the conditions, I would take Greg's truck and get down the mountain – or die trying. I didn't care if I slid off the cliff face; I'd never watch the sun go down in Colorado ever again.

It took about an hour for the adrenaline to wear off, at which point the beating I had taken began to register across my body. My bruised side now quivered with fresh agony, and my face sported two big welts. Ragged lacerations crisscrossed my torso, burning like fire with each movement. As I patched myself up with trembling hands in the bathroom, the voices returned.

They arose from far off in the woods, several of them at once, groaning and screaming their dark elegies to the night. It was all the same evil gibberish I'd heard a thousand times before, but now they made their way into the open field, and eventually, to just outside the cabin. Soon, a dozen voices, maybe more, babbled and shouted and cackled all around me. It was still too dark outside to see anything, but tiny pink and purple bands streaked the rim of the sky. It would be morning soon.

Fearing another confrontation, I limped around the house, ensuring that every window and door was locked. Not knowing what else I could do, I picked up the remainder of Tíwé's sage and set fire to it, wafting the smoke around in each room until my fingers burned.

I imagined the shattered dreamcatcher, and my crumpled corpse beside it. It may well have been warding off the Impostor all this time, and now there was nothing left of it to protect me.

The voices moved in circles around the cabin, whispering and wailing and weeping as they did. I imagined a Seussian procession of corpses marching around the perimeter, ritually celebrating the demise of another fool who had come to Pale Peak. Grim shadows moved across the curtains all around me. The pitter-patter of little feet echoed across the roof, layered with the sounds of children giggling.

Outside the front door, my own voice called out, "Faye! It's me! Let me in!" Seconds later, it called from near the bedroom door, "I'm so cold, Monkeytoes. Please, please help me." The Impostor was making his victory lap through my mind, allowing me a preview of what was to be Faye's ultimate fate shortly after he killed me. He wanted to terrorize me before the end, to make certain that I knew he had plans for her.

Windows shattered across the cabin. First in the bedroom, then the bathroom. The kitchen window burst behind me, showering me with flakes of glass and snow. The howling winds blew in, deafening me to all other sounds and granting cover to anything that crawled inside.

And then, as if heaven-sent, a blinding white light illuminated the entire building. All the window curtains at the front of the house lit up, and the sound of motors roared over the screaming wind. A hellish cry rang out in defiance somewhere down the hall. Someone had driven up to the cabin.

The wind ceased altogether as if banished by my fearful prayers, and I heard car doors opening and men calling out to each other. The footsteps on the roof thundered overhead to the back of the cabin, and the screams of children drifted off into the woods out back, reverberating across the mountain as they withdrew. The ranger bashed on the front door.

"Felix! Felix, are you there? Open up! It's William!"

I ripped a curtain open and saw five men. Four of them were rangers, and Nathan was the other. Behind them sat a humongous off-road snow plow, two snowmobiles, and a pickup truck. The men gathered on the porch and shined their flashlights all over the cabin. They had come to save my life.

I rushed outside and threw my arms around William. Snot and tears caked my face, and I did nothing to hide my childish comportment. I didn't even grab my winter jacket. He informed me loudly that they were getting everyone off the mountain because of a problem with the power grid, but when I looked up at him, he gave me a subtle wink. William glanced over to Nathan, who nodded back. The compassion of my friends overwhelmed me – not just the ones here, but also the ones looking after Faye back home. As we loaded into the plow, I took one last look at the shredded tires of Greg's truck. Without my saviors, there wasn't even a dream of escape.

The drive down the mountain would have been the happiest ride of my life, if not for the view. We snaked across slippery, white roads, and even with the truck's high beams on, I could still see the fading stars in the dawn sky. But beneath them, dangling in the trees, were scores of human bodies. They swung from their necks or wrists or feet, fastened with dark red rope – rope that looked much like the dreamcatcher's sinew. As they passed overhead on our downward crawl, I could barely make out their frozen faces, lifeless for years, maybe decades. Some of them were flayed or had missing body parts, and their black blood stained the trunks of the trees.

The ranger did not appear to notice, and so I kept my mouth shut. I'm not sure if these were the "spirits" Tíwé had spoken about, or if temporary insanity had poisoned my mind. Perhaps I'll never know for sure, but as I watched them drift past, I imagined what might have happened if the ranger had showed up an hour later than he did. I imagined my own corpse swinging there, and my bones strung up in a fresh dreamcatcher nearby. The faces of those mangled corpses will haunt my nightmares until the day I die.

The ranger took me to an emergency room, where he vouched to the hospital staff that I'd had a brush with a wolf. They gave me injections and stitches and antibiotics, and eyed me suspiciously as we left.

Twenty-four hours later, I found myself at the airport. I had no luggage, only the promise that William would ship my possessions to me. Right before I got out of his truck, he muttered,

"Tíwé's dead."

Although I already knew it, the words eviscerated my heart. That pain was reflected in William's face; he and Tíwé were dear friends and had known each other for decades.

"He got turned around in the blizzard," William said, barely able to force the truth out of his own mouth. "They think...think a bear might'a got 'im."

None of the typical anxiety troubled me on the flight home. No nausea, no claustrophobia. Only the memory of Tíwé's warmth, and of his unspeakable demise. The thoughts rotted me from within.

As I sat there with my head against the window, a constellation of possibilities presented itself in my mind. The Impostor *gave* Faye's ring back to me. He *wanted* me to destroy the dreamcatcher – the totem – whatever it was. The ring was an object of great sentimental value, both to Faye and to my family. The creature used it to invade her mind and control her thoughts. To weaken our relationship. To make us suffer.

But for some reason, the Impostor hadn't learned everything he needed to fully conquer Faye. So he gave up on that project and instead came after me. I believed that when the creature returned the ring to me, he gave up some of his influence over Faye – but he gained something else in exchange. By destroying the dreamcatcher, I gave him the keys to the cabin. I let him in. And when he came, his goal was to extract the meaning of the number five from me.

I'm not sure I'll ever unravel the truth behind that number, but I believe that my ignorance might have saved Faye's life. My ignorance, truly, is her bliss.

Walking into my home and seeing Faye light up nearly stopped my heart. An ineffable mixture of joy and sorrow overwhelmed me, and we wrapped each other up in a long hug – after which I endured a volley of angry slaps and kisses. I understood. She was furious that I'd spent so much time trying to take control of the situation, that I had treated her like a child and disregarded her feelings in my crusade to rescue her.

Tyler and Colin were delighted to leave our house and never look Faye in the eye again, although they did have some good news for me: she had not walked or talked in her sleep, or done anything out of the ordinary in a little under two days. This corresponded almost exactly with the moment when I had recovered the engagement ring. After an hour or so of reprimanding me for being an idiot, Faye forgave me, and we lay in bed together, holding each other in the silence of deep relief. At the end of the night, I took the ring out of my pocket and slid it onto her finger. The smile on her face soothed every bruise on my body and soul. The two little emeralds looking up at me sparkled, then disappeared behind tired eyelids. For the first time in what felt like forever, we slept without worry.

In the dead of night, Faye leaned over and kissed me in the dark, saying "Thank you for trying so hard for me."

And then she licked my face.

PART IV

Chapter 32

A few weeks came and went. Summer was upon us, and with it, the warm winds of change. Faye got a better job, and by the grace of some merciful power I completed my Qualifying Examinations, which meant that I was no longer obligated to attend graduate seminars or work as a teaching assistant at the university. I now embarked upon the final stage of my program: to finish my research and write my dissertation. In two years, hopefully I'd "get hooded" and revel in the snobbish honor of adding three little letters to the end of my name: *Ph.D.*

Luckily, I had secured a few generous research grants which enabled me and Faye to move a few hours north for her new job. We rented a nice condo in suburbia, slightly bigger than our home back in Faculty Housing, and both of us were delighted to find that the nearest forest stood miles and miles away. If the Impostor wanted to come after us here, he'd have to learn how to imitate a lawn gnome.

Faye seemed to be in much higher spirits too. Her playful demeanor had returned, along with much of her sarcastic wit. She talked at great length again – something she hadn't done in a month – and constantly engaged me in battles over everything and nothing. To me, her feistiness was the strongest indicator that this recovery was real. Best of all, that engagement ring never left her finger again. Our relationship remained alive, firmly clutched in Faye's vice grip. If anyone wanted to destroy it, they'd have to pry it from her cold, dead hands.

Ranger Pike had kept his promise and returned my possessions to me. Chief among them was my laptop, which held years of my research, as well as a lifetime of precious photos and unpublished stories. He told me that when he and Nathan visited the cabin to retrieve my things, there were signs of forced entry: shattered windows, marks on the doors, and a knob broken off. However, nothing was missing. The pile of firewood out back had been restacked. He made no mention of a cellar.

In the box William had shipped, I found a little piece of paper with a phone number written on it. It was Nathan's. I called it a few times, hoping to express my gratitude for his kindness and my anguish for his father's death. For weeks, I never received a call back. Then one day, as Faye and I unpacked in our new condo, my phone buzzed.

To my relief, it was Nathan. I immediately babbled a salutation and a few questions, which he ignored. His voice came through grave and low, and he said,

"Felix, let me speak to the one who followed you home."

I looked to Faye, who sat on the floor next to me in a pair of yoga pants, pulling books out of a box.

"Uhh...It's for you, I think."

Faye put the phone to her ear and said "Hello?" and then listened quietly for about a minute. I could hear Nathan speaking, but could not make out anything he said.

Suddenly, a volcano of black puke exploded from Faye's mouth. It sprayed across the carpet in a cone before her, and sent me nearly jumping out of my skin. She doubled over onto the floor like a ragdoll, coughing and sputtering. I leaped to my feet, panicking and asking if she was alright. I picked up the phone and screamed at Nathan, demanding to know what he had said to her.

"I *know* how to purge a drain clog," he said, chuckling.

"What did you do to her?!" I repeated, trying desperately to stave off the sympathy nausea that washed over me. My skin went clammy and tingly.

Faye staggered off to the bathroom to clean herself up. I fled to the backyard, shaking so hard I could barely command my muscles. Nathan spoke as I walked, but I barely picked up anything he said. The tunnel vision of fear protected me from all outside stimuli. My brain was trying to block the vomit out.

"You okay?" he asked. My mind settled enough to process his words. "You're out of breath."

"I'm phobic," I wheezed. "Can't...stand it...son of a bitch."

A cool breeze caressed my face. My lungs expanded. I could breathe again.

"We need to talk," Nathan said. As my awareness of the world returned, I suddenly worried that he was about to blame me for his father's death. How could I even begin to apologize?

"I...I wanted to...he was a good man," I said, trying to string my thoughts together into coherent sentences. "I'm so sorry."

Nathan was silent for a moment, then replied, "Yeah. I know."

"Do we know how it happened?"

I felt awful for asking, but some part of me had to know. Maybe he got lost and died of hypothermia. Maybe he fell and hurt himself. Maybe it was quick. My heart ached for a death other than the one my brain imagined; I couldn't bear the thought of gentle Tíwé meeting his end in the claws of the Impostor.

"He went off the road," Nathan said. "Up into the woods. Police think he was trying to avoid some of the snow collapses. They can push you off the cliff if they're big enough. Or bury you." His voice seemed incredulous, like he thought the idea was stupid.

"But you don't believe that," I guessed.

"No."

"Why not?"

"I don't know," he said, seemingly pondering another explanation. "A few days before, I was out hiking with friends, and I heard a voice in the woods. I'm the type to ignore those things, because of what I believe. But my dad...he was the kind of guy who saw the good in everything. If he heard a voice, he'd probably think it was someone in trouble. He'd go try to help them.

"They found him at the mouth of a cave. Something dragged him in, but he crawled back out. He died without his clothes."

"Oh my God," I breathed, leaning against the side of the house. "I'm so sorry, Nathan. He was on his way back from visiting me."

"The body was mutilated," Nathan stammered. "Someone took his skin and hair...took his teeth." He broke down and cried. I did too.

"I just want you to know," I said, trying to come up with anything that might dull his pain, "your dad saved my life that day. He pulled me back inside. I would have frozen to death if he hadn't been there."

Nathan seemed to take heart from my words. He calmed down a bit. His voice became firm and resolute.

"Pay it forward," he said. "That's the proper way to honor him."

I looked through the screen door at Faye, who now

scrubbed the carpet with frantic devotion.

"I will," I replied. "I promise."

Nathan and I spoke a little longer. I watched the clouds drift overhead and disappear behind the house as he talked. He told me that he'd met up with his best friend's grandfather, a man who still believed the old stories of their tribe, and learned a bit more about the *At'an-A'anotogkua.* Allegedly, the creatures hunt and kill at random, salvaging the human and animal parts they need to walk the earth as mortals for a short time – but their real pleasure derives from conquering a person from within. They become fascinated with certain people, and harbor special intentions for them. Faye seemed to be one of the unlucky few who are "chosen" in this way, and this Impostor's fixation upon her had probably festered for decades. After long enough, the continued presence of such a creature in the mind of a victim leaves a stain on the soul. This corruption necessitates a purge – hence the barf-party Nathan had just thrown for us. I prayed that the carpet stain was easier to banish than the creature, or else Faye would probably fly Nathan out here and force him to clean it himself.

"What did you say to her, anyway?" I asked.

"I just mentioned your famous tacos," he replied.

Chapter 33

Faye and I christened the new condo with our favorite tradition: we grabbed milkshakes from a nearby burger stand and held a movie marathon on the couch, awash in a sea of blankets. Instead of the usual horror films, we lined up a stack of mindless comedies, including Faye's all-time favorite: *Grandma's Boy.* About halfway through it, she got up to get a drink from the kitchen. On the way, she paused at the horrid gray stain on the carpet.

"It kind of looks like a person," she said.

She was right. The mark was about two feet long and looked a bit like a man with gnarled limbs and crooked shoulders. One arm reached up above his head, and twiggish fingers branched from his hands.

"I'll rent one of those carpet cleaning machines from the grocery store," I said, sucking down the last bit of my milkshake.

I stopped counting the nights since Faye had last walked or talked in her sleep. It had been a little more than three weeks, one of which we'd spent in our new place, and a feeling of cautious relief was finally settling over my mind. A few nights after the movie marathon, I rolled over in bed to put my hand on Faye's back. The second I touched the cold sheets, a thousand horrible thoughts rushed through my head. Faye hadn't made a peep since everything had settled down, so my brain immediately interpreted her absence as a sign that our visitor had returned.

I found her downstairs. She sat there in the dark, spine straight and neck craned to the side, facing the stairwell. Her eyes were closed. She ran her fingers across the stain on the carpet before her, whispering to it and giggling. I raced over and threw the light on. As I flipped the switch, Faye mumbled with a big grin on her face,

"How could I forget?"

She winced and threw her hands over her eyes, shielding herself from the light. When she came to, she looked around in confusion and then glared at me, as though she'd been woken from an unusually good dream. I asked if she remembered who she'd been talking to, but she shook her head and yawned.

I helped her to her feet. As we made our way up the stairs, Faye suddenly vomited again – this time all over the banister wall. My skeleton nearly leaped out of my mouth and bolted from the scene, but I somehow maintained my composure and got Faye to the bathroom. By the time we arrived at the toilet, she had nothing left to give. She climbed into bed, claiming she just needed to sleep.

For an emetophobe, cleaning up vomit is a diabolical form of punishment. I spent almost a half-hour scrubbing the wall, gagging all the while, scarcely able to still my rattling hands. But after a time, something distracted me from the horrid stench: this stain had an unusual shape that reminded me of a Rorschach test. From the angle at which Faye projected her dinner, the dark splotch ran across the wall diagonally, stretching nearly five feet. Like the mark on the living room carpet, this one also had the shape of a man – only this time, he was climbing or gliding through the air. His long, clawed fingers dangled out in front of him as though he could walk on them.

I had to take a boiling-hot shower to get the stink off my body, and by the time I crawled into bed, Faye was sleeping peacefully.

"Please don't do this again," I said, gliding my fingers across the small of her back. "I don't know if I can deal with it anymore."

Sleep never came that night.

I was awake when Faye climbed out of bed and wandered into the bathroom. I rolled over and buried my face in the pillows, shielding my eyes from the blinding light that outlined the door. She remained in there for a long time; I figured she was still feeling nauseous. Faye was usually sensitive to my phobia, and if she could help it, she'd sequester herself far away from me so as not to freak me out when she got sick. At this point, however, I wasn't sure why she'd even bother.

The light flicked off after a while, and the door creaked open. I waited for the feeling of her getting back into bed, but it never came. Finally, I rolled over and scanned the room. A strange form emerged from the bathroom, crossing into the peripheral of my blurry vision. It was Faye, standing there in the shadows so rigid and still I could have mistaken her for a department store mannequin. Her entire body was tree-stiff, with her head craned all the way back in a painful position. Her chin pointed straight up at the ceiling, and her arms stuck high in the air in a "hallelujah" gesture.

"...Faye?" I whispered.

She shushed me and wiggled her fingers, arms still outstretched. The contortion of her body reminded me of a

222

praying mantis in repose.

"What is it?" I asked, watching as her head swayed back and forth. She was looking up at something I couldn't see.

After a moment, Faye looked down at me with closed eyes and replied, "Did you know about her?" She balled her fists, leaving only one finger pointing upward.

"What?"

"There's an old woman up there," she whispered. A girlish smile grew across her face. "She lives in the attic. So friendly...She remembered my birthday!"

My skin crawled; it felt like a bed of worms writhed under the sheets with me. Before I could respond, Faye added, "She sleeps right above our bed."

Faye brought her arms down to her sides and her muscles relaxed. She stopped talking and wobbled toward the hallway. I intercepted her and gently tucked her back into bed.

For a long time I lay awake in the dark, staring up at the ceiling. I imagined the corpse of an old woman stuck up inside the drywall or dangling from the rafters in the attic. I couldn't shake the feeling that our unwanted guest had moved in with us, and was now pretending to be a friendly stranger to trick Faye. My imagination conjured a dark stain that spread itself out across the ceiling in the shape of a large man, just like the ones in the other parts of the house. And the longer I dwelled on it, the more I thought I heard something dragging itself around up there.

A man can only stare at the shadows for so long before they drive him insane. I shuffled around the house, trying to shake the heavy feeling of doom that weighed on my mind. I peeked through each window, trying to ensure that no strange visitors waited outside in the dark. All the ghastly memories of recent events flickered in my head on repeat. They lulled me into a hypnotic state that felt at once soothing and revolting. It was a strange feeling, like the calm of a soldier marching into a hopeless battle. Without even realizing what I was doing, I moved to a window, reached out my hand, and drew a backward '5.'

Chapter 34

Later in the week, I phoned a local carpet cleaning service, unwilling to devote any more time to removing the stains myself. A paunchy man showed up in the late afternoon, dragging in with him a big machine. He set to work in the living room while I hammered away on a research summary at the dinner table. After considerable effort, the man snorted his contempt at the stain, and moved to the one at the staircase.

"This ain't vomit," he called, prompting me to join him.

"What are you talking about?" I said, brushing my fingers against the wall. "I saw it happen."

The man shook his head and grunted.

"Ain't vomit. Vomit I can get out. You sure she didn't drink oil or some shit?"

Seeing that I wasn't laughing, the man cleared his throat.

"Need to be painted over, I reckon. You know how to sand and prime?"

"I'm almost a Ph.D.," I said, pointing at the mountain of books on the table. "I can't do anything that could even be *remotely* considered an employable skill."

The man laughed and slapped the back of his hand against my chest.

"I'll cut you a discount on today's rate, since I can't get this stuff out. If you want I can drop by on the weekend and fix this wall up for ya, nice and proper. Hunnerd bucks."

"I'll think about it," I said, wondering how hard it could be to do it myself.

"Try to keep the exorcism shit to a minimum until then," the man said. He lifted a cigarette from behind his ear and dragged his machine out the door.

Faye got home from work later than usual. The color was back in her cheeks, and she claimed she'd experienced no nausea throughout the day. She mentioned that her sister Becca had called and wanted to fly out to visit. Becca lived in Arizona with her husband and infant son Caleb, and hardly ever visited family. I figured it was probably a good idea that Faye spend some time with her sister, so I gave her the green light. Becca would sleep in the guest room, and I'd set up my office downstairs at the coffee table for a few days.

As we lay in bed, Faye snuggled up against me and tugged at my shirt.

"She's gonna bring the baby. Can you handle that?"

I laughed and shrugged.

"Just don't make me hold him. I'll drop him and he'll break into a million pieces."

"I think you'd be good with kids," she said. A big smile grew on her face.

"They throw up a lot," I replied. "Little barf factories. Don't need any more stains in this place."

Faye yawned and rolled over to her side of the bed.

"I'd like one," she whispered. "Just one. Maybe a mini-Felix. For some reason, I've always wanted a little boy."

My dreams have always tended to be elaborate and fantastical. They brim with surreal creatures, Dali-esque landscapes, impossible situations. To this day, Faye is the only other person I've known who experiences equally vivid dreams – and nightmares. On more than one occasion we've discussed their significance, and whether they are meaningful or merely the fragments of a semi-operational brain. I've never fully made up my mind.

But on this night, a dream came to me that felt like an urgent message, whispered into my ear by some potent being. In it, I was trying to clean the wall in the stairwell. It was night time, and for some reason I went about my task in the dark. Only a bit of moonlight seeped in from elsewhere, illuminating the scene in an eerie glow. As I crouched there with a rag, scrubbing fervently, the stain looked bigger than before. The shape of a disfigured man towered over me, desperately reaching a hand toward the second floor where Faye slept.

I worked quickly, commanded by a fear that something terrible was about to happen. The wall beneath the stain suddenly putrefied to a mush, and gave way to the pressure of my hand. My fist pushed right through the drywall. When I pulled it back, a beam of pale light came through the hole. Curious, I pushed more and more of the spongy wall away. It crumbled and plopped onto the floor like oatmeal. The hole widened as I dug into it, and in a moment, it was big enough to squeeze through.

It led to a familiar place. A dim room with a stone floor lay before me. Old wooden shelves lined the walls, each cluttered with dozens of dusty jars. The air felt cold and dank, and in the distance, the wind screamed. Although I had never been here before, I knew I was inside the hidden cellar beneath the cabin on Pale Peak.

I climbed to my feet and examined the jars. They brimmed with a brown, stringy substance.

227

Hair.

Others held bones and teeth and clumps of a pinkish substance.

Sensing that I was unwelcome in this place, I backed up to the hole – and bumped into a stone wall. The only other way out was up a short flight of wooden stairs that led outside. The cellar door had been ripped from its hinges, and now a gaping square framed the night sky. Trees loomed over the edges of the doorway, and snowflakes drifted down inside, frosting the steps.

As I moved toward the exit, something caught my eye, hidden behind the jars. It glimmered, as if calling to me, and suddenly I felt as though I was on the verge of a revelation. My hands reached out to grab the object, but the moment they touched its warm surface, a child shrieked in the distance. A hand fell on my back.

I woke up.

"Shhh," Faye whispered.

It was still dark. We lay in bed together, but she sat propped up against the pillows, looking down at me. I could make out faint dimples of a smile on her face, but she brushed her hand over my eyes.

"Sleep," she whispered. Her voice cracked.

Faye ran her fingers down my back, then up to my head, leaving a trail of goosebumps on my skin. Her hair dangled in such a way that it shrouded her face in shadow, but even in the gloom I could tell she looked different. Her body and slithering locks seemed familiar, but the bone structure in her face looked warped – the jaw too boxy, the cheekbones too low. When she tilted her head, I caught a glimpse of her skin. It had aged. At that point I noticed that her hand felt different, too. It was rough and heavy, like a man's.

I lay there motionless, paralyzed by the amalgam of familiar and unrecognizable features that comprised

Faye's visage. Dreadful memories of the Impostor lying in bed with me at the cabin raced into my mind.

"Where's Faye?" I asked, preparing for another brawl.

She abruptly climbed out of bed and stood in the middle of the room, tilting her head as if listening for a distant sound.

"There it is again," she said. This was unmistakably Faye's voice. The killer instinct within me faded. She walked to a wall and reached for a doorknob that wasn't there, then tried to flip on a light switch that didn't exist.

She's remembering the layout of our old bedroom, I realized.

Faye began arguing with someone, as a couple might in public – she kept her voice low but sharp:

"I already fucking told you, we don't know any of them. I don't know anybody."

"Is that you making all that noise? That's sick. You're sick."

"Who's with you? Let me see him."

As I crept out of bed to grab her, Faye shrieked at the top of her lungs, "Are you just gonna stand there and cry all night?! Why don't you just come up here already?!"

Her own screams woke her. She looked around in confusion and swayed. I caught her before she fell.

"Get off me!" she yelled, batting my hands away. I tried to hold onto her, but she squirmed loose and bolted into the hallway. There, she fell to her knees and vomited all over the floor.

For the third time since we'd moved into the condo, I found myself assessing a grotesque stain in the dead of night. Faye sat at the top of the staircase, leaning her head against the wall, looking at the hideous work of art she'd sprayed all over it a few days prior.

"I'm sorry," she said in a mousy voice. "I know you're

229

sick of all this."

"*You're* sick, Faye," I snapped. "We need to go to a hospital."

"After all this, you think that's the problem here?" she replied. "You think they're gonna give me a prescription and all this will just go away?"

I had no response. She was right.

"I know you tried to fix this," Faye continued, "and I know you feel helpless. I really do appreciate how much you've done."

I looked over at her. She traced a finger along the part of the splotch on the wall that looked like a gnarled hand.

"Maybe this is something *you* need to fix," I said angrily.

Without any response, Faye brushed past me and went downstairs, presumably to give me some space. While I cleaned up the mess, guilt for attacking her gnawed at my insides. I finished up and went downstairs to find her. She was lying on the couch under a blanket, trying to hide the fact that she'd been crying.

"I'm sorry too," I said, taking a seat next to her.

"I keep hearing a baby," she replied, ignoring my apology. "It cries and cries all night. It's driving me fucking crazy."

"A baby?" I repeated.

"Yeah. It freaks me out more than all the other sounds. I don't know why."

I glanced at the windows that flanked the living room on two sides.

"He wants to trick you, Faye. He's always trying. He tried to lure you with your grandpa's voice. Maybe he's going after your motherly instincts now."

She shuddered and tucked the blanket up under her chin.

"I'm exhausted," she said. "I feel like I can't fight him

anymore. I wish he'd just end it."

I leaned in and kissed her forehead.

"You're not licked yet," I said. "He's getting desperate. I saw it on the mountain. We just need to hold on."

"He wants something from me that I can't give," she said, finding my hand and squeezing it.

"Five?" I asked.

The hedges rustled outside. We both looked to the front door.

"I don't know what it means," she whispered. "I swear I don't."

"Maybe Becca knows," I said, getting up and looking through the peephole. Leaves blew across the empty walkway outside.

Faye elected to sleep on the couch for the remainder of the night. I didn't argue. As I sulked back to the bedroom, I noticed something about the stains: they all shared similar features and looked like a man. And each time Faye threw up, the man seemed to get closer and closer to our bedroom.

Chapter 35

Becca wasn't kidding about her intention to come stay with us. As soon as Faye told her I was fine with it, the two organized an itinerary and booked a flight. The short notice didn't bother me; I looked forward to having a full and lively house for once, and prayed the visit would distract Faye's mind from the darkness that possessed it. Becca was scheduled to arrive Friday night and leave Tuesday morning. Faye would pick her up from the airport while I ran errands and cleaned the house.

I spent the intervening time searching for information on Pale Peak, and for the last name of the family who had built the cabin. Since I didn't know Jennifer and Tom's surname, all I could find were brief mentions of the mountain and the weird experiences that campers had reported there. One forum, populated by enthusiasts of the paranormal, declared Pale Peak "one of Colorado's ten most haunted tourist destinations," but offered little more. Elsewhere, a user posted a story about her encounter with the "skin-thieves" of the Rocky Mountains, but other members of the community dismissed her as a phony.

I thought about calling Lynn, but then I reasoned that

she was just as likely to lie as she was to help. Instead I gave Ranger Pike a ring. He seemed reluctant to disclose Tom and Jennifer's last name, but with enough pestering, he caved. In exchange for the promise that I wouldn't "kick up the dust on that grave," William mumbled one word and hung up: *Ball.*

The search narrowed. I located Tom's obituary in a Las Vegas newspaper database, which only mentioned that he was survived by his wife and his brother, Neil. Finding Neil was easy enough. He owned a small business in Vegas, and answered my email within a day. I apologized for the odd contact and told him that I were seeking a Jennifer Ball regarding some old photo albums I'd found in the cabin. Neil responded that after his brother had died, Jennifer had remarried and moved to a little town in Washington. The two had lost contact after that – but he did remember her new husband's name.

Henry Schoeffer was a pediatric dentist in Greenhaven, Washington, as well as a small-time author of children's books with more than a dozen titles. The email listed on his goofy website was deactivated, so I took a chance and left a message at his practice, hoping that the sincerity and urgency in my voice would persuade him to return the call. I told him that the matter concerned his wife and my fiancée, and said that I needed to ask about a cabin in Colorado. Just after hanging up I realized how awfully creepy I must have sounded, and assumed that my little investigation was over.

The week slogged by, full of endless reading and writing in a quiet house. Faye worked during the day, so I spent that time alone, with nothing but the stains to keep me company. Thankfully, Faye slept without disturbance during that time, and nothing went bump in the night. In the wee hours on Thursday, the eerie singing of a child wafted into the bedroom from far away, but it did not precede a worse event. The dreary song caused Faye to toss and turn in her sleep, and nothing more. By the time Friday rolled around, I found myself giddy with excitement for Becca's arrival. Our dark visitor had not made a real appearance in weeks. Perhaps he would be dissuaded even further by a house full of people and noise and light.

"He's not a frickin' cheese platter, you goon!" Faye said, laughing at me as I held baby Caleb. She had just returned from the airport with Becca, and caught me walking out the door to pick up some steaks. "Tuck him against your arm. And arch your back a little so he's kinda nestled against your chest."

I had never held a baby before. I was the youngest child in my family, and all my friends with kids lived hours away in my hometown. Becca stood behind Faye, watching me with that hawklike stare that all new moms brandish. She looked a lot like her younger sister, but with a darker tan and chestnut brown locks that danced around her shoulders.

"Three points of contact, Felix," Becca added. She cracked up at my awkward fumbling.

"That's ladders," I replied, swaying back and forth. Caleb closed his eyes a bit.

"Is he having a seizure?" she joked to Faye. "He doesn't dance like that, does he?"

"His dancing is much scarier," Faye chimed in. "He needs to learn before the wedding."

"Caleb thinks I'm a natural," I said. His eyes were shut.

"He's been practicing this all week with a stack of books," Faye grunted, squeezing past me in the entryway. She lugged Becca's enormous suitcase, which probably weighed as much as her. "Jesus, Bec, is Kyle in here?"

"Was hoping you could help me bury him," Becca responded, taking the suitcase from her sister. She
234

followed Faye up to the guest room. I cringed as she examined the awful stain on the wall as they passed. Excited chatter and giggling echoed from upstairs, no doubt over the travel crib Faye had splurged on.

"Welp," I said, looking down at Caleb, "good to have another dude around here for once."

That night, Becca and I caught up over hot chocolate in the living room while Faye unleashed the full scope of her maternal instincts upon Caleb upstairs. She sang lullabies, laughed, cooed, and otherwise demonstrated several shades of mommy-crazy. I knew immediately that when Becca left, I was going to have to endure a long conversation about how starting a family doesn't necessarily have to wait until I finish my doctorate and get a job.

Becca, like her younger sister, was tough as nails. Her wit and sense of humor felt instantly familiar. I struggled to imagine her carrying on at a baby shower and shopping for miniature outfits; she seemed more the kind of person I'd find in a dive bar, engaged in a spirited belching contest. The best thing about the Spencer women, I suppose, is that they could happily do both.

Becca's roughness came from her upbringing in a stern military family, no doubt. But having a strict father also teaches girls how to be expert liars, and I wondered if Becca was selling me all sorts of bullshit when the conversation arrived at the cabin. She was five years older than Faye, and claimed that she had only visited the cabin at Pale Peak once. She said that mountain driving made her carsick, so whenever Faye and their parents took a trip there, she'd stay at a friend's house instead. I searched her eyes for any sign of deceit, but after an hour of thinly veiled interrogation, Becca had deflected each of my inquiries with a joke or a shrug.

235

When I knew that Faye had settled down and gone to sleep, I went for broke.

"All of this," I said, lowering my voice to a murmur, "the sleepwalking, the dreams, the talking – it's all related to one single thing."

Becca studied me. Her incredulous expression never changed.

"Like, some new medication she's on or something?"

"No," I said. "The number five. She has this weird obsession with it. She draws it in her sleep. Can't remember why when she wakes up."

Becca's eyes broke from mine, just for a second, then returned.

"Weird," she said flatly. "What do you think it means?"

"I was hoping you could tell me, Becca."

I knew it was a stupid thing to ask, and not only because the Impostor could be listening. I wondered if I could keep the secret as well as Faye had, or if the creature would force it out of me.

"Hell if I know," Becca said, shifting her legs on the couch. She yawned a few times, implying her desire to duck the conversation and go to bed.

"What *do* you know?"

"Nothing."

"Well, whoever Faye's talking to in her sleep," I said, not daring to look crazy by describing the Impostor, "he wants to know too."

Becca visibly shuddered. She asked me a bit about the man in Faye's dreams, always expressing a mixture of revulsion and morbid curiosity at my vague answers. I tried several times to turn the questions back on her, but Becca dodged me like a minnow each time. The more she learned about Faye's behavior, the more troubled she appeared. But it wasn't fear that I saw in Becca's eyes; it was denial. It was memory.

236

Chapter 36

That night, I woke up to the sound of a baby crying. Faye was gone.

A few weeks ago, she had accurately mimicked the voice of a child, so naturally I assumed the noises were coming from her. My skin crawled when the cries turned to shrieks. I imagined her huddling in the dark somewhere, channeling a demonic infant to lure me to my death.

I followed the noises to the stairs, and paused halfway down. Shadowy figures sat on the couch in the living room, one of them rambling to the other in whispers. I flicked the stairwell light on, illuminating the forms just enough to recognize them. They were Becca and Faye. In my midnight stupor, I'd completely forgotten our guests.

"Sorry Felix," Becca said, "we didn't mean to wake you. He was crying, so we brought him down here." After addressing me, she resumed telling a funny story about her husband.

Faye was seated on the couch with baby Caleb in her arms. She cradled him lovingly and hummed a song to him. Then, she looked up at me. Her eyes were pale white slits, and they burned into me with grim familiarity. When she saw the unease in my expression, she smiled a wicked little grin. Becca was so distracted with her own babbling that she hadn't noticed Faye was sleepwalking.

I stood motionless, too freaked out by the scene to do much else. Faye began humming that miserable lullaby, the one we'd heard so many times in the dead of night:

"Soouuul me aaahhh dooo...Soul me ahhhh dooooo..."

Caleb thrashed and cried as the song repeated. Faye simply held him tighter, raising her voice to drown his out. Becca moved to take him, and at the same time, I approached.

"Faye?" I called out. "Knock it off, babe. You're scaring him."

It was only then that I noticed a massive shadow looming over the window behind the two sisters. An enormous man stood there, cloaked in darkness, watching Faye and Caleb with such fascination that he didn't move a muscle. He looked more like a tree, and therefore my mind had dismissed him as an inanimate object. But as I reached the bottom of the stairs, his head snapped up at me, then he backed away from the window and vanished into the night.

"Son of a bitch!" I screamed, dashing for my shoes and ripping the front door open. "He's right there!"

The thunder in my voice silenced Caleb and wrenched Faye out of her hypnotic state. She glanced around in confusion as I ran outside. A hundred yards away, I caught sight of the colossal figure, barreling away from our house with an animalistic gait. He disappeared, but I could still hear his labored wheezing, and the smack of bare feet against the sidewalk.

I wasn't stupid enough to follow him. The bastard wanted to draw me out into the dark, away from the yellow glow of the streetlamps. Instead I investigated the place he'd watched us from, and there I found an oily black

238

puddle that looked like the ones Faye had recently puked up.

I heard Becca's terror and outrage before I walked inside. She yelled at Faye while clutching her son protectively, then turned her ire on me as I came through the door. Somehow, I managed to convince her that it was a couple of teenagers messing around with a Halloween costume, and she relented. We all retired for the night. Becca closed and locked her door without so much as a nod as we passed in the hall.

Faye was angry, too. She refused to speak to me when I brought up the obvious fact: our visitor had found us. We could run away, but no matter where we went, he would always track us down. His presence clung to our relationship like a dreadful shadow, and only by following him out into the dark could we make him leave our home.

Faye got into bed wearing her earbuds – something she only did when we fought. I scrolled through news articles on my phone, occasionally glancing over and wishing she'd speak to me, but each time she cranked the music a bit louder. Her anger died away to exhaustion, and eventually, sleep.

Devotion and hopelessness battled inside of me, yanking my mind back and forth across the landscape of my thoughts. I felt ready to die to protect her, and yet nothing I did kept her safe for long. Unlike the *At'an-A'anotogkua*, I could not always remain vigilant. I had to work. I had to sleep. The Impostor was intelligent enough to know this. His actions were purposeful. Patient. Calculated. Perhaps he had taken interest in baby Caleb – or perhaps he had merely discovered a new way to drain my energy for yet another night. Something eventually had to give, and it seemed unlikely that the monster who had stalked Faye for decades was going to be the one to quit now. To that end, the hopelessness I felt whispered into my ears: "*Give up.*"

Then, another voice whispered.

"I'm sorry."

Faye's head was turned toward me. One of her earbuds had fallen out, and gentle music seeped from it.

"About what?" I replied, trying to determine whether she was awake.

Her chest rose and fell in perfect rhythm. Her lips quivered and eyelids twitched. After a while, she said, "We don't talk enough."

I ran my hand down the length of her arm. Her skin felt cold.

"Oh, we talk plenty," I said, stifling a laugh. "You even talk to me when you're asleep."

"You ever think about...when we were little?" she asked in a slurred voice.

The question puzzled me.

"When we were little?"

"I can't remember," Faye said. "Hurts to try. Where were you?"

It took a moment to realize that Faye wasn't talking to me. Instead, she was having a conversation with her sister. I imagined Becca in the bedroom down the hall, fast asleep, carrying on the other half of the conversation in her dreams. The thought sent chills skittering across my body.

"Don't tell Felix," she whispered. "I didn't tell him. Didn't...wanna scare him."

"Didn't tell him what?" I asked, doing my best impression of Becca.

Faye's hand raised up off the bed and pointed at the door. It wagged a bit, then flopped back down.

"He's in the stains," she said, lowering her voice further, as if to tell her deepest secret. "He gets up and walks around at night."

240

The floorboards groaned beyond our bedroom door. Someone was on the staircase. Faye's head shot toward the source of the noise, then fell back down on the pillow.

"I feel like I'm starting to remember," she whispered. "Little bits."

"Faye...what do you remember?" I asked, not taking my eyes off the door. In that moment I wished I still had Greg's revolver.

Faye smiled and stretched her arms up over her head, issuing a pleasurable sigh. Her eyes never opened.

"He needs me..." she breathed.

Caleb's cries erupted from down the hall.

"...But he's a little corpse now," she added, then rolled over into a deeper sleep.

Chapter 37

Sleep never found me that night, but neither did our visitor. Caleb calmed down to the gentle singing of his mother, and the noises downstairs faded away. I felt like a zombie in the morning, but at least it was the weekend and I didn't have to stare at a computer screen.

Faye sat with Caleb upstairs, giggling and babbling along with him, while I made breakfast in the kitchen. Becca sat at the table behind me, watching everything I did in silence. Her mood was markedly worse; she seemed irritated by every little noise Faye made upstairs.

"Look," I said, cracking a few eggs into a pan, "I hope I didn't upset you with all the questions..."

"It's not you," she replied. "Trust me."

Instead of pressuring her to talk, I adopted the opposite strategy and remained quiet. After a few moments, Becca unleashed a torrent of angry mumbles in my direction. She complained about the fact that Faye rarely called her, but wanted a closer relationship now that Caleb was around. She admitted to being rough on her little sister, but explained that it was years ago, decades even, and Faye was harboring a ridiculous grudge over something neither of them could remember anymore.

"She's got a problem letting things go," Becca said. "If she's mad at someone, she's mad for weeks. If she's hurt, she hurts for years."

"I don't think she's mad, Becca," I said. "I think she's hurt...and it's exacerbating her sleep disorder. Being around Caleb seems to bring it out of her, for whatever reason."

"She's being selfish," Becca snapped. "She has *nothing* to be hurt about. *Nothing* happened to her."

Before I could reply, Becca pushed herself off the chair and headed upstairs to check on her son.

The three of us eventually gathered around the table. Caleb sat next to me in a little high chair that Faye had picked up. The two sisters ate in silence, barely making eye contact, and responding to anything I said with one-word answers. The tension was so high that it felt like static in the air, and Caleb seemed to pick up on it too. He glanced at his mom and aunt with quiet curiosity, then gazed up at me as if to say, "What have you done?"

Becca somehow managed to convince Faye to go shopping, probably with the intention of getting a bit of alone time with her. I spent the day learning the basics of fatherhood, scrambling to interpret Caleb's hundred different noises and checking his breathing every twenty minutes while he slept. I even tried my hand at changing a diaper – and nearly added a vomit stain of my own to our poor, mangled carpet.

When the two sisters finally returned home, Faye looked pale and exhausted, almost sickly, and trudged upstairs to bed. Becca refused to fill me in on what they had talked about, and instead retired with Caleb, leaving me downstairs to watch an *X-Files* marathon by myself.

243

Around 10 P.M., an ear-splitting noise sent me nearly flying off the couch. A cacophony of shrieking and thrashing boomed from the upper floor. The image of Faye being thrown around by the creature rushed through my mind. I raced upstairs to find her in her underwear, screaming and pummeling the guest bedroom door with her fists. She rambled incoherently and slammed her head against the door, then tried to rip the knob off with her hands. Becca and Caleb cried out in fear behind it, probably just as confused and horrified as I was.

I bear-hugged Faye and lifted her off her feet, pulling her back. She shoved me with unnatural strength, sending both of us careening to the floor where she wrestled free of my grasp. Once Faye had the advantage, she mounted me and jammed her face against my neck, trying to bite me. I managed to hold her back by the throat, but her rage made me weak with fear.

"I'll put you up in the trees," she growled. Drool ran down her mouth onto my hand. She landed a tiger-palm to my crotch, stunning me, and lunged once more with bared teeth. Just before she reached my face, however, she collapsed. The dark presence that commanded Faye's body had suddenly vacated it.

She looked around the dim hallway, regaining consciousness. Becca poked her head out from behind the door, and as Faye beheld our terrified expressions, she burst into tears and retreated into our bedroom.

"I'm so sorry," she whimpered, shaking visibly as she moved. "I'm so sorry, you guys. I'm sick. I'm really sick. I want to die."

The lock clicked. I looked to Becca for answers, but she scowled at me and slammed the door in my face.

I approached the master bedroom, at a loss for what to say, but wanting to offer some sort of consolation. We were both at the end of our rope.

244

"Faye? What's going on? Are you okay?"

"Go away," she called out in a shaky voice. "You're not safe."

"I'm... I'm gonna call Nathan," I said. "He'll know what to do."

I pulled out my phone and headed downstairs. As I passed the stain on the wall, it looked bigger than before.

Chapter 38

Nathan answered his phone as I stepped into the garage. His voice was dull and dreary, as if he'd been awake for hours, contemplating some terrible thought.

"Tell me about the child, Felix."

The question caught me off guard.

"How'd you know?"

"I had a nightmare," he replied. "I went to check on the cabin, and ever since then, I've been seeing a child in my dreams. Always different ages...but I know it's the same person. I figured he's got something to do with you guys."

Nathan told me that he and a group of friends from his community went back up the mountain to investigate the circumstances of his father's death. They camped for a few nights, and even stayed in the woods next to the cabin. Nathan heard Tíwé's voice calling for help, crying and speaking in their native language. After learning about my experiences in the weeks prior, he was convinced that this was not his father, but something else trying to lure him into the woods.

They also heard children weeping in the forest. One of Nathan's friends left the tents to take a piss, and when he returned, he claimed to have seen a young boy with grayish skin. The child stood a few yards out, facing away, staring up at something in the trees. His body was stiff and corpse-like, propped high up on the balls of his feet, and the calves were shredded and bloody. The sight of the boy frightened Nathan's friend so deeply that he returned to the camp and grabbed his belongings. He wanted to hike back down the mountain – in the dark, in the cold, by himself. Nathan and the others tried to stop him, but he insisted. The man never made it back to Nathan's community.

"I hope you find him," I said, already convinced that he'd met a terrible fate. "Faye's sister is here now. Her son Caleb is with her. He's only a few months old, and he's never been to the cabin. I don't know if it's him you're dreaming of, but Faye and I heard children on the mountain too."

"Strange," Nathan replied. "Maybe it's a different kid. And there's something else. I spoke with one of the elders of our community – one of the few who would speak to my father about your situation."

"Tell me everything," I said.

"The one who followed you home," Nathan said, "he has killed many people with ease. So why is he putting such great effort into tormenting both of you? Clearly, there is something he wants, and he cannot get it from Faye if she's dead."

"I've asked myself a million times," I snapped. "Neither of us knows. It's something about the number five. It doesn't make sense that he can go into her mind like he does, and yet he still can't figure out what it means."

Nathan's voice lit up, as if he'd solved an ancient math problem.

"But what if the *At'an-A'anotogkua* can't read minds, Felix?" he said. "What if he can only read dreams?"

The notion explained much about Faye, and about our experiences at the cabin. When the creature had Faye's ring, he seemed to be able to enter her body for brief periods while she was awake, causing her to behave strangely. But now, he appeared to infiltrate Faye's mind only while she was unconscious, taking advantage of her sleep disorder and commandeering her body. As before, his power over her was always tenuous. Always fading. To control her permanently, he would need deeper access.

At the cabin, the creature mimicked Faye's grandfather Alfred, and my mother. Perhaps there wasn't any particular reason he had selected those specific people. Perhaps we'd merely dreamed of them, so that was what he used. The Impostor had also mimicked Greg's buddies from the army – the ones he'd seen in his nightmares. The ones that made him wake up screaming over and over. And the cabin's former owner, Jennifer, swore she'd heard her daughter's voice in the woods at night. Who wouldn't have dreams of her own child after such a terrible loss?

"Son of a bitch learns about his kills through their nightmares," I said. "That's why he's always standing outside the windows. He's not watching us sleep. He's *listening.*"

"Sometimes when my dad and I went hunting," Nathan added, "we'd use calls to lure the animals. If you do it right, they come to you."

All the voices we'd heard in the forest, all the tongues the Impostor spoke with – they all belonged to other victims, and the people in their dreams. That wretched thing wandered around in the dark, sharpening his skills and practicing his speech. And now, he had perfected his impressions of the people Faye loved. He was getting closer to the information he so desperately sought. He was going to discover *what makes five.*

248

"Whatever that number means," I said, drawing it on the wall with my finger, "Faye isn't dreaming about it. She only dreams of the number itself."

Nathan paused to consider my words. My finger dragged across the drywall, tracing the number backwards and forwards. It was almost soothing to do so.

"I think that's what makes Faye so fascinating to this being," Nathan said at last. "Her mind is mysterious to him. She's a puzzle...a challenge. And most of all, when he speaks to her through her dreams, she speaks back. I guess you could say he has a very dark fixation on her...maybe even love. A putrid form of it, anyway."

My hand clenched into a fist. What Nathan said was true. Faye mirrored the Impostor's darkness; when he gazed into her, he didn't find all the hopes and dreams and fears he could see in others. Instead, he saw a pitch-black well – and he craved to know what was hidden at the bottom. '5' was simply the candle he needed to look inside.

Cold sweat matted every inch of my skin during the conversation. I pressed the phone tighter to my ear so as not to miss a word.

"Why does he need to get the answer from Faye?" I asked. "Her parents probably know what that number means too. They're definitely hiding something."

Nathan sighed into the phone.

"They haven't slept in that cabin for years, right? Maybe the Impostor establishes his connection to people through the land. That's how it works in our tradition, anyway. The mountain anchors the spirits and people together."

"She's getting worse, Nathan," I said. "She's slipping away. Becca's son is like... driving her insane. I can't figure out what it all means."

"Maybe it's best you don't," he responded. "If you discover the truth, this being could steal it from you in your sleep."

"I know," I said. "I worry that I'll—"

A door creaked open somewhere in the house, followed by the muffled sounds of movement.

"I've gotta go, Nathan," I said. "I need to keep an eye on Faye. Are you gonna be alright? You sound awful...I mean, understandably so."

There was a long pause. Another door opened in the house.

"It's not just the child," Nathan mumbled. "I'm dreaming of my father too."

"Of his death?"

"No. It's the cabin. Every time I shut my eyes."

"What do you see?"

Nathan's voice wavered. He tried to hold back tears.

"It's sitting there in the dark, and there's a bad storm. I'm standing in the distance, near the edge of the woods. A light turns on inside the cabin. I walk toward it. As I approach, the front door opens, and something in my heart tells me not to step inside. But I do. Every time, I do."

My heartbeat sped up. Memories of that miserable place flooded through me.

"As I enter, the light cuts out," he continued. "It's so dark. From the living room I can hear my father...he's calling out to me from the bedroom. He's speaking in our language, and sounds happy and peaceful. He tells me to come to him, and that he wants to see my face before he goes to be with our ancestors. He calls me *Ha'an'tue* – 'my light' – the nickname I was given as a child. But when I go to push the bedroom door open, I wake up to the sound of that child crying. Every time."

"Jesus," I blurted out.

"I want to go back," Nathan said, voice cracking into sobs. "I know he's not there, but it feels so real."

Someone screamed inside the house. Heavy footsteps thundered across the upper floor.

250

"I gotta go," I said, throwing the door open. The knob pinged against the wall. "Do not go inside that goddamn cabin."

Chapter 39

"Where is he?!" a woman shrieked. It was so primal I couldn't tell if it came from Faye or her sister. As if in response, a baby's cries resounded throughout the house. I raced up the stairs to find Becca rifling through each room with murder glinting in her eyes. Caleb's crib was empty. His little blanket lay on the floor.

"What's going on?!" I shouted. "Faye! Where are you?"

"I went to the bathroom," Becca replied, tears of rage and fear rolling down her cheeks. "I was gone for two minutes!"

The pieces fell together in my head, and a terrifying picture took shape from them. Faye had sequestered herself in our bedroom, waiting to snatch the baby.

"Where the fuck would she go?!" Becca yelled in my face. A gust of cold air licked the back of my neck.

She'd take Caleb outside – to him.

Without a word, I headed back to the first floor. Becca moved even faster, shoving me aside and bull-rushing past me. If the back door hadn't already been open, she probably would have kicked it down. Caleb's agonizing cries filled the night air, but the yard was so dark that I couldn't tell where he was.

Then, a branch snapped. Something moved in the trees that formed a wall around the perimeter of the backyard. Becca rushed out into the grass, causing the automatic lights to flood the scene in a blinding white glow.

Baby Caleb lay on the ground, trying to roll himself away from the blades of grass that poked his face. Faye stood beside him, reaching both arms up at the trees – as if a child herself, waiting to be lifted into the arms of a loving mother.

"Caleb!" Becca screamed. She strode across the grass and snatched her sister by the hair, then threw her to the ground with tremendous force. Faye gasped as she collided with the earth and then lay still. Becca scooped Caleb up and burst into wailing cries, matching his in volume and fear.

I ran over to help Faye. As I did, a huge mass leaped out of the trees and landed in the neighbor's yard, then darted off into the night.

"Are you out of your fucking mind?!" Becca shrieked at Faye. Lights flicked on all around us, and concerned neighbors peeked out from their bedroom windows.

Faye groaned as I helped her up, but she nearly fell again when I freed an arm to block Becca from coming any closer. Even with her son in hand, Becca looked like she was about to break her sister's neck.

I guided Faye back into the house. She staggered and stumbled as if she'd never walked a day in her life. She asked, "Did you hear the little birdies? They sing like angels."

Back inside, I tended to Faye on the couch while Becca stomped around overhead. Within minutes, Becca descended the stairs, luggage in one hand and Caleb in the other, and summarily exited the house. It was only after I heard the screeching of tires that I realized she'd driven off in Faye's car.

It wasn't long before a police cruiser lit up our driveway. A fist pounded on the door, and two burly officers greeted me with stoic gazes. The commotion had upset the old lady who lived across the yard. She claimed to have heard one of us rummaging around on her side of the fence. For her sake, I hoped she kept her doors locked.

The officers were under the impression that a drunken argument had taken place on the back patio, so I went along with it. What else could I have said? I explained that my fiancée had taken a few too many shots and had started a fight with her sister, and that Becca had stormed off and returned to her hotel. Faye sat up on the couch and woozily reassured the cops that her sister was sober as a judge, and that they need not worry that she was out driving drunk. They asked Faye if she was alright a few times, then eyed me sternly and left.

I wanted to scream at Faye. I was so tired of the creature's relentless intrusions, and I felt the urge to blame her. But at the last moment, I held my tongue. Faye looked up at me with dripping eyes, and in them I could see a misery more profound than anything I'd been through. Her exhaustion was betraying her. While unconscious, Faye was highly suggestible, almost childlike. The Impostor took advantage of this by manipulating her dreams, trying to convince her that he was a friend. The creature was grooming Faye to believe that he could take her away to a beautiful place. But in reality, she was being coaxed out of this world.

After draping Faye in blankets and securing all the doors and windows, I went upstairs. Thoughts of surrender and death swirled in my mind. I couldn't take it anymore. I pulled out my phone and called Angela, begging her to come and see with her own eyes what Pale Peak had wrought upon us.

She agreed.

Chapter 40

Faye and I spent Sunday out of the house. We window-shopped, saw a movie, and ate at a nice restaurant. I tried my best to cheer her up, but she was still devastated over what had happened. Being away from home, however, seemed to distract her, and that night, she didn't budge in her sleep.

On Monday morning, I woke to find a missed call on my phone. To my surprise, it was Jennifer's second husband, Henry Schoeffer. He sounded old and tired, and not at all happy to inform me that Jennifer had passed away more than ten years ago. I hit redial and spoke with a receptionist who reluctantly promised to have the dentist return my call at his convenience. By lunchtime, my phone buzzed again, and a grumpy man interrupted me when I answered.

"I'm trying to run a business here, Felix," he said. "I don't need your pictures, or your phone calls."

"Henry," I pleaded, forgoing the charade about the old photo albums, "I'm sorry about Jennifer. But I need your help. I think what happened to her is happening to my fiancée. Do you understand what I mean?"

The man paused in contemplation, as if considering

whether to open the old wound of his wife's passing.

"I don't know what you're talking about," he finally said.

"The mountain, Henry. The cabin."

Henry paused again.

"Please," I continued, "I need to know what happened. Jennifer sold that place to my in-laws. Now something terrible is happening to us."

"The Spencers," he grumbled.

"Yes. Their daughter and I stayed at Pale Peak. Now she's losing her mind. Please."

"I can't help you," Henry said. "Take her to a doctor. My wife was ill. Plain and simple."

"Did she ever do anything unusual?" I asked. "Sleepwalk, hear voices, things like that?"

A muffled crackling noise emitted from the phone, as if Henry were trying to crush it in his grip.

"Leave me alone!" he shouted. "Don't ever waste my time again!"

The phone clicked, and he was gone.

A few hours later, I received a series of text messages from Becca. She had gone to a hotel the night of the incident, then booked an earlier flight back to Arizona. She left the car at the hotel and taxied to the airport. We'd have to go pick it up.

Becca's final message read simply, *Ask our mom about 5. She knows.*

The message infuriated me. I knew Becca was hiding something, but the fact that Lynn bore the knowledge of what drew the Impostor to Faye was outrageous. Her duplicity had endangered her own child. I picked up the phone and called her immediately. When she didn't answer, I called again. And again. And again.

After some time, she answered with a frightened

"What do you want?!"

There was no irritation in her voice. Only guilt. She'd lied to me about something in the past, something important – and had been dreading I'd discover the truth ever since.

My words came out sharp and unmeasured.

"I flew all the way out there to hear your bullshit."

She didn't make a sound.

"I took time off work," I continued, "time I didn't have. I risked my life up at that cabin. And you knew something all along. Something you didn't tell me."

"I told you everything," Lynn said meekly. The show had ended; she couldn't act anymore.

"You know something about that mountain, and about Faye, and why this is all happening. Why you'd go this far to protect your lies is beyond me. Your daughter's *life* is in danger. At *best*, she's going to end up in a nuthouse."

"N—No," she replied, "I don't know anything about the mountain – I swear to God. I know bad things happened to Tom and Jennifer, but I don't know what it is. I'm telling the truth, Felix. I swear."

"What makes five?" I demanded. "You know what that means. Your daughter draws that number all over everything in her sleep, and she can't remember doing it when she wakes up. You're a liar, Lynn. Look what it's cost us."

Lynn whispered something, and then I heard Greg's voice.

"Oh just tell him already for Christ's sake," he grumbled. "He's family. He needs to know."

They bickered for another moment, Lynn trying desperately to conceal what she was saying from me. Greg became upset. His voice rose.

"You were *pregnant*, Lynn. Just tell him, okay? She was pregnant, Felix."

"You fucking asshole!" she yelled. A door slammed, and then her voice calmed. After a moment she took a deep breath and said, "Felix...I'm going to overnight a box out to you. Call me when you get it. And whatever you do, keep it between us. Don't let Faye see it. She doesn't need to know."

I didn't have time to express my shock. The sound of Greg thumping on the door came through the phone, and then Lynn promptly hung up.

Chapter 41

Hiding this revelation from Faye proved to be a difficult task. She was naturally perceptive and could read me like a book, so I decided not to masquerade as though nothing was wrong. Instead, I pretended to have a bad stomach ache and went to bed early to avoid talking with her altogether. Millions of questions swarmed my mind as I lay in the dark. Did Lynn have a miscarriage? An abortion? Did she give the baby up for adoption? Was it not Greg's child? The possibilities were myriad, and my desire to know kept me awake for hours.

A day and a half later, a package arrived in the mail. As I carried it inside, my phone beeped from upstairs. I hid the little box behind the TV stand and raced up to the bedroom, hoping that Nathan had tried to reach out. My heart sped up when I saw that the voicemail was from Henry.

His melancholy words seeped out of the phone. He slurred and paused from time to time, probably drunk, and seemed on the verge of tears. He apologized for attacking me and proceeded to mumble bits and pieces of a ghastly story.

"My wife lost her child to cancer," Henry reflected. "You never move on from a thing like that. She never talked about Kayla, or kept any photos around...that's why I didn't want the albums you found. I guess I figured if Jennifer wouldn't have wanted 'em, I shouldn't take 'em either. Outta respect, that sorta thing.

"But then after a couple years, she started dreaming about Kayla. She'd dream of her ex-husband Tom, too. Really bad nightmares. Jennifer never told me what was in the dreams, but she'd wake up screaming. We got her back on her old medications, but over time it only got worse. One morning she was talking about hearing their voices, Kayla and Tom's, out in the woods. Hearin' 'em while she was awake. They wouldn't let her sleep, she said. They were calling to her all the time, trying to get her to come out. But she knew it was wrong. Scared her to death.

"One evening I came home from my office and she was gone. Just gone. The back door was open, but all her stuff was still here. She didn't take a jacket or shoes or anything. And it's all woods up here, Felix. Hundreds of miles of it. They searched for a month and found nothing. They investigated me...accused me of murdering my wife. I thought about killing myself. I swear I never hurt her. She just left. And she took my world with her.

"Then one day, I got a call from the sheriff's department. Some campers found Jennifer's remains, about forty miles away from our home, way up in the mountains." Henry paused to choke back tears. "She'd been buried upside down with her legs stickin' out of the ground. Some animal chewed 'em all up."

Henry apologized once again, and asked me not to return his call. I understood, and sat there on the bed in silence for a moment, mourning all the people the Impostor had brought to ruin. Although I tried to resist it, a horrible thought took root in my mind: I imagined Faye's slender legs caked with soil and jutting from the earth.

Since learning of Lynn's mysterious pregnancy, I

struggled to act normal around Faye. I kept my lying eyes averted whenever she was near, and hoped she wouldn't notice the fact that I was hiding something big from her. I had no idea why Lynn would be so secretive about the pregnancy, but she had endangered her own daughter's life to hide it. That night, I worked late into the night on my laptop, and got into bed only when I felt certain that Faye was sleeping.

Her body was stiff beneath the sheets. As I slid under the covers, I noticed her legs contorting in an awkward position.

She rolled her head toward me and smiled with her eyes closed, then asked if Caleb was still awake. I hesitated.

"Ugh, he's crying again," she went on. "I'll get him."

Faye tried to sit up, but I gently pulled her back down. She offered no resistance.

"He's fine, sweetie," I replied.

She furrowed her brows and pursed her lips, as though she'd just realized I was lying.

"He's...not here," she said. She gazed around the room, eyes still peacefully closed.

"Who *is* here, Faye?" I asked. "Do you know?"

She paused for a long moment, then let out a sigh.

"You."

"Who am I?"

"Felix."

"And who are you?"

"...Faye."

Her head cocked to the side. She listened for something.

"What do you hear?" I asked. "Is there someone else here?"

"There's someone outside," she said, "...hanging something up in the trees."

I wanted to get up and look out the window, but I feared it might wake Faye.

"Is it a dreamcatcher?" I asked. "Do you know what they're for?"

She smiled and laid her head back on the pillow. Her eyes were open now, and rolled back in her head so that only pale white showed.

"I found one outside the old house," I said gently. "I never told you. It was made with your hair, Faye. Did you make it? Do you know who makes them? Is it *him?*"

Faye's eyes rolled forward and her little green irises finally showed. Even in the dim light, I could see the fear that glinted in them. Her gaze snapped to the door that led into the hall, and she said, "No. No. He's listening now." She began hyperventilating. "He'll find out. He'll hear."

"It's okay, sweetie," I whispered, brushing her chin with my fingers. "It's alright. Just calm down."

Faye's breathing slowed and her eyes fell shut, but her body still trembled.

"He's gonna kill you," she whispered back. "I saw him. He's gonna hang you up in the trees. Real soon. Just a little longer now."

My phone vibrated on the dresser, igniting the room in a blueish glow. I reached for it, wondering if Nathan or Dr. Schoeffer was trying to get a hold of me. It was after 2 A.M. Whoever it was, I knew it was bad news.

Lynn's voice came through the speaker.

"I'm outside," she said. "Please, let me in."

Chapter 42

The walk downstairs felt surreal, as if I were lost and wandering in a dream. My body was weak and my mind felt clogged with mud; the long months of anxiety and insomnia worked in concert to grind what remained of my spirit into dust. When I looked through the peephole and beheld Faye's mother standing there under the palm trees on our walkway, my head felt even lighter.

I cracked the door open a few inches.

"What the hell are you doing here?" I whispered. I couldn't even begin to imagine what Lynn was up to, but her presence here – and the look on her face – signaled that she came bearing grave news.

"I took a red-eye," she said in a mousy voice. "Greg doesn't know I'm here. Not yet, at least."

Satisfied that this wasn't some trick by our *other* unwanted guest, I pulled the door open. Lynn followed me inside, carrying only a modest suitcase and a grocery bag.

"I'll wake Faye," I said, turning toward the stairs. Lynn nabbed my arm and spun me around.

"We need to talk alone," she whispered. Her wide eyes screamed the point.

We sat on the couch, where she quietly apologized to

me for everything: for constantly being evasive, for lying, and for letting us stay at the cabin in the first place. I waved away her ramblings and demanded to know the purpose of her visit.

Seeing my frustration, Lynn produced a photo album from the grocery bag.

"Felix," she said, clutching it in her arms as if to protect it from me, "I told you the truth. Faye was about five years old when something happened at the cabin...when she developed her sleep disorder. But that isn't what the number five means."

Lynn stared at me for a moment, struggling to force up the words she thought she'd never speak. The mask was off, and beneath it lay only a barren sadness she'd hidden for decades. My gaze fell to her lap, where she opened the photo album. Its tattered spine groaned as if disturbed from centuries of rest.

As she turned the pages, I realized that it was actually a scrapbook – a very elaborate one that had taken years to construct. Inside lay photos, drawings, designs, letters, handprints, and even a garland of pressed flowers. There were pictures of Faye I'd never seen before. Her glowing smile poked out from beneath little strawberry locks in photo after photo. She looked exactly the way I imagined our daughter.

"This is what I wanted to show you," Lynn said. "I don't know how to talk to Faye about it."

I was so amazed by the elaborate craftsmanship and the touching photographs that her words didn't almost register with me.

"You made this?" I asked.

She flipped further into the scrapbook and revealed a few old pictures of herself in the later stages of pregnancy. The centerpiece of one of the pages was a Polaroid of Lynn, big-bellied and bearing a youthful smile, with little five-year-old Faye curiously resting her ear on her mother's tummy. It was a priceless image, and one that hadn't seen the light of day in decades. The elegant script above it read, *Listen to him kick!*

"Faye and I put this together, actually," Lynn replied. "When she was little."

It made sense. Faye was one of the most talented arts and crafts hobbyists I've ever known. She must have gotten it from her mom.

"So...uh," I mumbled, unsure of how to broach the topic, "what happened?"

Lynn looked over her shoulder to the darkened staircase. She feared her daughter would wake up.

"His name was Christopher," she whispered. Her lips quivered as she spoke. She turned the page, revealing a photo of herself undergoing an ultrasound and giving a thumbs-up. "He was stillborn a little under a month before the due date."

I had no idea what to say. Between her loss and Tíwé's death, I had discovered the true poverty of the words "I'm sorry." I remained silent, and the stillness in the room spoke for itself.

"Placental abruption," she continued. "It's rare. But it happens." Lynn scooted closer to me and put the scrapbook on my lap, then grabbed my wrist. "Felix, Faye doesn't remember any of this. We've never spoken of it."

I raised my finger to my lips, signaling her to be as quiet as possible. It wasn't just Faye who might be eavesdropping.

"How is this possible?" I asked. "Five is old enough to remember something like this. I have memories from when I was two."

Lynn explained that the emergency occurred while Greg was out with the girls. The paramedics rushed her to the hospital, but the baby could not be saved. When she and

265

Greg finally decided to break the news to their daughters that Christopher had died, Becca was heartbroken, but Faye didn't react. It was as if their words simply didn't register. Lynn would say, "Do you understand that Christopher is never coming home?" And Faye would respond, "Yes, mommy," with a blank expression.

This went on for weeks. Faye would occasionally ask about Christopher as though he'd be here soon, and then suddenly she'd forget all about him, as if he never existed. She began to act out at school and would throw violent tantrums. A child psychologist warned that Faye was not handling the situation well, so Greg and Lynn decided to spend a few days with her up at the cabin, in hopes of separating little Faye's mind from the heavy event.

That's when it happened. Whatever it is that lives in the forest up there, up in the trees or down in the hole, took notice of Faye. It found her fascinating. And it wanted to learn more about her, but her little brain shut down in terror when it got too close.

"After that day," Lynn said, "Faye never spoke of Christopher again, and seems completely unaware that he ever existed. We didn't know what else to do, so we played along."

"You've kept this from her all these years?" I whispered.

"Her therapist wanted us to tr—"

Suddenly, Faye's voice erupted from behind us.

"Mom?"

My head snapped toward the sound. Faye stood there at the bottom of the stairs – for God knows how long. I slammed the book shut. The air went out of the room. An agonizing moment of stillness ticked by, during which we all exchanged looks of shock. A shit storm was upon us. This much I knew.

"What's that?" Faye asked gently, pointing to the book

on my lap.

I was dumbstruck. My limbs ceased responding to my brain's commands. Lynn jumped up between Faye and me.

"Sweetie, we need to talk," Lynn said, opening her arms for a hug. She tried to obscure Faye's view.

Faye pushed her mother aside and walked over to the couch. Her fiery eyes locked onto the scrapbook and didn't blink. She reached down and tore it from my frozen hands.

Then she opened it.

The page she revealed bore a colorful cutout of the number 5. It was one of the final pages of the book. Her jaw trembled and her eyes became slick with welling tears. A look of excruciating pain fell over her face, and she cupped her mouth with a hand. Lynn reached out to assuage her, but Faye evaded her and raced back upstairs to the bedroom, taking the book with her.

Lynn tried for an hour to convince Faye to open the door, but it remained locked. During that time, Faye only spoke once, and she said,

"Go home."

Eventually, Lynn surrendered to her daughter's command and hugged me goodbye. I tried to get her to stay, but she seemed downright terrified of what her daughter might say when she finally emerged from the bedroom.

I spent the rest of the night alone, too afraid to go to sleep. I feared the Impostor might walk in my dreams, plucking bits of today's events like flowers in a meadow. By now, he had almost everything he needed to conquer Faye's mind.

Faye never came out of the bedroom, and wouldn't speak to me when I knocked. I played video games and watched TV shows to distract myself from the horrible knot of stress in my stomach. I even texted with Tyler and Colin about the new developments. But the night wore on slowly, and each passing minute compounded my worry. What would this news do to Faye? Would it finally break her?

As dawn crept over our home, I heard the bedroom door click. She was finally ready to let me in.

Chapter 43

Faye looked like a cemetery statue when I pushed the door open. She sat there on the bed, perfectly still, with the scrapbook resting on her lap.

I didn't speak, but the look in my eyes asked, "You want to talk about it?"

The paths of a thousand tears streaked her face. Her skin was pale, and her bloodshot eyes seemed wrung of all their sorrow. A few tear-soaked locks of hair clung to her cheeks.

"I remember now," Faye muttered.

I stood there in the doorway, afraid to move. I had no idea how she'd react to the knowledge that I'd conspired with her mother to uncover the secrets of their past. This was new territory for both of us. I worried that Faye might try to hurt herself.

"Mom and I spent all summer getting the nursery ready," she said, tracing a finger over one of the photos. "Dad was so excited that he was finally going to have a son. So we did a sports theme."

I sat down beside her, quiet as a lamb. Talking to Faye in this state seemed a bit like handling a bomb, so I opted to just listen. She kept her hands pressed on the scrapbook as though she were feeling for a pulse, and closed her eyes in search of distant memories. A colorful '5' rested at the center of the page, overlaid with various photos. One depicted a baseball mural painted on the wall with five players, and another displayed a toddler onesie in the design of a basketball jersey. It bore the number five.

"I always wanted to be a big sister," Faye said. "I used to lay on my back in that room, staring up at the ceiling and wondering what kind of person he'd be. What he'd look like. I fantasized about all the adventures we'd have."

I rested my hand on her back. Her skin blazed with warmth.

"You'd have been the world's greatest big sister," I offered. "I'm sure of it."

Faye turned a few more pages. Some were unfinished, and then the rest were blank.

"I never got to see him," she replied. "That number was how I always thought of him. Christopher was going to be the fifth member of our family."

We sat there for a long time. I listened quietly as a deluge of ancient memories surfaced within Faye. Sometimes she could barely speak. Other times she shook her head and said it was all a dream. Her denial rose and fell in waves. She grasped at all the faded images in her head and tried to describe them to me with great strain. A tomb had been unearthed from the deepest catacomb of her mind, and despite the pain it wrought on her, Faye was excavating it. All I could do was hold her hand and listen.

After our conversation, Faye asked to be alone. I nodded and kissed her forehead. As I left, I took out my phone to call Nathan, wanting to update him on all the new developments, but then realized it might be a bad idea. The more people who knew what the number five symbolized, the more opportunities the Impostor would have to discover it. Nathan had told me about his dreams of the cabin and his father. Perhaps the creature was already inside his head.

As I came down the stairs, my eyes fell on the TV stand, and I suddenly remembered the package I'd hidden behind it the day before. Perplexed, I retrieved it and brought it to the dining room table. Lynn mentioned she would send a box out to me, but she ended up visiting instead. So who the hell sent this?

I ripped the thing open and discovered a jar of something that looked like tea leaves. A little note attached to it read:

My friends,
This is Calea, the dream herb. It's used by Native cultures in Mexico, but some folks in my community make tea from it to ward off nightmares and promote good sleep. In case you find what you're looking for, may this protect you.
An-we hite'anei,
Nathan

I opened the jar and sniffed the leaves inside. They smelled bitter and earthy, and I guessed that the tea made from them probably tasted horrible. But, I trusted Nathan's judgment. Perhaps it could shield us from the Impostor's nightly intrusions – or at least prevent us from dreaming about Christopher and the scrapbook.

Night eventually fell, and I slogged up the stairs, barely able to keep my eyes open. Faye had taken the day off work and spent most of it texting with her family, probably getting everyone's version of the tragedy. Surprisingly, she was receptive to Nathan's gift, and said she'd try anything to stop herself from having any more bad dreams.

I brewed up enough of the tea for both of us. The look on her face as it touched her lips confirmed my suspicion that it tasted awful. As she forced it down, I said,

"Actually, I lied. We're sending you on a vision quest. This is going to be intense."

She laughed. And it sounded like heaven.

We slept like corpses that night. Colorful dreams washed over my mind, bringing with them a dizzying euphoria. I soared over fairytale landscapes and met bizarre creatures. I wandered through a bright green forest whose trees stretched up to the sky, and discovered Faye at the edge of a glowing pool of water. She stood there nude, fiery hair billowing in the gentle breeze, and beckoned me to follow. I watched as she slipped beneath its surface. Inviting warmth crept up my feet as I dipped them into the pool. The feeling rose up my body, almost to my neck, so pleasurable that my vision faded into a soothing darkness.

But then, a familiar cold licked my neck and ears. It pushed through my hair and forced its way into my nostrils, jarring me from the calmness of the dream. I rubbed the darkness from my eyes and opened them.

A yellow light glimmered high up in the air against a black background. It cast a pale beam down to the ground, where beneath it, a blurry figure stood.

"Faye?"

A sharp, green thing poked against my bare arm. The sensation jerked me from my stupor. It was a palm frond. Short trees lined the sides of my vision, and a little stone path stretched out before me toward the yellow light.

I stood on the walkway in front of our condo, looking out at the street. It must have been very late, because most of the lights of other houses were off. A few crickets chirped, and in the distance, sprinklers hissed.

There, across the road, standing under a street lamp,

was a man. His body glowed in the yellow light, but his face remained in shadow. Even with a hunched comportment he looked about seven feet tall. One of his shoulders arched noticeably higher than the other and his head cocked to the side, reminiscent of the way Faye looked when she sleepwalked. The figure swirled a bony finger in the air as if conducting a choir of ghouls, then dropped his hand when he realized I'd woken up. It seemed that the tea had stopped me from dreaming of the awful things I'd learned about little Christopher, but it did nothing to prevent the Impostor from seeing whatever came into my mind while I slept. For the second time now, the monster led me right to him with my own dreams.

"I thought I told you to *fuck off!*" I roared. I don't know what possessed me, but I strode toward him, fully prepared for round two. To my surprise, instead of clawing me to death right there in the street, the figure turned and ran. Against my better judgment I gave chase, screaming at the top of my lungs to stay away from my family and my house.

He moved faster than I could, even with his freakish limp. I'd always imagined the Impostor as some hellish mockery of a man, but the longer I watched him move, the more I realized he was more of a patchwork of *things*. My mind tried to comprehend what exactly I was looking at; I envisioned a rail-thin creature made of oily black parts, squeezing into the costume of a human and gracelessly lurking around in it. His movements looked animalistic, his strides far too long. He wheezed the night air like an old accordion, and the stench that dragged behind him singed my nose. It smelled like wildfire.

"No woods for you to fuck around in out here!" I screamed. Lights came on in houses all around me as I chased the creature. He practically galloped, and was always twenty feet ahead.

273

I chased him down for two blocks. He rounded a few turns and finally bounded over a chain-link fence into the nearby community park, where there were no lights. Unable to climb the fence, I ran all the way around and found him standing perfectly still in the grass.

Only the hideous silhouette was visible. The figure stood there in the empty field, shrouded in the night, gazing up at the moon. One of his hands reached into the sky, twitching wildly, and the other hung at his side like gnarled driftwood. My adrenaline faded as I realized how far away we were from help. Out here, no one would hear me scream. But I approached the figure still, committed to ending this nightmare tonight, one way or another.

As I neared him, the creature issued a rumbling growl. The sound was so deep I felt it in my ribcage as much as I heard it. I stopped in my tracks, but still managed to push out the words,

"You will *never* have her. *Never.* Go back to that goddamn mountain and bury yourself in a mine."

The figure growled again, then gurgled up a wet laugh.

"What is your name?" he asked – in my voice. He'd been practicing. The impression was perfect now. "May I come in? Open the door, Faye."

I didn't know how much of human speech he could truly comprehend, but my tone must have communicated whatever my words could not.

"You *will* leave us alone and go back to the mountain," I said, louder than before. "Faye will *never* be yours."

The Impostor emitted the shrieking of an infant. The sound mortified me, not just because of its accuracy, but because my brain refused to match that noise to a person this large. Then he said, in the voice of a child, "You go down in the hole. That's where he'll put you."

"Look at me, you piece of shit," I said. I tried to sound menacing, but my flight instinct was beginning to kick in.

274

There was little doubt the Impostor sensed it too.

Then, he said something I did not expect. The words felt like a fist bashing against my skull, and upon hearing them, everything started to spin.

"Tell me about the child, Felix." Nathan's voice wafted effortlessly from its throat. "Tell me about the child."

Before I could speak, the Impostor whirled around and glared at me. My knees came straight out from under my body and I collapsed onto the wet grass.

Staring down at me, boring into my soul with lidless eyes, was the face of Nathan – my friend, my protector, the son of a man who had given his life to help me. Now his skin was hard and bruised, his scalp flayed, his eyes tormented. His features didn't quite fit the skull they'd been stretched over, and the whole mess was propped up by a body that rattled with loose, collected bones. A slimy black liquid dribbled out of the mouth and spattered onto my chest when he cackled. As the creature loomed over me, a familiar little pouch bobbled around his neck, emptied of its former contents and now overflowing with severed fingers.

The creature spoke a phrase in the language of Tíwé's people – the same one Nathan had uttered over the phone to make Faye sick – and I began vomiting profusely as I lay there on the ground.

"Tell me about the child," he said once more. The lips spread in an expression of malevolent joy, baring the rotten maw of a long-dead wolf. Nathan's calm voice seeped out of it. "Let me speak to the one who followed you home."

I gasped for air but couldn't impel my body to move. The creature took a few steps toward me, and I slammed shut my eyes, expecting to feel those hideous fangs in my neck. Instead, I heard his footsteps approach, and then recede in the opposite direction. I smelled his stench as he passed over me. When I opened my eyes, he was already in the distance, moving quickly. Back toward my neighborhood. Toward my house.

"Followed you home," he repeated, voice echoing in the cold night air. "Followed you home. Followed you home."

Chapter 44

When I was three years old, my parents took my brother and me to Yosemite for a vacation. We were joined by two other families that my mother knew from work, so we all stayed in a giant cabin together. At some point during our stay, one of the other kids came down with some kind of stomach bug. It didn't take long for the illness to spread to all the children, and eventually I began vomiting uncontrollably. My father could not hide his disgust, and refused to come near me. This made me cry. A lot. My mother came to the rescue and consoled me, but the damage was done. My dad's horrified expression imprinted itself on my mind forever, and taught me that there is something to fear about being sick.

I'm twenty-eight years old now, and I've spent years of my life being paranoid about throwing up. Emetophobia controls much of my existence. It makes me afraid to share someone's drink, afraid to eat without washing my hands, afraid to get on rollercoasters, to fly in planes, to try new things or go to new places.

At some point after decades of living with this phobia, I've almost forgotten what causes me to regard all those things with fear. The *possibility* of vomiting becomes subconscious; I don't really think about it anymore. I simply fear everything that could cause me to be sick, and yet I have no immediate explanation for why I am afraid anymore. I just *am*.

That possibility no longer lingers at the precipice of my conscious thoughts. But the Impostor found it anyway. He reached deep into my nightmares and pulled out what terrifies me the most. He brought it out and used it against me. Repeating Nathan's spiritual purge didn't just disable me there in the field; it was a reminder. A reminder of his remarkable power to turn my own flawed humanity upon me. A reminder that he was planning to make me suffer in the most personal of ways. The *At'an-A'anotogkua* was designing a personal hell for me, and was nearly ready to drag me down into it.

And so the world collapsed on me. I lay there on the ground, puking my guts out, knowing that Faye was asleep and unguarded while a terrible being strode toward her through the dark. He beckoned her in every voice she knew, calling out her name in all his stolen tongues. He whispered things that would make her happy. He made her promises. He begged for help and mimicked the cries of children. He capitalized on her innate motherly instincts, on her buried memories, and on the vulnerability of her unconscious state. And all I could do was stagger around and wait for the thrum of my death-gripped heart to subside.

After a few blurry moments, the first light of morning poured into my vision, illuminating my way out of the park. My pulse recovered from its frenzy, and the numbness of my limbs faded. The acrid taste in my mouth, for once, didn't paralyze me. I tore through the streets to get back to the house. I had no plan.

Many lights were on in the homes that lined our street, and the sky over the eastern foothills blazed dawn-red.

A few of my neighbors had heard me shouting, and were now standing on their driveways with cell phones or flashlights in hand. I ran past them, telling them to look out for a prowler, and ducked into the walkway of our condo. I hoped that their watchful gazes would discourage the creature from making another appearance.

The front door sat wide open. I couldn't remember if I'd left it that way while sleepwalking, but I assumed that the creature was somewhere inside the house. I entered, squinting through the darkness and calling out to Faye.

The bed was empty. Its sheets lay across the floor as if Faye had been dragged from them. I shouted her name and searched the rooms, growing more frantic with each passing second. When I couldn't find her anywhere, I leaped down the stairs, hoping to catch one of the neighbors and ask if they'd seen her. Just as I reached the front door, a person's silhouette appeared in the corner of my eye.

It was Faye. She stood in front of the sliding glass door that led out to the backyard. She remained perfectly still, except for her hand, which gripped the door handle so tightly it trembled.

"Thank God," I sighed, slamming the front door shut and ensuring it was locked.

Faye muttered something, but I couldn't hear it. All I could see was the featureless outline of her body, and her breath that fogged the glass in front of her.

"Are you alright?" I asked, moving toward her.

"I saw him," she whispered. The door frame shuddered under the strength of her grip.

"He was here."

"Where is he now?" I asked, looking over her shoulder and surveying the yard.

"I saw him," she said again.

279

Faye backed into me and stumbled. I caught her before she fell. She looked up into my eyes with a panic I knew too well. She'd finally met her biggest fan.

"I saw his face," she whispered, pointing a shaky finger at the glass. *"I saw his face."*

There, streaked across the glass where she'd been standing, was an oily black handprint.

Faye and I forced ourselves to stay awake through the next few hours. We communicated only with pen and paper, for fear that the creature might still be listening somewhere outside. During that time, we heard three distinct sets of footsteps across the roof, and two different knocks on the door. Children laughed all around the perimeter of the house. Occasionally there were long periods of silence, but even then, I could not relax. The image of Nathan's eyes staring into me with otherworldly malice haunted my thoughts. The ache of his loss gnawed at my heart so hungrily that I could not even speak it to Faye.

We waited until the sun climbed high in the morning sky. As the noises faded and the world brightened, Faye went to the window to look outside.

"I've got an idea," she said, confidence rising in her voice. "I know what to do."

Chapter 45

Faye's new boss was generous enough to give her the day off, so we had a long weekend to set her plan into motion. We sipped Nathan's awful tea after concluding that it did more good than harm, and Faye spent her time furiously drawing, journaling, and texting with her mom and sister. She explained little, but I could tell by her demeanor that everything she did had a purpose. Angela called me to set up her visit, and seemed genuinely disturbed by the fact that I refused to talk about our situation over the phone. I asked her to bring sage, to which she replied, "I'm not that kind of Indian."

Over the next two days, I periodically heard Faye crying in private. She had certainly entered some kind of mourning process, long-delayed by years of denial, and I now bore witness to the lifelong impact of her loss. She sobbed for hours on end, and stared at the scrapbook all the while. Never have I seen a person in so much pain. But, she assured me that she'd be alright, and simply asked that I trust her. I obliged. Faye knew herself better than anyone, even me, and seemed confident in her ability to rid us of the shadow that loomed over our lives. And so, I put my faith in her judgment.

I cried too. Nathan never answered any of the thousand calls I made to his phone that weekend. Neither did Ranger Pike. My heart was certain of Nathan's ghastly fate, but my brain still had to know for sure. The wait was agonizing.

Finally, on Saturday night, my phone rang. I was in the middle of heating soup for Faye. When I saw that it was the ranger, a sudden dread washed over me. The phone felt like a twenty-pound brick in my hand.

"Hello?" I said. It came out almost a plea.

William skipped all pleasantries and said, "You better sit down."

"Just tell me," I begged. "Just tell me." My heart pounded so hard it shook my vision.

William cleared his throat and tried to speak with composure, but I could hear the sorrow in his voice.

"We got a call from one of Nathan's relatives," he said. "Told us he'd been missing a few days. Thought he went camping with his buddies, but none of them knew where he was. On my route yesterday morning, I dropped by the Spencer cabin—"

There was a long silence, which told me more than words could say. A jolt of desperate rage flashed through me. I'd warned Nathan not to go back there.

"We got city cops everywhere up here now," William continued. "Whole mountain's shut down. Weren't no bear this time. They're up here lookin' for a murderer."

The ranger heard my muffled sobs.

"That's enough then," he said. "They were my friends too, Felix. Family to me."

"Tell me," I repeated. "I have to know."

"I can't, Felix. It just don't make any sense yet. Maybe if we wait for an official—"

"Tell me what you know," I demanded.

William sighed.

282

"Somethin' happened up there at the cabin. They did somethin' to him. I don't understand it. Our coroner up here's deferrin' to the boys in Denver, so we gotta wait some more. He ain't ever seen anything like it. It's horrible. Just horrible."

The news singed every nerve in my body; pain radiated up from my stomach across every limb. My scalp tingled. Fuzzy gray static began to form around my vision. I felt like passing out.

"I called for backup right when I got there," William said. "Went inside, found a hell of a puzzle. Bathroom window been forced open. Don't get why, though, because the front door was unlocked. That's how we came in.

"Seemed like two people been in there recently. Bedroom door was locked from the inside, but the door leadin' from that room out to the back was open. Wide open. Somebody'd been stayin' in that bedroom for a few nights. Food and all kinds of weird shit in there. Some dead rabbits and a chipmunk or somethin' too.

"We found Nathan's satellite phone on the couch in the living room. Your number was the last one he dialed, Felix."

The static pressed closer to the center of my vision.

"I never got a missed call," I replied, exasperated. "I never heard from Nathan at all. I called him a hundred times."

"Might notta gone through," the ranger replied. "I found his buck knife jammed into the wall outside the bedroom door. He'd been carvin' symbols and words all over the house. Took pictures of 'em, but nobody in his community ever seen anythin' like 'em before. Specialist at Boulder says some of 'em are Hopi and Zuni words, but Nathan didn't speak them languages. Neither did Tíwé. Nobody on their reservation does.

"There was a big carving of a dreamcatcher on the outside of the bedroom door, and non-lethal amounts of blood spattered on the carpet and the wall there in the hallway. If that ain't weird enough, on the inside of the bedroom door, we found little marks everywhere. Like someone been poundin' and scratchin' on it."

William explained to me what the sheriff and his men had hypothesized: that Nathan had been sitting on the floor in the hall for a day, maybe even two. Someone was in the bedroom, but the door remained locked. Whoever was in there, it was possible that he and Nathan were having some sort of conversation. At no point was the electricity or heat functioning in the cabin, because it had been shut off after I was rescued on my second visit. This meant that however long Nathan had stayed, he remained in the dark and in near-freezing weather each night.

The K-9 team found two pairs of tracks leaving the cabin, one from the back door in the bedroom, the other from the front door. They both headed into the woods across the field. The tracks joined together, indicating that although the two people had left the house separately, they had walked side-by-side into the woods.

They found Nathan's body approximately a quarter-mile in, buried upside-down with his legs erupting from the soil at the knee. Upon exhumation it was discovered that his face and scalp had been flayed. There were deep lacerations in his back that appeared to be claw marks, and carvings on his arms that looked self-inflicted. The unofficial cause of death, however, was suffocation. He'd been buried alive.

If it is true that we have souls, I felt mine die in that moment. I remained in the kitchen, speechless, watching as Faye's soup boiled over and splattered across the stove.

"You ever go down into that cellar?" William asked, shaking me from my stupor.

"N—no...it...it was locked."

"Must'a been," he replied. "Both 'em doors been ripped

off. Whatever was inside is gone now. Taken."

The rest of the night slipped by in silence. If the Impostor made any noise outside, I was oblivious to it. Faye slept soundly, thanks to the effect of Nathan's final gift. I sat at the living room table with a single lamp on, wistfully remembering the warmth of Tíwé's smile, and the liveliness of his eyes against his weather-beaten face. I recalled the feeling of camaraderie that Nathan had always made me feel; from the day we met, he treated me like his brother. The wicked grins they donned while worn by the Impostor still haunted me – but my heart knew that those were petty torments. They faded and gave way to the memories I had of the *real* Tíwé and Nathan.

I didn't know what to do. I went online and made the largest donation I could afford to their community, to help cover some of the cost of their funeral ceremonies. Afterward, I wrote a long letter to both of them. I intended to read it at their place of burial someday, when all this was over.

For now, we had a pest to eradicate.

Chapter 46

It was Sunday. Angela arrived at our home just before nightfall, immediately hugging Faye and demanding to know what was going on. She looked deeply unsettled, and I wondered if she knew about Tíwé's and Nathan's deaths. In that moment I remembered what Nathan had told me on Pale Peak: "We don't speak the names of the dead for some time." I decided to avoid the subject altogether unless Angela brought it up. Her green eyes reminded me of his, and it only struck me then that she might have been his mother.

I took Faye's drawings outside and scattered them around the yard on Faye's instruction. She had sketched more pictures of her own nightmares, and of memories from when she was little. She had even drawn a man that looked like Christopher – or at least how she imagined he might look, had he survived and grown up. Many of the pages contained annotations, and some even had stories from Faye's childhood. At our front door, I placed my favorite of the bunch: a portrait of five-year-old Faye holding a baby.

The sky darkened. Back inside, Faye dimmed the lights and lay under a blanket on the couch. She had the remarkable ability to nap at any time of day, and was even more prepared to fall asleep quickly due to our recent all-nighter. She refused Nathan's tea this time, and instead told me, "Wake me up when he gets here."

In under a half hour she was out cold, leaving Angela and me to discuss the situation at the dining room table. I explained my hypothesis on Faye's grief.

"She buried that pain so deep that she didn't even dream of it," I said. "She totally erased Christopher from existence. I just don't get how."

"It makes sense," Angela replied, keeping her voice low. "Extreme denial might force something way down inside, but there's more than one way for it to get out."

"Do you believe us?" I asked. "Do you believe her?"

We looked to the couch. Faye's chest rose and fell rhythmically. Her face looked serene.

"I believe something remarkable is happening here," Angela offered.

"He's real," I said. "I've seen him. I've *touched* him. He did this."

I pulled down my collar, revealing the scars on my chest.

"Well," she said, after a moment, "I'm here, aren't I?"

"What are you doing?" Faye blurted out. "You need help with that?" Angela and I listened intently, but after a few more strings of babble, I realized that Faye was dreaming about her coworkers.

An hour passed. I could tell that Angela was beginning to regret making the drive.

"Maybe we need to take a more direct approach," she said.

"Like what?"

"She talks to him, right?"

"Yes."

"Well," Angela said, moving to the kitchen window and peering outside, "what makes you think he always comes to her? Maybe she calls out to him."

I opened my mouth to protest the ridiculous idea, but then a memory disrupted my thoughts. It was a familiar song, ringing so clearly in my mind that I thought I was actually hearing it.

I approached Faye, and began to hum the dreary elegy we first heard from the mouth of a child outside the cabin.

"Sooouuul me aaahhh doooo...Souuuul meee aaahhh doooo..."

Faye's eyes darted around behind her eyelids. She rocked her head back and forth a few times. Her arms jerked.

Angela's voice rose behind me, carrying the same tune. Faye grit her teeth, then began to mouth the words we sang. Her breathing grew louder and faster, and a timid humming escaped her lips, joining us in chorus.

Suddenly, Faye jolted upright, the sudden movement silencing me and Angela. A few seconds ticked by, and then she fell backward onto the couch, twitching periodically.

"She's fighting it," Angela said, kneeling beside her.

"Faye?" I asked. "...Are you alright?"

"Yes," she murmured.

"Do you know where you are?" Angela asked.

"I'm with you."

Faye's breathing settled into a slow and shallow rhythm. I knew it well; I'd heard it every night for the past several years. She was dead to the world.

Angela looked to the windows, then to the darkened staircase. I followed her gaze, suddenly very aware of the shadows that swallowed up most of the house.

"Who are you with, Faye?" she asked. "Do you know?"

"Felix. Angela... Erica." Her voice barely penetrated the air in front of her, forcing us to lean in close.

288

"Who's Erica?" Angela whispered to me.

"Her boss," I replied.

"Sweetie," Angela said, touching Faye's hand, "Erica isn't here. Is there someone else here?"

Faye looked puzzled for a moment and rolled her head around, taking in the space around her like a satellite.

"No," she replied.

"What about the one who follows you?" Angela pressed. "The one who calls out in the night. Is he here?"

"No."

"Where is he now?" Angela asked.

Faye's head craned from side to side as if she were emptying water from her ears.

"...Across the dark."

"We need you to call out to him," I said.

"No," she replied.

"Bring him here," Angela said, squeezing Faye's hand, "and I promise we'll protect you."

Faye whimpered. The more we prodded, the more resistant she became. She started to cry, at first in her own voice, and then in the voice of a small child.

"Please no," she begged. The sounds that came out of her mouth should have come from a five-year-old girl. Angela looked up at me wide-eyed. Goosebumps rippled down my arms.

"Sooouuul me aaaahhhh doooooo," Faye sang. *"Amma neta soouul me aahhhhh dooooo..."*

Suddenly, Faye's body stiffened and her eyes rolled forward. They landed squarely on me, then looked over my shoulder and focused on something a thousand miles behind me. Her mouth opened slightly, and a gurgling sound came up from her throat. She spoke in a wet and guttural voice, *"Wachu...Wachu..."*

Faye leaped off the couch and shuddered as though she

289

was trying to throw something from her back. Her body remained rigid, and she turned to face away from us. Every joint in her limbs popped and cracked in sickening symphony. She bent her head back and stared up at the place where the ceiling met the wall in front of her, balling her fists so tight her knuckles crackled like twigs. She snarled again, *"Wachu, wachu, wachu."*

Angela jumped to her feet, ready to stop Faye from hurting herself or dashing off into the night. I played safety a few feet away, knowing how quick she could move in this state.

"Tell us where he is, Faye," Angela commanded.

Faye put her finger to her lips and shushed us. She placed her fingers against the wall, like she was feeling for a pulse. She breathed hard through gritted teeth and forced out the word *"Bedroom."*

I looked over my shoulder at the stairwell. I couldn't see anything, but somehow, the darkness up there felt full, like it concealed a thousand terrible eyes peering back me.

"Is he talking to you right now?" Angela asked.

Faye grunted, trying to resist the force that contorted her body.

"His mouth is always moving," she whispered, "but I can't hear him. He's facing the other way."

I went upstairs, wading through the darkness of the hallway. Terror pushed back against me as I advanced. I could *feel* him now. As my hand touched the bedroom doorknob, I heard a window open on the other side.

The bedroom was empty, disturbed only by the cool night air that wafted in from the window near Faye's side of the bed. The dim glow of the backyard's automatic lights poured in. I approached and looked outside.

At the far end of the yard, just beyond the reach of the lights, stood a huge figure. The shadows smoldered around him, but his size betrayed him and outlined his wretched body against the blackness. He looked taller than ever before, and faced away, staring up into the trees that lined the property. His arms lay pressed against his sides, and his fists were balled, tightly clutching pieces of paper – Faye's drawings.

"Wole my...wole my..." he growled.

I locked the window and raced back downstairs. Faye was now sitting on the couch, head still craned up toward the ceiling, Angela rubbing her back and whispering to her.

Outside, a voice howled. It sounded like a little girl crying out for her mother. Another voice erupted – Lynn's – shouting "Greg, we need to take her to a hospital!"

Faye began to convulse. Angela wrapped her hand around Faye's forehead and whispered into her ear, but I couldn't hear what she said.

An infant shrieked in the backyard, and then slowly moved down the side of the house to the front door. There was a loud, slow knock, followed by more voices. The knock repeated again and again, and Becca's voice called out, "Faye? Where are you? Help me, please help."

Angela shouted something I could not understand. At last, Faye sucked in a huge breath and leaned back on the couch. Her head returned to a normal position and she frantically gasped for air. The pounding on the door grew louder, and the voices began to overlap, as though several people were standing in front of our house, crying out in the dark.

"He's here, he's here," Faye stammered, clutching herself with shaking hands. Her eyes shrieked louder than a scream ever could.

A man's sobs filtered through the door from outside. Greg's voice bellowed, "He was *my* son too. *My son.* Did you think a weekend in the goddamn mountains would make us forget?"

Faye covered her ears, trying to block out the wicked

lures that snared her. The words were so clear that I nearly believed Greg stood on our doorstep.

"Don't you fucking dare!" Lynn's voice cried out. "Just let her forget. This doesn't have to be her burden too."

Faye burst into tears and wobbled to the door. I followed just behind, ready to block her from opening it. The wails of a baby echoed through the house, followed by a little girl saying, "It's Faye. *Faaayyee.* What's yours? I can't see you."

Faye crumpled to the ground. She leaned her back against the door and brushed a handful of tear-soaked curls out of her face. There came another knock. My own voice followed it, saying, "May I...come in? It's freezing out here. Looks like another storm's coming."

Faye looked up at me. Our gazes locked, and time slowed to a drip. I saw an abyss of terror and uncertainty in her eyes, mirroring my own state. But then, a look of conviction fell over her face. The fear seemed to dissipate from it.

"I have to tell you something," she said, gently knocking on the door. Her eyes never left mine. "I know what you really want."

The voices fell silent all at once, and only an uneven wheezing remained.

"I had a baby brother," she said. "His name was Christopher. He was number five."

The breathing cut out.

Faye knocked on the door again. After a minute, something knocked back.

"I remember now," she continued. "I couldn't remember for years. Or I guess I didn't want to. It's easier for me to just pretend it never happened. Some kids make things exist. Friends, monsters, places. But I made Christopher not exist. That way I didn't have to lose him.

His death was just make-believe. And eventually, so was he."

A long, slow scratching noise crisscrossed the door. The thing outside was dragging a claw over the wood, drawing symbols or pictures. Faye put her palm on the door, feeling the weak vibrations of the scratching.

"For a long time," she said, "that number was all I could remember. I knew it meant something more, but every time I thought about it, my whole body would hurt. I'd feel sick. And then I'd just fall asleep. Or, if I was dreaming, I'd just wake up. I always knew it meant something more. But I wanted to forget."

The doorknob rattled and a wet, clunking sound emitted from it. The Impostor was gnawing on it from the other side. The clatter of a hundred jagged teeth rose in vile symphony throughout our living room.

"He was stillborn," Faye said. "Do you know what that means? He died inside my mom. All this time I've avoided burying Christopher. I couldn't imagine him going into the ground, down in a hole where he'd never see the sun. But you've finally helped me realize why it's time I laid him to rest."

"Faye, come hold him," Becca's voice called from outside. "I don't get it. He falls asleep so fast when you've got him. You want her to be your new mommy, Caleb?" The scratching noises persisted.

Faye wiped tears out of her eyes and took a deep breath. "Now you know everything. I wanted you to know. And now you can leave. I'm not going with you."

A chorus of voices rang out in the night. An infant screamed, a toddler laughed, Greg and Lynn and Becca and Tíwé and Nathan and the ranger all spoke at once. Decades of pain washed through the door; words of anguish and sorrowful cries drowned out the world. Angela and I exchanged horrified glances, but Faye remained

293

motionless at the door, staring up into my eyes. She didn't blink.

The knocking on the door swelled to violent pounding. The entity used every possible trick he could. He tried to hit her right where the wounds were fresh, tried to tear open the oldest scars. But Faye never budged. She held her ground, and never took her eyes off me. They were filled with a knowing calm, as if to say, "*Enough.*"

When the Impostor got no response, he stomped from the front door to the nearby window. Angela shut off the light so she could see his silhouette on the curtain.

"*Wole my, wole my,*" he bayed, rolling his nails across the glass.

Faye's lips quivered, but she said nothing. A titanic scream erupted from the creature, and he slapped the side of the house with an open hand. The sounds shook the room and struck a lightning bolt of terror in the pit of my stomach, but Faye did not react. She didn't even flinch.

Then, the entity said something I did not expect. Instead of assuming the voice of someone we knew, he spoke in several I did not recognize. He uttered only one labored sentence, but each word was formed with a different tongue:

"*I...walked...a thousand...years...across...the dark...to find you.*"

The message petrified me. The finality, the sheer longing of it seemed incomprehensible. But Faye just shook her head.

"*Go,*" she said.

The creature howled. His shadow receded from the window, coloring Faye's body silver with the dim kiss of moonlight. Sullen footsteps lurched across our yard and vanished into the backdrop of cricket songs. Angela and I looked down at Faye. A relieved smile spread across her face. She wasn't crying anymore.

Epilogue

Faye has finally laid her demons to rest. Several days have passed since she made her confession to the Impostor, and he appears to have given up on his sinister quest. He returned only once since that night, merely to sing his morose lullaby. Faye slept right through it. I didn't mention it to her.

A dreadful weight has been lifted from her shoulders, allowing her to mourn properly. At night, she sleeps soundly. During the day she cries. She cuddles with me and talks about her childhood. She has long calls with her parents and sister. They cry too. I have shed many tears with her, and for her loss, but now I finally understand why she did what she did.

As a child, Faye repressed the pain of her brother's death so completely that Christopher himself disappeared with it. The number five became the lockbox in which he was hidden. The coffin she buried him in. And she buried him so deep that she couldn't even dream of him anymore. That is why the Impostor never fully understood what she was hiding: he learned his prey through their dreams.

I believe that Faye's lifelong sleep disturbances were her brain's attempts at keeping that pain repressed. But by talking in her sleep, Faye invited dark attention to herself. I suppose that if you speak long enough into the void, someone is bound to start listening. Someone, or something, heard her pain and saw it as a weakness. He saw those cracks in her heart as a passage into her soul, and so he chose her. The Impostor became transfixed with Faye not because she was an easy target, but because she was a monolithic challenge. A worthy opponent.

But Faye's brain is not just a factory of denial. It is also a work of art. She is able to see the world in ways that I cannot, and her vision granted her insight into the monster. Faye realized that the Impostor could tug on her puppet strings by invading the darkest parts of her mind. In all those hidden places, he found weapons to use against her. To wear her down. But instead of burying her secrets deeper, Faye unearthed them and brought them into the light. By moving Christopher out from the depths of her subconscious and into her waking thoughts, she unleashed a tidal wave of anguish upon herself. But at the same time, she took away the Impostor's power over her. She cut off her own puppet strings, and now there was nothing left for the creature to grab onto. And so he left.

This catastrophe has taught me what it means to grieve. I've found the time to mourn for my dear friends, Tíwé and Nathan. Their deaths are terrible wounds on my heart, and I will always bear the agony of their loss. But I want it to hurt, as a permanent reminder. They gave so much to me and asked nothing in return, spare that I preserve the goodness of their people in my memory. By writing about their altruism and sacrifices, I am trying to fulfill that promise. May their spirits live on in the sacred land they protected.

Angela and I have spoken a few times since that night, mostly about the dreamcatchers, but the conversations go nowhere. We may never know for sure who built them. Perhaps they were crafted by the people who live on Pale Peak. Perhaps they wanted to protect fools like me who venture to that mountain without understanding its history. Maybe they were creations of the Impostor himself. Or maybe they had nothing to do with us.

We have also discussed the engagement ring: what the Impostor wanted with it, and what it enabled him to do to Faye, remains a mystery. Once the creature had possession of it, he slowly gained Faye's trust and the ability to influence her — even while she was awake. After I retrieved the ring, he ceased visiting her for several weeks, and could only possess her through dreams. Angela has advised us to get rid of it for fear that it could be cursed. But to Faye, that ring symbolizes everything we've been through, and she refuses to part with such a meaningful thing. It still rests on her finger, and glitters like her smile.

There is a terrible being that still lives up there in those woods on Pale Peak. Some people believe him to be an Old Evil, a progenitor of the bad spirits that wander the Southwest and the Rocky Mountains. Others call him a *soul trader*, a demon who takes his victims out into the endless dark to feast on their suffering. Tíwé and Nathan thought of him as an apex predator with a remarkably effective hunting style. But when I think of the *At'an-A'anotogkua*, I can't help but think of another animal: Carrot. The Impostor reminded me of a parrot: always watching, always imitating, always practicing. And just like Carrot, he could only ever approximate the people he watched. He could never fully become one of them. But whatever the Impostor truly is, I have stopped trying to understand.

Faye and I plan to head back to Colorado in a few weeks to reconcile with her parents. I will return to the mountain alone to pay my deepest respects to Tíwé and Nathan's community, and to witness the bulldozing of the cabin. In distant days I may regret not investigating it further. I may wonder. I may dream. I don't know if it is better that we should remember, or forget. But I know that we have an obligation to help protect future visitors to the mountain. Whatever secrets that cabin on Pale Peak still hides, let them be buried deep beneath the rubble and the snows of decades to come.

A Word on Natives in Fiction

How should a non-Native person write about Natives in a work of fiction? Does he have the right? Is it unethical to do so?

These questions wracked my brain throughout the entire process of authoring this book. My fear was that I would misrepresent Natives, like so many Hollywood films have over the decades, and portray them as something other than what they are: people. Like anyone else, they are people with cultures, beliefs, histories, and ideas about how the world should work. They can be just as interesting or boring as anybody else, except they are lesser-known, and therefore somewhat mysterious to outsiders.

Why should I care about misrepresentations and stereotypes? Many books and films, widely regarded as masterpieces, portray Indigenous people (or black people, or women, or LGBT people) as flat and one-dimensional, often to terrible ends. And they do so with waning impunity. I care because Indigenous peoples are especially vulnerable to the effects of misrepresentation. They are perhaps the most submerged, marginalized, and underrepresented ethnic community in the United States

301

(and in many other countries around the world). By this I mean, among other things, that Indigenous peoples do not have the public station they would require to combat or correct these misrepresentations. They are often ignored by the media. They are reduced to brief mentions in history classes. They are not cast in any significant number as actors or elected as politicians. They are mostly reflected through other lenses, like movies and TV shows – and books like this one. Historians refer to them sometimes as "peoples," by the way, to indicate that they are not just one group.

I spent a long time debating whether it was unethical to write a horror story centered on a creature inspired by Native American lore. In graduate school, while training to become a history teacher, I worked with an Indigenous professor and had the rare privilege of hearing from this person's own mouth the many plights of Natives inside and outside academia. I studied the ways in which the Western paradigm of knowledge production (ethnographies, archaeological digs, research trips, interviews, etc.) conflicted with Indigenous conceptions of knowledge (which is often sacred, private, powerful, and therefore worth protecting from outsiders). Today, there is an effort among historians to "decolonize Native studies" – meaning to critically examining the ways Indigenous histories and cultures are taught, who is teaching them, why this information is being taught, and what effects this education has on the relationships between Native and non-Native populations. The premises of this movement are that:

1. Most of the knowledge we (non-Natives) have of Indigenous people was gathered in ways that might have injured the communities it was extracted from;

2. There are very, very few Natives actually teaching this knowledge to the public. It is instead being taught by non-Natives and is therefore more susceptible to misinterpretation and misrepresentation; and,

3. Natives are limited in their ability to combat these problems in our education system or to mitigate the potential negative effects this style of education might have on their communities.

This is a hot-button subject. There are strong opinions on all sides of the debate.

I went about making this decision carefully. I asked a few colleagues of mine, and their hesitation about including Native characters in this book was unanimous. Some of them were concerned that I would do a poor job in my portrayals. Others were simply fearful that I would offend somebody, regardless of the quality and accuracy of the writing. After all, we grad students operate at the physical epicenter of this debate: on university campuses, where social justice and its conflicting interpretations are on the lips of every student.

After much deliberation, I decided to write the characters I wanted to write. It is, after all, impossible to satisfy every person's expectations when it comes to representing a group, or even describing a single member of one, and there seems to be a great diversity of opinion on whether fiction authors should channel the sociopolitical zeitgeist. Thus, I have little doubt that someone will be upset by the inclusion of Natives in my story, and conversely I suspect that someone else would be outraged had I excluded Natives entirely for the purpose of political correctness.

Ultimately I decided to write about Natives simply as people, and tried to avoid the common stereotypes that

303

harm their communities. First, I chose to fictionalize the names of the people groups that my Native characters belonged to, so as not to mischaracterize the beliefs, cultures, or histories of any real tribes. Second, I tried to texturize the characters such that they were not one-dimensional caricatures of real people. I did not want the Natives in my story to be expert advisers on all things spiritual. I did not want them to use mystical powers to ultimately banish an evil that only they understood. I did not want them to have all the answers. As a fan of horror, I've seen these caricatures before, and frankly they are boring, not to mention potentially harmful. Instead I wanted Tíwé and his family to struggle with their memories and heritage, and where those things fit in with their everyday experience of the world – something we all endure to varying degrees. I wanted their world and experiences to make them forget some things. Important things.

I also feared to head too far in the direction of the vanishing Indian. It would be remiss of me to articulate these characters as relics of a forgotten past, lost in a modern world they do not recognize as their own. They should not appear as a dying species of aliens on the precipice of extinction, ready to be consigned to the annals of history. In reality, Indigenous communities are suffering in manifold ways which deserve more than a brief mention at the end of a horror novel, but they are also thriving in other ways. Cultural and language preservation efforts, though hotly debated (and often managed by outsiders to those communities), often do help to ensure that precious elements of Native lifeways do not vanish forever. Too many have already, and most of us will never know about it. Indigenous rights and recognition movements, although constantly faced with structural opposition, racism, and the legacy of centuries of violent oppression, are experiencing moderate success in directing badly needed attention to policy issues that affect Natives across the United States. Native professors have constructed entire academic departments and authored award-winning books to introduce the many histories of Indigenous peoples to the public, and they do so with this "decolonization" in mind and practice.

The road will always be arduous and full of pitfalls for them, but my point is that Indians are hardly a single idle people waiting to disappear – or mystical spell-casters, or foolish alcoholics, for that matter – and should not be portrayed so flatly in fiction. They are many peoples, with many histories, many cultures, many languages, and many adversities and triumphs. And while I did not have the creative space to describe the disadvantages that likely plague Tíwé's reservation, nor its probable efforts to overcome them, I tried at least to write what I think is a dignified and complex set of characters who offer something to the reader other than mere amusement.

I'm glad I made the choice I did. My first large audience, thousands of Redditors, were overwhelmingly receptive of Tíwé and the little bits of history he shared. It has been over a year since the release of the original story, and I still receive emails to this day from readers interested in learning more about the plights of Indigenous people groups. As a writer who believes that fiction can be educationally valuable, this is extremely heartening.

This digression is not to serve merely as a defense of my decision to write Indigenous characters. It should also serve as a think-piece to be grappled with by readers. I wanted to write about people, and I have done that. The people in this story are all colored by my experiences, my personal interests, my desires and perceptions, and do not represent anyone but themselves. They were, however, developed with the aforementioned problems and debates in mind. As a person who has trained for the past several years to be a teacher, I think we should be bringing attention to the experiences of Indigenous communities in a multitude of mediums – in the classroom, in the political forum, in the arts – instead of avoiding them and creating worlds of education and entertainment where Natives simply do not exist. My way of doing this, of writing horror, is not nearly the most effective way. But perhaps it will have some positive effect on someone, and perhaps that person will choose to read further on these issues. If you do find this subject engaging, I personally recommend the book *Wisdom Sits in Places* by Keith H. Basso, which is a short and moving ethnography on the Western Apache that has had great influence on me as an academic and as a member of the human race.

About the Author

Felix Blackwell emerged from the bowels of reddit during a botched summoning ritual. He writes novels and short stories in the horror and thriller genres, and draws most of his inspiration from his own nightmares.

For more creepy things to keep you awake, visit
www.felixblackwell.com

Connect with the author at
facebook.com/felixblackwellbooks

Made in the USA
Monee, IL
21 March 2024

55408915R00185